The Trouble with Skateboarding

Chris Ashley

Editing, book design and cover design by Emily Jacques (emily@trafford.com).

Note for Librarians: a cataloguing record for this book that includes Dewey Classification and US Library of Congress numbers is available from the National Library of Canada. The complete cataloguing record can be obtained from the National Library's online database at: www.nlc-bnc.ca/amicus/index-e.html

ISBN 1-4120-2367-X

TRAFFORD

This book was published on-demand in cooperation with Trafford Publishing. On-demand publishing is a unique process and service of making a book available for retail sale to the public taking advantage of on-demand manufacturing and Internet marketing. On-demand publishing includes promotions, retail sales, manufacturing, order fulfilment, accounting and collecting royalties on behalf of the author.

Suite 6E, 2333 Government St., Victoria, B.C. V8T 4P4, CANADA
Phone   250-383-6864   Toll-free   1-888-232-4444 (Canada & US)
Fax   250-383-6804   E-mail   sales@trafford.com
Web site www.trafford.com TRAFFORD PUBLISHING IS A DIVISION OF TRAFFORD HOLDINGS LTD.
Trafford Catalogue #04-0195   www.trafford.com/robots/04-0195.html

10   9   8   7   6   5   4   3   2

Contents

Foreword

This book was written at the request of my son Benjamin and my daughter Emily. He really likes to skateboard and was interested in reading a book involving some sort of skateboarding adventure. We checked our local library and there didn't seem to be that many options. My daughter, son and I felt we could come up with our own entertaining story.

This book offers a multi-dimensional story that is designed to be entertaining and educational. The intended audiences are girls and boys (approximate ages 8-14) who like skateboarding and/or solving mysteries. While the reader does not have to skateboard to enjoy the story, a majority of the book involves activities that relate to the group of skateboarders.

There is a glossary of terms at the end of the book in case you are not familiar with some of the language.

This is a fictional story. Any resemblance to real characters is unintentional. Use of any trademarked names in this book is done recognizing the right of the company holding the trademark. Redistribution or copying of this manuscript requires prior and written author consent.

Chris Ashley can be reached by email at chrisashley903@shaw.ca. Special thanks to McNally-Robinson Booksellers (www.mcnallyrobinson.com) and Draft Skateboards (www.draftskateboards.com) for your support.

Dedication

With the help of the ones I love
I have achieved a dream

The Friends

Three years ago…

It was a hot July day in Exton, Pennsylvania. Mike and his best friend Clay Osgood were practicing their staircase tricks. Mike was really getting good grinding the rail. Clay was very good already. He could kick-flip and land on the rail and slide down to the bottom. They were both practicing their landings.

Mike had just completed a clean run and had asked Clay to tape it for a video they were making. Clay had the video camera all setup and ready to roll for Mike. Most of the video so far was Clay doing tricks. Clay could land pretty much any trick you asked him to do. JuiceMan Drink Corporation already sponsored Clay in a sweet deal. JuiceMan not only paid for all of Clay's skating equipment but they also covered his travel and expenses for each of the 10 competitions that he entered every year.

Clay was trying to hook up his best friend to the same deal. He had recently gone in twice to the President of JuiceMan to tell him about Mike and show off Mike on video. JuiceMan was always looking for talented new boarders and had asked one of their assistants to make an appointment to talk to Mike. When Mike had heard the news, he was stoked. They decided to celebrate by finishing off their video. If JuiceMan signed Mike, he would need to show the company president a tight video with several landed tricks. Even though Clay had turned pro first and was making lots of money he didn't forget his friends. Mike always promised himself that he would be not forget the people who helped him after he turned pro.

As Mike looked over his board, a guy named Nick Leland was leaving O'Sullivan's bar just up the street. Nick had had a bad day at work and was having a drink before he went home to his wife. One drink lead to a second drink and then a third drink.

Instead of calling a taxi or his wife to come and pick him up, Nick decided he was not drunk, even though he was feeling pretty good. As Nick got up, he was surprised to feel his feet wobble a little beneath him. "I should have had lunch," he thought to himself. Nick opened the door to leave and daylight poured into the dark bar. He shielded his eyes and tried to remember where he parked his car.

At the same time, Mike was cleaning some dirt out of his wheels. "I don't want this grit to get in the way of a perfect run!" Mike laughed.

Nick found his car and struggled a bit to get the key in the lock. Nick forgot that his car had keyless entry. He put the key in the ignition and fired up the engine. Nick loved the powerful noises of his car. "What a beauty she is!" thought Nick. "God I love this car. No one can catch me in her."

Mike lined up about 50 feet back from the stairs. The handrail was on the right-hand side of the stairs only and went down at a 45 degree angle for 10 feet and then straightened out for 3 feet, then went down another 10 feet at 45 degrees. At the bottom was a wide sidewalk that gave Mike and Clay more than enough room to land the trick safely before reaching the street.

Mike ran forward a few steps, threw down his board, jumped and landed on it perfectly. He gathered speed.

Nick backed out of his parking spot just barely missing the car next to him. He exited the parking lot without looking properly. When he pulled into traffic, he cut off a city bus. The bus driver slammed on his brakes and everyone in the bus was thrown forward quickly. The bus driver leaned on his horn.

Mike approached the stairs at just the right speed and executed a flawless kick-flip onto the top of the handrail. Clay was capturing it all on video. "Go for it, man!" whooped Clay. Mike was trying not to smile. You don't smile on your videos until you complete the trick.

As Mike was sliding down the first handrail doing a 50–50, Nick was weaving his car back and forth in the lane next to the sidewalk. Instead of keeping his eyes on the road, Nick was searching the floor under his stereo looking for his favorite CD. Nick never realized he was veering towards the sidewalk until his front wheels bounced over the curb.

Clay heard the bang as Mike slid by him on the rail. "What was that?"

Mike could see the whole scene playing out in front of him. The car seemed to climb the stairs towards him like a hungry beast. Before Mike could react, he had left the end of the rail and was heading straight for the hood of the car.

In an instant Mike's dreams of turning pro were over. The impact of the car hitting Mike knocked him backwards 15 feet. Mike landed back on the cement stairs, opening up a cut across his back that would require 38 stitches to close. The worst of the impact hit Mike's left side.

The accident broke Mike's leg badly and he was in the hospital for two months. The doctors put six metal pins in his leg to help pull the bones back together and he had to wear two different casts on his leg for a total of 11 weeks. When the cast was taken off, the bones had healed but Mike had to go through months of physiotherapy to be able walk and run properly again. Even though the bones had healed well, they were not strong enough for Mike to continue to do skateboarding tricks, so he had to retire early. He was really sad to give up boarding so he decided to open his own skate shop right there in Exton.

At the time of the accident, Clay had immediately called the police on his cell phone. When the police arrived, they found the driver still sitting in his car wondering how his car had ended up on the stairs. Nick was arrested at the scene for Driving Under the Influence (DUI). He didn't even realize that he had hit someone on a skateboard.

When the police told him what he did, he said, "That's the trouble with skateboarding," and pouted to the cops. "What was someone doing sliding down the rail anyway?"

The policeman just shook his head and led Nick away to the cruiser. "Why would someone who had been drinking get behind the wheel of a car?" the cop said to himself and shot a look of disgust at Nick.

Mike and Nick now had one thing in common. After today their lives would never be the same.

Many of Mike's skateboarding friends who had turned pro helped Mike set up his new shop and often came by to visit. It was awesome to see some of the best skateboarders in the world come into the shop to talk to Mike. You never knew whom you were going to see next.

Clay was there as much as he could. When he was not at an event or on tour, he was flying back to Exton to help with the shop. Clay organized all the suppliers and worked out really good rates on supplies. Clay even showed Mike how to design the store in the style of the shops he visited in California. Mike was so happy to have Clay there to help him.

It was hard at first for Mike to get around but Clay continued to make regular visits to the store over the first several months. On one of those visits Clay brought someone with him. Her name was Julie Jones. Mike thought she was the most beautiful woman he had ever seen. Mike thought that Clay was pretty lucky to have her as a girlfriend and he said as much to Clay.

Clay laughed, "Mike, Julie is not my girlfriend. She's my agent. She sets up all my events and promotions. Sure, I would love to date her but she has a rule that she doesn't date her clients."

"Too bad!" said Mike.

"Too bad indeed!" said Clay. He was only down for the weekend before heading on to his next competition. Julie wanted to come to Exton to meet Mike and to see the new store. Clay had talked so much about Mike that Julie had to meet this guy. Julie and Mike hit it off immediately.

Julie was born and raised in Victoria, British Columbia. Victoria is a beautiful Canadian town on Vancouver Island that is a two-hour ferry ride from the city of Vancouver. Over the course of a few hours Mike spent almost all his time staring at Julie while encouraging her to tell more about herself. Mike loved to hear stories about how amazing the scenery was in Victoria.

Julie's parents used to own a maple sugar bush factory but now owned a restaurant called Hunter's Steakhouse. Julie's family was very hard working and Julie knew that Mike would fit in well. Julie wanted to take Mike one day to Victoria and to meet her parents at the restaurant. There was this special booth in the restaurant that was very romantic and she wanted to enjoy a dinner there with him.

"I'm sure you take all your boyfriends there!" joked Mike. "Who said you were my boyfriend!" Julie said back with a funny look.

12

Clay had decided he was not needed and would take a drive out to see his parents who lived not far away in Scranton. "You kids be good!" said Clay as he left.

A month later Julie decided to give up being an agent and head back to Exton to be with Mike at the store. When Clay heard the news he couldn't believe what she was saying.

"I can't believe you are going to give up a successful career as an agent to…" Clay's voice trailed off.

"To…what?" asked Julie.

"Nothing," Clay said quietly. "Are you sure you want to do this?"

"Absolutely!" said Julie.

"Then I am happy for you," said Clay.

After several months of hard work the shop was doing brisk business. Mike was organizing the Mayor and City Council to help fund Exton's first skate park. Mayor Carter was supporting Mike because it gave the young people of Exton a place to go and have fun and to stay out of trouble. The Mayor had said that the City could come up with half of the money if Mike could come up with the other half. That meant that Mike had to raise $250,000. Mike needed help to do that and was looking for ideas.

Today…

Jim sat on his front porch waiting for his best friend Ben to show up. Jim should have been happy but he wasn't. School was out and all his friends were coming over to go skateboarding, the one thing they loved the most. From the sound of his voice on the phone, Jim knew something was up with Ben but he didn't know what. When Ben had called Jim about hour earlier, he had said he would be over shortly with some important news. Jim had no idea what Ben had on his mind. Jim thought about his friend and wondered why Ben was always so secretive.

Jim and his four closest friends all lived nearby and hung around together. Ben Holt was the oldest of the five friends. Jim and Ben were looked upon as informal leaders of the group because they were the best boarders. Christyn Middlehurst, who was twelve like Jim, was a ripper on a skateboard and had once done a darkslide. Scott Wilson was 11 years old and incredibly tall for his age. Scott could ollie higher than anyone Jim had ever met. Billy Brandt was only nine years old, but was allowed to hang around with the group because he was Jim's brother. Jim's mom also said he had to let him. Billy was OK. He was annoying a lot but he loved skateboarding as much as any of them so they put up with him.

It would have been hard to choose who was the best boarder in the group. They were all good in different things. Jim knew he was probably the best but there were many tricks he was still learning that the others had already done before him. It didn't really matter who was the best, as long as they all got to practice together and have fun.

Ben was 13 years old and in Grade 8. He was a year and a grade ahead of Jim. Ben was the funniest guy in the group. He loved to play tricks on the others and was always telling some sort of bad joke. Jim remembered the time that Ben put this fake dog poop on the seat of his teacher, Mrs. Creepen. Apparently she almost fell onto the floor trying to avoid sitting on it. Ben got a week of detentions for that one. Everyone in the group liked Ben even though he often played tricks on all of them. Speaking of tricks, Ben tried hard to learn new skateboarding tricks and he typically ended up with more bandages on his legs and arms than anyone else.

Ben had an older brother named Mike who owned the only skateboard shop in Exton. The shop was called Boardzone and had been open for almost two years. Ben worked part-time after school and on weekends to help out his brother. His brother was an awesome guy who gave all of Ben's friend's great deals on decks, trucks and anything else they needed for their boards. Mike was a great skateboarder who was going to turn professional but couldn't because he was injured in an accident.

Jim had met Ben on the day Jim moved to Exton with his family three years ago. Ben lived two streets away on Frazier Drive. Jim can remember sitting on the curb watching the men unload the moving van. Jim was not happy about leaving his friends behind where they used to live in Riverside, California.

Riverside was the best place ever. They had the greatest skate parks and everyone was into boarding there. There were five skate parks close to his house and he spent most evenings and all weekend visiting them. He remembered his favorite skate park was called Darkslide. They had this vert wall that was 14 feet tall. Jim had never been able to go down it without falling. It was so high that he felt like he could reach up and touch the clouds.

Then Jim's dad was transferred to Exton where they had exactly zero skate parks. As a matter of fact, he hadn't seen one kid on a skateboard since they arrived that morning. As he watched the men unload their refrigerator he finally saw a kid on a skateboard coming up the street. As the kid came closer Jim could see he was wearing a Spitfire t-shirt and bright orange cargo pants, the kind of pants that unzip to become shorts. "This was a kid that I want to meet," thought Jim.

Jim put on his Quiksilver hat and grabbed his skateboard. Jim hadn't packed either on the moving van because he didn't trust anyone to take care of his board. He had worked hard raking leaves and doing chores in his Riverside neighborhood to afford his board. It was an Element board with Independent trucks, Flip wheels and Swiss Bones bearings. It was a smooth ride and he had quickly learned to ollie and kick-flip with it. Not many people put Flip wheels with Independent trucks on an Element board because that combination was stiff and made it harder to do tricks. Jim had read that his favorite professional skateboarder Erik Worth used that combination and while it was harder at first, you could get more height on your ollies once you got the hang of it.

The kid looked up and stopped. He seemed interested in the activity around the moving van. "Hey there. What kind of board do you have?" said Jim. The kid looked up and after a moment said, "This is an Element board with Independent trucks and Flip wheels – just like Worth."

Jim couldn't believe his ears. "Someone else who liked Erik Worth!" he thought. Jim knew that he and this guy were going to become friends. And he was right.

Three years later, Jim was sitting on the same street waiting for Ben. He had done this a million times since that first day. Sure enough a figure appeared on a skateboard from around the far street corner. It was Ben wearing the same worn blue hoody that he wore everyday. The way he wore his hat sideways, you could tell him a mile away. His Quiksilver hat was practically stuck to his head. Rumor had it that Ben wore it to bed each night.

"Hey Jim! Jim!" said Ben as he came rushing up on his board. "You aren't going to believe this!" Now Jim was really curious and bounded down the stairs to meet his friend.

"What is it Ben?"

"I overheard my Dad and my brother Mike talking this morning about the skate shop and Mike was saying that for the past two months hardly anyone has been buying new skateboards from him."

"Maybe it has just been a couple of slow months," countered Jim.

"No, May and June are normally busy because everyone wants their boards for summer break. Mike says that if people don't start coming back to his store then he might have to close down!"

"Oh no!" exclaimed Jim. "What would happen to the skate park Mike is planning?"

"We can forget about that park!" groaned Ben.

"We have to do something!" they both exclaimed at the same time. Ben and Jim had a habit of saying the same thing at the same time. It was kind of weird that it happened so much and freaked out Jim's parents a bit.

"What should we do?" asked Jim.

"Let's get the others and we'll go down to see Mike at the skate shop. Maybe he will tell us more."

Bad News

While Jim went in to call Christyn and Scott, Billy came out wearing Spiderman pajamas and eating toast and peanut butter. Like always, Billy's hair stuck straight up and he had most of his meal around his face or on his clothes. Ben just shook his head at Billy. "You know Billy, if you got half of your meal in your mouth you might already be a foot taller." Billy didn't get it.

Billy asked, "What's all the commotion? Why is Jim running around the house yelling and looking for the cordless phone?"

Ben told him what was going on. Billy ran back inside to get changed so he could go with the others. He wanted to help too. And he didn't want to be left behind!

While Ben was waiting, he was thinking about the problem. Ben was worried about his brother. His brother loved Boardzone. Ever since Mike had to retire from boarding, the skate shop had allowed him to remain close to the sport he was so good at. Mike really liked helping kids learn how to skateboard responsibly. That was why he wanted to build the skate park. He wanted to make sure that there was a place for kids to go and ride without worrying about getting hit by cars in the streets.

Without the shop, what would Mike do? Ben didn't know yet but he knew that he and his friends were going to help his brother.

Jim ran out the front door, sending the screen door banging into the wall. From inside the house Jim's mother yelled something about "doors don't grow on trees" which was kind of strange because it was a wooden door.

"I called Christyn and Scott," said Jim. "Christyn will be on her way as soon as she finishes her visit with her grandmother. I woke up Scott. He's now getting ready and will meet us at Boardzone right away." At that moment, Billy came charging out of the house, sending the screen door banging into the wall. Again, Jim's mom, Clarice, started yelling from inside the house. This time there were clear cries for assistance from Jim's dad, Felix.

"Uh oh, I think it's time we took off!" called Ben.

"What about Christyn?" said Billy.

"Well Billy, we can either wait here for Christyn and give your dad time to come downstairs or we can go towards her house and meet her halfway. Your choice?" questioned Ben.

"Since you put it that way, let's move," said Jim with a bit of a grin.

The three of them grabbed their boards and headed down the street towards Christyn's house.

At that moment Felix came rushing out of the house to have a little "chat" with his sons. In his haste to catch them he lost his grip on the screen door as he pushed it open and he too sent it crashing into the wall with a loud bang. Clarice came upstairs from the middle of doing laundry and was not happy to see her husband standing next to the screen door trying to fix a new dent he had made in the outside wall.

18

"Oh…it's you Felix! I blamed poor Jim for that racket!" she sighed. Standing next to the fresh dent, Felix knew that it was futile to protest with Clarice when she was this angry.

"Not to worry," he thought to himself. "I will have a little chat with those sons of mine when they came home. They have to come home sooner or later and I have a lawnmower with their name on it!"

As the three boys approached Christyn's house they saw her grandmother's unmistakable 1970s station wagon. It was gold-colored with fake wood paneling. In a word it was hideous but they loved that car. The boys had a few opportunities to ride in it, usually when Christyn's grandmother took them for ice cream or bowling. The cool thing about the very back of the station wagon was that it had two bench seats that faced each other. Four friends could face one another on those trips. Everyone always wrestled to see who would get in the back. Christyn almost always won, she was pretty strong…for a girl.

They walked up to the door and rang the bell. Christyn's mother came to the door and they could see Christyn in the living room talking to her grandmother.

"Please come in," said Mrs. Middlehurst. Christyn was sitting there in a dress with a blue and white checked pattern. When the boys saw this they all burst out laughing, not even trying to hide it from their friend.

"Christyn's in a dress! Ben, I wish we had your dad's digital camera!" Jim could hardly talk, he was laughing so hard.

Christyn was a girl but in many ways was more of a boy than the others. She was the strongest in the group and she was certainly the toughest. She wouldn't back down from anyone. They knew they were taking a risk in laughing at her but they couldn't help themselves. It was too funny.

Christyn was getting red-cheeked she was so mad. Mrs. Middlehurst knew what the boys were laughing at but was happy to see her daughter dress a little more like a girl than a skateboarder. Christyn's grandmother understood her embarrassment. Christyn was her favorite grandchild. She always made time to visit her grandmother and every year made her birthday and Christmas cards.

Her grandmother reached into her purse and said out loud, "Christyn, thank you very much for visiting with me today. I have a little present for someone who is dressed up so nicely." She reached into her purse and pulled out a crisp new $20 bill and handed it to Christyn. "Why don't you take this and spend it on some new skateboarding magazines for yourself," she said looking directly at the boys who were not laughing any longer.

Christyn's eyes opened as wide as a half-pipe. "Thanks Gram. You're the best! Mom, can I go and get changed?"

"Well Christyn, I was going to ask you to come to a film this afternoon with Gram and me. The film is called "The Wonderful World of Carbon Dioxide". I think it is a scientific film." Her mom, Alice, answered. "Since your friends are here I guess it would be alright for you to go with them instead."

Before another thought could enter her mom's head, Christyn raced up the stairs to her room.

While Christyn was changing, Mrs. Middlehurst asked the boys where they were going. Ben told her about Mike's problem and she thought that was very nice of them to want to help. "But listen carefully to the problem before trying to figure out what to do," she said.

Christyn thumped down the stairs wearing jeans, white Roxy t-shirt and her faded red jean jacket. She put on her black high-top running shoes and grabbed her Girl skateboard from the closet.

"Bye Mom, bye Gram. Have fun at the movie. Wish I was going!" she said with a wink to her grandmother. Her grandmother thought back to the days when she was younger and every day was a new adventure and smiled.

As the kids ran across the lawn and hopped onto their boards, Mrs. Middlehurst yelled, "Have fun Christyn, and stay out of trouble." But she was pretty sure that warning had fallen on deaf ears.

As they rode down Pine Street towards Mike's shop, Jim teased Christyn. "That was pretty nice of your grandmother to give you $20. Maybe you can use that to get yourself a nice new dress?" Jim laughed. Billy and Ben also started to hoot.

Christyn replied, "I owe you a couple of punches already so don't push it. At least I didn't have to stay and go to that movie. It sounded like a snooze fest."

19

"So what is the big deal? Where are we off to in such a hurry?" quizzed Christyn.

"We're meeting Scott at Boardzone and we'll fill you in there," replied Jim.

Boardzone

When they turned the corner on Canyon Drive they could see the Scott's familiar figure standing in front of Mike's skate shop. Scott was tall and thin. By the time he was 11 years old he was almost six feet tall. He weighed only 120 pounds and the group of kids always kidded him that his parents put sand in his pockets to make sure the wind didn't blow him off his skateboard.

Scott was kind of quiet. He was an intense person and did very well in school. He was one of those kids that didn't have to study much to get good grades. Everything at school seemed to come easy for him.

He was also the ollie king in the group. He could ollie over anything. Once, he had even ollied over a shopping cart in a Safeway parking lot, which made him a legend in the group.

When Scott saw the group coming up the street he waved his arms wildly – like they wouldn't see him otherwise! It should be noted that Scott was a waver. It took him about five minutes to walk away from his house each morning. He would turn around every 10 feet and wave to his mom and baby sister who were watching him leave while standing on the front step. He would keep waving until he was out of sight of his house. I don't know who needed to do it more, him or his mom.

He always said he did it to make his mom happy but there he was, once more, waving like he was bringing a 747 into a hangar.

"Hey Scott!" said Jim. "Glad you could make it".

"Sorry if we woke you, I know how important it is to not interrupt your beauty sleep!" said Ben with a laugh. Billy and Christyn snickered.

Scott responded, "Very funny Ben. I can see that you are long overdue for a big nap." Jim looked over at Ben and said "Ouch!"

"Before we go in," Christyn said, "I want to know what's going on."

"Yeah, since you guys got me out of bed for this," said Scott.

Jim and Ben started to tell the whole story again. When they were done, Billy was already thinking that there must be some sort of secret government plot to force Mike out of business. Billy had such a vivid imagination. Scott was trying to make it add up in his head and quickly laughed off Billy's theory.

Scott said, "There must be a logical reason why no one is buying skateboards from Mike."

"We know that he has the best selection of gear, we know he carries the highest quality of equipment and we know he offers the best advice on what to buy," added Jim.

"He gives us sweet deals too," Billy reminded them. They all agreed. Each one of them had been able to buy their skateboard stuff at very good prices because Mike would give them a break. Making a ton of money for himself and his girlfriend was not the reason why he owned the shop. Mike owned the store because he loved skateboarding.

"Now someone was trying to take that away from Mike," said Ben.

"Let's go talk to Mike and see if we can find out more about this from him," said Scott.

They picked up their boards and walked single file into the skate shop. Each time they walked into the place, they were impressed. Mike was always changing things and putting up new displays of the latest equipment.

When you walked in, the first thing that caught your eye was the giant glass counter. It was actually made up of four individual counters linked together in the shape of a square. Each counter was 15 feet long. They were shiny and had chrome edges that reflected the light like rainbows. There were three glass shelves in each counter. Mike kept those counters polished and clean. No matter how many kids came in and put their dirty hands all over, each counter always looked clean.

Mike had never been a clean freak, but since meeting his girlfriend, Julie, she had taught him that being clean was not only healthy but it could lead to more business. Julie worked full-time helping Mike run the skate shop. She was the one who had the floors and counters shining all the time.

The top shelf of each counter held a huge display of trucks. The middle shelf held the wheels and bearings. The bottom shelves had things like stickers and grip tape.

All along the back and sides of the shop, Mike had placed each of the decks that he had for sale. There were almost 450 decks when fully stocked and today looked pretty close to being full.

In between the counters and walls there were racks of clothing on display: t-shirts, hoodies, plain sweatshirts, jackets, pants and shorts. Mike carried all the national brand names including Spitfire, Ocean Pacific, Element, Flameboy, Girl and Hook-ups.

Lots of posters from the different skateboarding manufacturers hung from the ceiling. Ben loved those posters and each time Mike got some new ones, Ben would take down the old ones and give them to his friends. Each of them had several in their rooms. Mike could have sold them because everyone wanted to buy the posters but he knew how much they meant to Ben and his friends.

There were other racks that Mike had setup to sell magazines, sunglasses, watches, wallets, videos and miscellaneous stuff.

The one part of the store that everyone went to sooner or later was the wooden half-pipe cage at the back of the store. The half-pipe cage was a typical six-foot high wooden half-pipe that was 35 feet in length. Mike had wrapped wire mesh around the entire half-pipe to prevent anyone from coming out by accident. He also installed a lot of padding on the mesh so no one would get hurt. Many, many inexperienced riders tried a shot in the half-pipe. The padding got a regular workout.

Riders were always excited about the boards they bought here because they could try a board on the half-pipe before they put out the cash. Putting a half-pipe right in the store so customers could try out something before they bought was an idea that was common in the West Coast but was something not typical on the East Coast.

The half-pipe, and the fact that Mike was a fair and knowledgeable businessman, made Boardzone the place to go for skateboarding gear for the last two years. Mike had seen steadily increasing sales each month, until the last two months when sales dropped right off for no apparent reason.

When the group walked in, they made such a racket that Mike looked up from the skateboard he was working on. He immediately smiled to see his favorite group of friends.

"Well, well, well!" said Mike. "Here comes trouble with a capital T."

Billy smiled at Mike. Mike always said that.

"Hey Mike!" said Jim. "How's it goin?"

"Not bad," Mike lied. Julie was wiping down the counters and looked up when Mike responded.

"Hey Julie!" said Ben.

"Hi Ben! Are you planning on being in here early on Saturday? Mike is holding a special sale to try and bring some customers back. We need you here by 8:00 a.m. sharp."

"I sure will be!" Ben said enthusiastically.

"Mike, can we go sit in the cage and have a talk with you?" Jim asked.

When the cage was not in use, it was a good place to sit and talk. There weren't many other places in the store to sit down and Mike couldn't leave the store. It was quiet and Mike agreed.

23

"Julie, I'll be in the cage with these rodents for a few minutes. If you need me, just holler," said Mike.

"Will do!" said Julie as she went back to cleaning some fresh handprints on her glass.

Everyone went into the cage and Scott closed the door carefully. He would rather have been in the cage alone on his board but he knew this discussion was important and put his own personal thoughts out of his mind.

Ben started. "Mike, I overheard you and Dad talking last night about the lack of sales over the last couple of months and we all want to help. I hope you aren't mad that I was eavesdropping on your conversation."

Mike smiled, "I'm not mad Ben. I appreciate the fact that you guys are worried and want to help. I am worried a bit too. I'm not sure why sales have dropped off but I need to find out soon."

"Maybe that is where we can help you, Mike," said Jim.

"We could try to figure out where people are buying their equipment?" suggested Scott.

"I'm not aware of any new skate shop that has opened up within 100 miles of here," said Mike. "At first I thought I had a new competitor who was taking my customers but I checked and there are no new stores open."

Billy had been quiet but finally spoke up. "Mike, yesterday when I was at L&J's convenience store getting some milk for dinner, I saw two friends of mine, Bradley Horton and Cody Smith. Bradley had a new World Industries complete. He said he got it a few days ago. So you are at least selling some boards."

Mike had a strange look on his face. "I didn't sell Bradley a new board."

Mike went on, "He was in a week ago looking at a new World Industries board and said he was saving up to buy it but he only had half of the money saved so far."

"I wonder how he got it?" piped up Christyn.

"And I wonder where he got it?" demanded Mike.

"You don't suppose that he…no, Bradley wouldn't have done that," said Mike.

Mike walked over to the wall where the World Industries decks were on display. Everything seemed in order.

He yelled, "Julie, can you do me a favor and tell me how many World Industries decks we should have in stock?"

"Sure hon, just a second," said Julie.

She put down her cloth and grabbed a binder. She opened up the binder and quickly located the World Industries inventory totals.

"We should have 18 decks on-hand," she said.

"Thanks sweetie," said Mike.

Mike counted them out loud. "Six, twelve, fifteen, sixteen, seventeen, eighteen. Yup, they're all here."

"Well at least I know it wasn't stolen from the shop," Mike said, breathing a sigh of relief.

"That is kind of good news and bad news at the same time," responded Christyn.

"Yes, it is," said Mike.

"I'm really at a loss here. Any help you guys can give me would be greatly appreciated," pleaded Mike. "If we don't find out quickly what's going on, I won't be able to hold the Boardzone Competition that I planned for July 31 and I certainly won't be able to afford the $1,000 prize money."

Julie came over and said, "If we don't find out what's going on quickly, we may not have enough money to continue to pay the rent on the shop and that means we would have to close the doors forever."

Everyone looked over at Julie. This was serious!

"You can count on us!" said Ben and Jim at the same time.

Christyn rolled her eyes. "Would you two stop doing that!!"

Billy Gets a Lead

The group felt like they were on a mission. They reassured Mike that they would begin their checking right away. As they left the store, Jim looked back at Mike and noticed that Mike actually looked happier. Jim knew that everything Mike had worked so hard to build was at stake and having help was making it easier on him.

When they got outside, Ben was the first to speak. "OK, I have a plan."

"Let's go over to L&J's and grab a hot dog and drink and I will tell you what I think we should do."

They crossed the road and went down a block to L&J's convenience store. It was a typical convenience store that sold everything a kid could ever want. Mr. Asad who ran the store was very cool. He would always give the kids free chew candies and gum. He worked the store with his two sons, Mohammed and Mubarak, and his wife, Fasal. One of them was always working at the store. It was open 24 hours a day, seven days a week.

Mr. Asad had lots of light in his store and had put in video cameras to help keep his family safe. Everyone knew Mr. Asad and his family and they also knew they were kind and fair.

When they walked into the store, Mr. Asad and Mohammed were working. Mr. Asad was counting lottery tickets behind the counter and Mohammed was cleaning out one of their six slush drink machines. Mohammed had once quietly confided to Ben that he hated that part of the job. Everything was sticky and he often went home smelling like one of the fruit flavors of the day. He especially hated blueberry and water-melon.

Mohammed was a good son and never complained to his parents. When he finished high school in June, he said he would gladly pass on college so that he could stay and help out his mother and father.

Mubarak couldn't have been more opposite to Mohammed. Mubarak was lazy and didn't like to work at the store. He would often get Mohammed to take his shift at the store so that he could go out with his friends. Mubarak was one year older than Mohammed and used that as a reason to bully Mohammed, who would never say anything against his older brother to his parents.

Mohammed thought the world of his older brother and even though he had to work harder to come up with a cover story for the both of them on many occasions, he never got angry with Mubarak.

Mubarak seemed so successful. Even though he didn't work much, Mubarak always had lots of money in his wallet. Mubarak was always buying things and he had lots of friends hanging around him. He would drive up and down the streets in what seemed like a different shiny sports car each month. Mohammed always dreamed of being successful like his brother. Mohammed wondered if maybe Mubarak had a second job.

Mohammed acknowledged the group when they came in. "Good day Ben," said Mohammed in his typically happy tone. What are you all looking for today? Something cold on this hot day?"

"Yes, Mohammed. We are here to grab a hot dog and drink. How are the dogs looking today?" asked Ben.

"Fresh and tasty as always," said Mr. Asad still counting the tickets. "When was the last time we ever sold you an old hot dog?" Mr. Asad laughed.

"OK then Mr. Asad, make it two dogs and heavy on the mustard!" called Ben.

"I'll take one as well!" said Jim.

Billy only had $2 and asked Jim to loan him some money. Jim had just received his allowance so covered his brother.

"Make that another dog for Billy, Mr. Asad."

"Wait a second guys, I can't keep up!" groaned Mr. Asad.

"How can you guys eat that stuff? Do you know what's in a hot dog?" wondered Christyn out loud.

"Miss Christyn, these are all-beef hot dogs, nothing but the finest meat available," responded Mr. Asad.

"All-beef can mean a whole bunch of things!" exclaimed Christyn.

"I'm going to stick with this healthy tossed salad. Do you have any ranch dressing?" asked Christyn.

Mohammed answered, "All the dressings are in the last container next to the pickles…and I don't know how they eat those hot dogs either. Give me a veggie dog any day!" Christyn and Mohammed laughed.

The other kids ignored them and they added gallons of ketchup and relish to their food.

Scott, of course, was not eating a hot dog or a salad. He was busy loading up on Twinkies.

"How did he ever get to be so tall eating that junk!" thought Ben.

"Hey, Scott!" Ben bellowed. "Have you ever read the label on one of those things?"

Scott, who had just finished paying Mr. Asad, ignored the comments from Ben and hungrily ripped open the package. He slid half a package into his mouth in one large bite and turned to face Ben. In a semi-muffled voice Scott said, "Maybe you had better not look – it's not for the faint of heart!" With that he stuffed the other half of the package into his mouth at the same time.

Ben thought it was disgusting but you had to admire someone who could jam so much cake into his mouth at one time without dropping a crumb.

The group paid for their food and one by one left the store to sit out on the front step. Billy was the last to leave because he was having trouble opening those little packages of ketchup. Mohammed came by and asked if he needed help. Seeing the group starting to leave, Billy gratefully accepted. As he watched Mohammed open the ketchup he mentioned they were on a mission to help save Mike's store.

29

"Mike is cool. Helping him is a good thing," replied Mohammed. "What is it that you are going to do to help him?"

"I dunno yet. We are going to work out our plan outside," replied Billy. "Say, Mohammed. The other day when I was in here buying milk for my mom, do you remember seeing Bradley Horton about the same time?"

"Why yes, Billy. I saw him in here twice that day. The first time I saw him was when I started my shift. When I came into the shop, Bradley was with Devin Snively and my brother Mubarak. They were talking about some sort of deal. Bradley gave Devin some money and left a few minutes later carrying a garbage bag," recounted Mohammed.

"Did you see what was in the garbage bag?" Billy asked.

"No. It was not my business to ask. But later in the day, I saw Bradley again in the store. You came in around the same time. Bradley was asking for Mubarak but I told him that Mubarak was not there. Bradley told me he had a new World Industries skateboard and that it was going to give him the winning edge when he entered the 2nd Annual Boardzone Competition."

"Mr. Billy, he let me hold his new skateboard but something didn't seem right. I see a lot of skateboards each day and while I am not an expert, the board seemed different for some reason."

Billy was really excited. Finally, there was some real information to share with the group. He grabbed the hot dog and headed for the exit. Over his shoulder he yelled, "Thanks Mohammed, you've been a great help."

Mohammed replied, "It was nothing, Mr. Billy. Those little packages can be quite hard to open."

"Guys! Guys! Guess what I found out!" exclaimed Billy.

"Let me guess, you finally realize that slush is not a food group?" joked Ben.

Billy thought about that for a second and then said "No, I was talking to Mohammed about Bradley Horton."

"What did he say?" asked Jim excitedly.

"Mohammed said that Bradley was in the store on the same day I was there getting milk."

"Go on…" Ben said impatiently.

"Well, apparently Bradley was talking with Devin and Mubarak about some deal and Bradley gave Devin some money and Mubarak gave Bradley a garbage bag with something secret inside."

"Hmm…interesting. Anything else?" asked Christyn.

"Yes!" said Billy, trying to munch down bites of hot dog between sentences. "Later in the day, Bradley came back looking for Mubarak and was showing off his new skateboard to Mohammed and he said that something about the board seemed odd," said Billy.

"Did he say what seemed odd?" questioned Scott.

"He didn't know exactly what seemed out of place, but there was something," said Billy as he polished off the last of his dog.

Jim spoke urgently in a loud voice. "I think it is time we paid a little visit to our friend Bradley Horton. I have some questions about this new skateboard of his!"

The group gathered up their garbage and put it in the large container that Mr. Asad had placed outside the store. Mr. Asad was watching the kids put away their garbage. "If only all the kids were so careful to clean up after themselves," pondered Mr. Asad, noticing a lot of garbage scattered around his parking lot. No matter how many times he cleaned that lot, more garbage showed up each day from careless customers.

The kids jumped on their boards and headed towards Bradley's house. It was almost two miles away. Mr. Asad was not the only pair of eyes watching them. In a dark blue 5.0 liter Mustang sports car parked beside the dumpster at the side of the store, two people had been watching the kids every move. The driver was smoking a cigarette and blowing smoke out his nose. A cloud of bluish gray tobacco smoke hung in the air. The passenger was uncomfortable and breathing in the smoke made him want to cough.

They had been listening to the kids' conversation. The passenger asked nervously "What are we going to do?"

The driver, who was older, snarled, "Quiet. Get Bradley on my cell phone, NOW!" The passenger, who was shaking, quickly dialed a number.

Bradley Gets a Visit

The group of kids left the convenience store, formed a single file line and boarded down Canyon Drive past Mike's store and along Cliff Road. Cliff Road was a narrow road that ran along the top of Bishop's Hill and ended up cris-crossing the hill four times as it made its way to the bottom. The road was perfect for getting good speed on a skateboard.

The only problem was cars. Jim's mom and dad did not like the idea of Jim racing down the hill but they knew he always wore his helmet and pads when he did. The only time they would let Billy go on the hill is when Jim was with him and the others made sure there were no cars coming.

Cliff Road was about two miles long and descended vertically down Bishop's Hill about 340 feet. It was such a great hill for cruising. The group ripped down Bishop's Hill without encountering one car. This was the same place that Mike had used for the 1st Annual Boardzone Competition last year.

As Ben and Jim passed the place where the finish line had been, they looked at each other and smiled. "Just you wait, Ben! I'll be coming after you this year," laughed Jim.

"Bring it on!" chuckled Ben. "The champ is ready to take on all challengers!"

They all continued past Bishop's Hill onto Riverglen Street. Bradley lived on Lindenway Place that was at the end of Riverglen Street. It was a nice street with new blacktop. It was so smooth to board on. Scott was ollie-ing over every manhole cover and Christyn was trying to do heel-flips, but not with much success.

Ben yelled over to her, "Make sure your left foot is further back on the board, before you start the trick. It'll be easier."

"Thanks Ben!" Christyn yelled and immediately completed the trick.

"Wuh hoo!" yelped Christyn. "Did you guys see that?!!!"

"See what?" Scott and Billy responded, knowing that would make Christyn mad.

"She was getting pretty good. She will be one of my biggest competitors in the Boardzone Competition this year," Jim thought with some surprise.

As they reached the end of Riverglen Street they turned right and headed up one block to Bradley's house. As they approached the house, Ben and Jim were in the lead with Scott and Christyn back about 50 feet. Billy was another 25 feet behind Christyn trying to keep up.

Ben was pretty sure he remembered which house was Bradley's. He was looking for a yellow house with blue trim windows. A few houses away he could see a yellow house. As he turned to indicate to the others which house it was, a blue Mustang roared to life and jumped forward, squealing its tires.

The sudden noise caused Ben's heart to race. Jim shot to the left to get out of the way of the car. Ben turned back to see the car bearing down on him and the only thing he could do was fling his body to the right. He crashed onto a lawn and narrowly missed a fire hydrant. His skate-board continued straight and went right under the car in between the front wheels and out the back. Luckily the car did not hit it.

The car had tinted windows so Christyn and Scott could not see who was driving. It all happened so fast that no one thought to remember the license plate number.

Jim turned around to see Billy, Christyn and Scott standing safely by the curb. He was so relieved.

"Is everyone alright?" asked Jim.

"OK, here," said Scott.

"I'm fine," said Christyn.

"I'm good!" said Billy excitedly. "What about you, Ben, are you OK?"

"Yah. What an idiot driver that guy was! I wonder why he was in such a hurry?" said Ben.

"I think it was a woman driver!" said Jim.

"Ha Ha Ha!" said Christyn. "Based on the noise, speed and total lack of regard for safety, my money is on a male driver," Christyn retorted.

Both Jim and Ben knew she was probably right.

They picked up their boards and crossed the street to Bradley's house. He lived at number 146 Lindenway Place. It was a small house but well kept. There was an older car in the driveway but it was clean and shiny.

As Ben rang the doorbell, Jim lingered a moment by the sidewalk in front of Bradley's house. He was looking at something in the street.

Christyn came up to him, "What is it Jim?"

"Look at these tire marks, Christyn. They start right in front of Bradley's house," said Jim.

"That means the person in the car may have been visiting the Bradley house before we arrived!" exclaimed Christyn.

"This day is getting more interesting by the minute. Let's go have a word with our friend Bradley," said Jim.

"Lead the way!" said Christyn.

Ben rang the doorbell of the Bradley house and the front door opened. Jim and Christyn walked up to the bottom of the stairs. Only Ben was at the top of the stairs. Billy and Scott stayed back on the sidewalk still looking up and down the street for other cars.

Bradley Horton looked very shocked to see Ben standing on his front step. Ben noticed through the glass in the door that Bradley had a scared look on his face even before he recognized Ben.

"Hello Bradley!" Ben said in a challenging voice. "We've come to have a talk with you."

"I can't talk right now!" responded Bradley in a quiet voice.

"Who's there now, Brad?" Bradley's mother came to the hall. Bradley looked really scared now.

"Are you going to invite your friends in?" his mom asked in a pleasant voice.

Mrs. Bradley was a nice lady. She often helped at the school when they needed a substitute teacher. She was also a heck of a good cook and won the baking contest each year at the State Fair. Her Chocolate Chunk cookies were killer.

Bradley didn't seem happy with the prospect of having Ben and his friends come into the house.

"We were just going outside, Mom. Back in a little while," said Bradley as he slipped on his runners and headed for the door.

"Don't forget your new skateboard!" said Ben.

Bradley looked up in horror. Bradley's mom stepped forward, "Sorry dear, Bradley hasn't saved up enough money to get a new skateboard yet. He keeps spending his allowance on candy instead."

Bradley looked like he was going to die. He was white as a sheet and had a pained look on his face like it was hard to breathe.

Once outside Bradley gulped several deep breaths of fresh air. He walked over to the picnic table they had in their front yard and sat down.

Jim was the first to speak. "Spill it Bradley! Tell us about the skateboard."

Bradley said, "I don't know what you are talking about."

"Don't lie Bradley, we know something is going on," said Ben, who had placed his face only a couple of inches from Bradley's ear.

Bradley was looking scared again. Christyn felt sorry for Bradley. He was normally a shy, quiet kid who never got into trouble. He obviously didn't do well when confronted by an angry group.

Christyn spoke up, "Guys, can you back off and let me have a word with Bradley?"

Ben and Jim knew that Bradley didn't stand a chance with Christyn. She was tough and wouldn't take lies from anyone. Bradley was going to sing like a canary in a few seconds all courtesy of a tongue-lashing from Christyn.

Jim, Ben, Scott and Billy all winced, waiting for the yelling to start but Christyn surprised them all. In a quiet and controlled voice, Christyn began to ask Bradley a few questions.

"Bradley, we have a problem and we're trying to find a solution. We think you can give us some help. Are you willing to try?"

Bradley was caught off guard but more than willing to talk to Christyn who was being so nice compared to the others. Bradley began to relax a bit.

"Sure, I will do my best," stammered Bradley. "What do you want?"

"Tell us about your new World Industries skateboard," Christyn said casually, almost as if she didn't care about his answer.

Bradley wasn't sure what to do. He looked puzzled and concerned at the same time. Bradley spoke.

"W…W…World Industries? I-uh don't have a World Industries board." Bradley was looking more confident.

Christyn spoke again, "Oh, maybe I have that wrong."

"Y-Yes…I think you do!" said Bradley with a bit of an attitude building in his voice.

Christyn smiled her sweetest smile. Jim was thoroughly confused at the way his friend was acting. Had she lost it?

"Bradley dear, tell me something…" she let that thought hang out there for a few seconds before exploding: "If you don't come clean about this World Industries board right now, I'm going to drag you back in to your mom and you can explain to her about the board, Mubarak and your friends in the sports car that just tried to run us down!"

Jim sighed with relief to himself, "Well, Christyn's back!"

You could practically hear Bradley's teeth begin to chatter at the prospect of explaining to his mom about the new skateboard and those people who had just visited the house.

Christyn didn't like coming down so hard on someone like Bradley but they needed answers fast and they didn't have time to fool around.

Bradley began to toss out information like an active volcano spewing lava. He began the whole story from the beginning and didn't stop until he gave them every last detail. It was like he was waiting to tell someone the story so he could feel better.

He had been in Mike's shop looking at a World Industries board that he was saving up for. When he left the shop, a guy in the parking lot of L&J's asked him if he was looking to buy a new board. Bradley had never seen this guy before and was a little suspicious of him. When the guy started to talk about skateboarding tricks, Bradley thought he could be one of Mike's friends.

Bradley told the guy he was saving to buy a new World Industries board. The guy said he had a friend at the factory that could get him any complete he wanted at half the regular price. A complete is the name for a complete skateboard that consists of a deck, trucks and wheels.

Bradley couldn't believe his luck. He had only been able to save just over half of the money needed to buy the board at Mike's shop. Now he had enough to buy from this guy and he would be able to use the new board in the upcoming Boardzone Competition.

Bradley asked the guy, "Where is your friend's shop?"

The guy had just laughed at Bradley and said that his friend didn't have a shop. That is part of the reason he was able to sell new boards for so little money. The guy told Bradley to meet him at the convenience store tomorrow at noon and to bring $60 cash for the complete.

"What happened next?" said Jim.

Bradley went on, "I went home and put the money in my wallet. The next day I came back to the store just before noon. At the side of the store, next to the dumpster, I could see the guy I was talking to the day before. He was standing at the back of a blue mini-van with Mubarak and a kid from Grade 6 named Ryan Thornwell. The man was handing a skateboard deck to Ryan and slipping some money into his shirt pocket.

As I approached the man, Mubarak walked away towards the front of the store. The man looked strange. He was looking around from left to right.

"Hey, kid! You got the money? I got your board," he called.

Bradley was nervous but in an excited way. He reached into his pocket and pulled out the wrinkled bills. The twenty he received on his birthday from his grandfather still had the writing on it:

"To Bradley,

We're proud of you.

Love Grandpa and Gramma"

Bradley didn't feel so proud for some reason but wanted that skateboard so badly. The man stuck his cigarette in his teeth and reached into the van. He pulled out a board and handed it to Bradley. Bradley quickly surveyed the board and saw that it was indeed the same World Industries board that he had been eyeing in Mike's store.

Bradley handed the money over to the guy who quickly stuffed it into his shirt pocket.

"Thanks, kid. Enjoy the board."

With that he slammed the van door shut and walked around to the driver's door. Bradley was still admiring his new board when he remembered to ask about a warranty. Bradley rounded the corner of the van as the guy started the engine with a roar.

"Excuse me, sir. If I have a problem with this board, who do I call?"

Bradley wasn't sure if the guy heard him or not over the blare of music coming from the CD player. He always hated hard rock and this guy was listening to it...loud.

The only thing the guy did was laugh and gun the mini-van out of the parking lot in a cloud of dust and gravel.

Coughing, Bradley looked at his new board. Bradley thought to himself, "I guess the guy didn't hear me. At least I got the board I wanted."

On the way home, Bradley soon began to realize that his parents were going to wonder where he got the board and where his money had gone. Bradley didn't like to lie and had a sickening feeling in his stomach about what he had done.

Christyn spoke next back in her soothing calm voice. Bradley was not sure she would stay that way but he certainly liked it when people weren't yelling at him.

"Bradley, it's OK. You made a mistake and no one is mad at you. Maybe you can help us out," Christyn said.

"As long as my parents don't find out," whined Bradley.

Jim interjected, "Bradley, you've done something stupid by buying a skateboard from a stranger in a van. That guy could have robbed you, kidnapped you or worse."

"Bradley, you seem like a nice person who really does feel sorry for having done this. Telling your parents the truth is going to be hard but it will make you feel better in the end and they can maybe even help you get your money back," said Ben.

"I guess you're right. I haven't been able to sleep well at all since I brought the board home," confided Bradley.

"Where is the board, Brad?" asked Ben. "We'd like to see it."

"I hid it in the attic of the garage. I'll go and get it," said Bradley.

While Jim and Ben waited for Bradley to return from the back of his house, Scott and Billy got into a separate discussion of their own.

Christyn was listening to their conversation and was shaking her head in disbelief.

"Billy, if you take a dog and wag its tail with your hand, does the dog get happier?" Scott asked Billy. Billy was thinking about it. Christyn couldn't believe her ears.

"And these two represent the future of Exton! Oh my god," Christyn murmured to herself.

Bradley came back around the corner carrying a skateboard. The group ran over to Bradley. At first glance it looked like a World Industries complete. The deck appeared normal. The trucks looked like Grind Kings and the wheels were also from World Industries.

Ben asked to get a close look at the board. Bradley handed the board to Ben and upon taking the board in his hands, Ben immediately got a quizzical expression on his face.

Christyn asked "What's wrong, Ben?"

Ben replied, "This skateboard is so light. I have been putting completes on display for the past year and I know how much a World Industries complete weighs. This board set is way too light."

Jim asked to see the complete. He carried it over to the sidewalk and placed it on the ground. He jumped on it and jumped off. He picked it up, turned it over and said "Hmmm..."

He then placed it on the ground again and jumped on it again. Then he did a kick-flip and landed on it hard. He picked up the board one more time, examined it and then placed it back on the ground.

He then looked up and down the street and made sure no cars were coming. He then vaulted off the edge of the sidewalk onto the blacktop with a bang and raced up the street about 100 yards. He then came to a stop by hitting the curb. Then he turned around and came back to the group.

He also had a puzzled look on his face. Ben asked him what he was thinking.

"What did you notice?" said Ben.

"You're right about the weight, Ben. I did a couple of hard jumps on it to see how it handled my weight. I noticed it starting to form little cracks after only two jumps," said Jim.

"Anything else?" said Billy.

"Yah, when I was racing along the blacktop, the bearings were not smooth at all. It was like they were rubbing together. When I hit the curb I also noticed chips fly off the board. That should never happen to a brand new board," said Jim.

37

"And look at the World Industries logo. Those aren't the right colors," Billy said, excited to be of help.

"Are you thinking what I'm thinking?" said Ben.

"Are you thinking about chocolate cake?" said Scott.

"No, I think this is a counterfeit complete!" said an exasperated Ben.

"Counterfeit? Do you mean fake?" said Billy.

"Yes," said Jim. "Bradley has been taken by a guy selling bogus boards."

"But the board says World Industries," protested Billy. "Doesn't that mean it came from the World Industries factory?"

"Not always, Billy," said Ben.

"Every year, people open up factories to make goods that look and feel like regular name brand items but they aren't. They put stickers and labels on the items so people will think they are the regular name brand items," said Ben.

38

"What is wrong with that?" said Billy. "If they give you a good deal on it, who gets hurt?"

"The company that makes the real item gets hurt. People buy the fake items sometimes not knowing it is counterfeit. The fake is never made to the same high quality as the original and when the fake breaks, it gives the original company a bad name. Also when the fake breaks, people get hurt in accidents," said Ben.

"Take a look at this board, for example. Not only was it built with cheap materials but after just a couple of moves it is already starting to come apart," said Scott.

"Billy, how would you like to be coming down Bishop's Hill on this board when the trucks decide to split in two?" said Christyn.

Billy shuddered a little thinking about that. "We have to tell someone and stop this from happening!"

"You are right Billy. I know just the person we should go and see," announced Jim.

"Uncle Frank!" said Ben and Jim. They looked at each other and smiled. Christyn was really getting tired of them doing that.

Uncle Frank was Jim's uncle and he lived on Peterson Avenue. Uncle Frank was a former Philadelphia police detective. He had moved back to Exton to get away from the hustle and bustle of big city life after he retired two years ago.

Uncle Frank sometimes helped out the local police when they needed help in solving local crimes. Exton was a pretty safe place and not many big crimes occurred. This was different and Jim knew that his uncle would take a special interest in this case.

They asked Bradley if they could take the board with them and Bradley readily agreed. He wasn't too keen on having it around the house any longer. He also knew that he was going to have to tell his parents about spending the money foolishly. He wasn't looking forward to that.

The group grabbed their boards and headed back down Lindenway Place towards Bishop's Hill. Now they would have to go back up the hill on foot. As luck would have it, Randy Carver was driving by and offered the kids a lift. Randy owned a local gas station and everyone could fit into his Ford F-150 Extended Cab pick-up truck.

"Thanks Mr. Carver! You are a life-saver," Jim said enthusiastically.

"Well, Bishop's is a lot of fun to come down but not as much fun to walk up," said the kindly Mr. Carver.

It only took a few minutes to make it to the top of the hill. Ben didn't bother to explain what was going on to Mr. Carver. He was going to save the story for Uncle Frank.

At the top of the hill, Mr. Carver let them off as he was going in a different direction than Uncle Frank's house.

"Thanks Mr. Carver," they all said in unison.

As they watched Mr. Carver drive away, Ben yelled, "Let's go." One by one they hopped on their boards and zoomed off towards Peterson Avenue.

It would take another 10 minutes to reach Peterson Ave and Scott was getting tired and hungry. They passed Charlie's Chicken Barrel and the smell of fried chicken made their mouths water. It was just past lunchtime so they decided to grab a bite to eat.

Christyn offered to use her $20 to buy the group some chicken and Coke.

"How come you can't be nice like Christyn?" Ben joked to Jim.

After the group had eaten their fill of chicken, Billy and Scott were trying to see who could burp the longest.

"What's your record, Billy?" quizzed Scott.

"I can make it all the way to L," Billy announced proudly.

"L...that's kids stuff," laughed Scott. "I can make it to Z and start again."

Billy was thoroughly impressed with that. "Show me, Scott!" Billy demanded.

Christyn moved out of the way. "I don't want to be around when his chicken reappears," she said as she backed away from Scott.

Scott took a final long gulp of his large Coke, placed the cup on the outdoor patio table and began.

"Braaaaaaaaaaaaaaaaaaaap!!!!" bellowed Scott. People in cars driving by turned quickly to see what happened. In the distance a car alarm went off.

Even Ben turned around. "That was truly one of your best," said Ben.

"That's nothing," said Scott. "Fried chicken always gives me gas. Wait'll later and I'll give you a real treat."

Billy was already looking forward to the show later. "When it came to cool stuff like that, Scott was the best," thought Billy.

Christyn was thoroughly disgusted with Scott. "Note to self," she said out loud. "Do not feed these guys any more greasy food!"

"We had better get going," Jim said. "Put away your stuff."

They put away their used plates and wrappers and continued on to the house of Jim's Uncle Frank. Peterson Avenue was about four blocks away. They had to take a right on Wellington Crescent and go about two blocks before taking a left at Peterson Avenue

40

"Say Jim, did you ask Bradley about the blue car that almost hit us?" asked Ben.

"That's right!" exclaimed Jim. "In all the excitement, I forgot to ask Bradley if he had any visitors before us. Remind me tomorrow to talk to Bradley about that."

1ˢᵗ Boardzone Competition

Wellington Crescent was the oldest street in Exton. It ran along the river and anybody with money lived on this street. The homes there were huge and each yard was gigantic compared to most other neighborhoods.

As they were boarding down Wellington Crescent they passed a large house hidden behind some trees and a large stone fence. The fence had to be ten feet high. On the top they could see chunks of broken glass sticking straight up that were embedded right into the stone. No one would try climbing over that.

"That's a good way to discourage visitors," pondered Ben. He then noticed a series of video cameras setup along the wall and by the long driveway. There was a massive iron gate that prevented anyone from driving onto the property and as they went past the driveway they could just make out a blue car parked by the house.

"Isn't that Devin Snively's house?" Christyn asked no one in particular.

"Yup! His mom came from a family who owned a bunch of steel mills in Pennsylvania. They have more money than they know what to do with!" said Jim.

"Wouldn't that be a nice problem to have," said Scott.

"Then we could help out Mike!" said Billy.

"Yes we could," said Ben. "But we don't have much money so we have to help Mike the old fashioned way, using our brains. We're almost there."

Devin was watching the kids go by them from the balcony in his room. Devin was the only one home that day. His parents were out somewhere doing something without him and he was alone again. He felt envious of those kids. "Where are they off to in such a hurry?" he wondered to himself. "It would be cool if they stopped by to see if I wanted to join them. I could show them the new Blind complete I got straight from my new friend who has a contact at the factory."

The group continued on down the street and out of sight. No one was going to stop at Devin's house that day to ask Devin to hang with them.

Jim was getting tired of carrying the extra skateboard and asked Ben to hold onto it for the remaining few blocks. Ben had no problem assisting his friend.

"Hey Jim, want to stop in and see if Devin can come out and board with us?" laughed Scott.

Jim choked, "Not likely! Anyone who just wants to show off what they have and is not interested in anyone else is not someone I want to hang out with."

"He's a cheater too!" chimed Billy. "Don't forget what happened at last year's Boardzone Competition."

That thought had never left Jim's mind. He was going to make sure that he beat Devin this year, fair and square.

42

* * * *

There were 65 competitors that day, all of them trying to win the $1,000 first prize. The prize went to the skateboarder who could come down the hill the quickest while completing three different tricks along the way. Each rider got points for how fast they came down the hill and they also got bonus points for each of the tricks they did. The better the trick, the more points they could add to their score. They could do up to three bonus tricks along the way but they could only do the tricks where a race judge was positioned. The race judge watched the trick as the skater zoomed by and decided how many points to give to the rider. Each judge had a list of tricks and how many points it was worth. An incomplete trick was not worth any points so a racer had to be careful which tricks they attempted. Doing tricks meant slowing down and some riders took the option of not doing any tricks so they could get a faster time. That was OK to do.

For the 1st Annual Boardzone Competition, the three race judges were Julie, Mike and Mohammed. Mike was the first race judge and was sitting on a lawn chair about half way down the course. Julie was the next judge and she was 400 yards further down the course from Mike. Julie was also on a lawn chair and had rigged up a large beach umbrella to protect her from the hot sun that day. Mohammed was the third and final race judge and he was positioned near the bottom of the course. He would also make sure that each boarder had an accurate finish time.

Riders started the race on a raised ramp. There was room for four racers to start side by side. Each racer had a lane. The ramp gave each racer a good burst of speed to start the race.

Jim and Ben had made it to the final after Scott and Christyn had wiped out in the semis. Jim had been assigned the first starting position. Jim had not yet been assigned that position and was unfamiliar with how to handle the first curve from that lane. In each of the qualifying races, Jim had started in Lane 3 or 4 and had figured out which line to take on that important first corner.

Devin Snively had been given starting Lane 2. Jim did not like Devin Snively at all. Devin had always been a mean kid. His parents had a lot of money and gave him everything he wanted. Devin spent all his time making fun of other people and showing off new things his parents had bought him.

Devin didn't have many friends and was very hard to talk to because he only wanted to talk about how wonderful he was. Jim felt sorry for Devin. Jim was glad that he had good friends to hang around with like Ben, Christyn, Scott and Billy.

While there was no video evidence, witnesses say that Devin won the final two qualifying races by pushing the leading rider off their boards.

Ray Wilson was in the third starting position. Ray was an all right guy. He was 13 years old and was always tinkering with something in his dad's workshop in their garage. Ray was pretty good on a skateboard. He could go faster than most people but his tricks were not as good as his speed.

Ben was in the fourth starting position. He knew that Jim and Ray were his biggest competition. Jim was going to be hard to beat because his tricks were pretty solid. Ben knew that if he could make good speed he could stay ahead of Jim and Ray, and, as long as his tricks worked perfectly, he might have a chance.

As the four riders lined up at the starting gate, Devin was already planning to reduce the competition. He had taken a small piece of duct tape and had rolled it into a small sticky ball about the diameter of a quarter. As the starter was counting down from 5 to 1, Devin flicked the tape ball and it landed just under the nose of Jim's board.

When the starter fired the pistol to begin the race, the four boarders began to race down the raised starting platform towards the hill. Before Jim could even begin to get going, he realized that something was horribly wrong. Just as he was trying to place his foot onto his board, the tape ball grabbed the front wheel and prevented it from moving. In what Jim only remembered as slow motion, he heard a loud scraping noise as his wheel slid down the ramp without turning. Next Jim remembered his body flying forward and landing on the ramp with a painful thump.

Everyone saw Jim's head hit the ramp and watched his body slide down to the bottom. As Jim crashed down onto the ramp, Jim's arm flew to the side and almost upset Devin who was in the next lane. Devin didn't

43

look angry, however there was a little smile on his thin lips.

"One down, two to go!" snickered Devin.

Jim's dad and Christyn came rushing up to Jim who was a crumpled heap at the bottom of the ramp. The other three skateboarders were now a distant blur.

"C'mon buddy!" cried Jim's dad. "Get back on your board and try to catch up!" he implored.

Jim was a little groggy after whacking his head on the ramp. Jim was thinking, "Thank goodness I always wear my helmet."

"What happened?" exclaimed Christyn. "I've never seen you crash in the starting gate!"

"I don't know!" said Jim. "I think I hit a rock or something. My wheel felt like it was stuck on something."

44

"A rock on a raised starting platform? That doesn't make sense," said Christyn.

It didn't make sense to Jim either. He picked himself up and dusted off his pants and shirt. In the distance he could hear some cheering. The racers were well down the course now.

As he picked up his board to head towards the finish line, he finally saw it. "What is that?" Jim said out loud in a puzzled voice.

"What is what?" responded Christyn.

Jim reached down and pulled something gray and sticky from his right front wheel.

"I think I know what happened," Jim said to himself.

"What did you find?" asked Christyn, impatiently this time.

"A rat named Devin!" Jim hissed.

The race was almost over. Ray was in the lead but Ben and Devin were close behind. Ben had completed all three of the required tricks so far – a kick-flip, a 360-flip and a heel-flip. Ray had only been able to land two of the three tricks so Ben might be able to win on points if he could just stay close to Ray.

Devin had been having trouble landing his tricks and only had one good one. If he were going to win, both Ray and Ben would have to wipe out. "That can be arranged," Devin thought to himself.

Devin got down into a crouch and even though his board started to wobble a bit, he started to move in behind Ben and Ray.

"Perfect! I'm drafting them," Devin thought.

Ben didn't notice Devin creeping up behind him. Ben was intently watching Ray and could begin to make out the finish line that was approaching in the distance.

"If I can just stay close to Ray, I may just win," thought Ben with a smile.

Ray knew that Ben was right on his back wheels. Ray also knew that his tricks were not so good today. He was guessing that Ben was able to land all of his tricks. Ray knew that he had to win by at least four or five seconds to generate enough points to win.

That momentary lapse in concentration was enough to cause Ray to miss the pebble on the course in his path. Like Jim before him, there was a high-pitched screech as Ray's spinning wheel ground to a halt. The sudden drop in speed of the board caused two things to happen. Ray was launched forward like a space shuttle taking off from Cape Canaveral. The second thing was more curious. With Ray shooting forward, his board shot backwards towards Ben. Ben knew exactly what that screech-ing sound was and had immediately swerved to the right to avoid the same rock. In doing so, Ben had moved out of the way and Ray's skate-board flew backwards right into the path of Devin.

45

The board hit Devin square in the stomach with a tremendous "Whump!" Devin had the wind knocked out of him and his legs turned to Jell-O. He crumpled to the ground and skidded to a halt 100 yards from the finish line. With Ray and Devin both down, Ben cruised to a first place finish. Everyone was cheering; the loudest being Jim, who thought that what happened to Devin was a perfect punishment for his earlier ac-tions at the starting gate. Jim was very happy for his friend Ben.

Devin lay on the ground trying to catch his breath and muttering to him-self, "What happened? My plan was so perfect. How could it go wrong?"

On his way to the finish area to congratulate Ben, Jim walked by Devin who was still lying on the ground. Ben tossed a little sticky, gray ball at him. "I think you dropped something back at the starting gate. Sorry to see you ran into a bit of trouble yourself."

As Jim walked away laughing, Devin was scowling as he tried to free the ball of tape that was now stuck to his hair.

Uncle Frank

Jim forgot about Devin for the moment as Ben turned onto Peterson Avenue and only a few houses up they found Uncle Frank's house. Peterson Avenue was quite different from Wellington Crescent. The homes on Peterson were average in size with small yards. A lot of older people had moved into this area to retire.

Jim wasn't sure if Uncle Frank was 44 or 45; he was the older brother of Jim's dad by five years. He had been a policeman in Philadelphia for 27 years and had retired recently back in Exton. Frank was still a cop to Jim. His whole house was like a museum dedicated to the police. He had pictures, banners, medals and books everywhere showing the history of police in Pennsylvania. Whenever the local paper wanted some background on the police service, they would contact Frank for information. He was always glad to help promote the local law enforcement agencies.

Jim knew that Frank would really be interested in helping with their situation. Frank loved being a detective and was sad he had to retire. The Philadelphia Police Service was going through a tough couple of years and they were forced to reduce the number of cops on the streets, including detectives. Since Frank had been on the force for so long, he was offered early retirement with a full pension.

As the group approached Frank's house, Jim noticed that Frank's car, a 1969 Cadillac Brougham, was not in the driveway. That car was easy to spot a mile away. Frank loved that car more than anything. You could always find Frank on the driveway rubbing some sort of wax product onto that car while listening to the police scanner. Frank liked to hear what was happening on the police frequencies and could even pick up the calls that came from his old precinct in downtown Philly.

"I wonder where he is?" Jim said.

"I'll ring the bell," said Christyn as she did a kick-flip over the curb and onto the sidewalk.

Billy tried the same but his board didn't quite clear the curb. As he flew off his board he caught the toe of his runner on the top edge of the curb. The force caused his leg to fold underneath his body and he was headed for a faceplant. From out of nowhere, Ben was there to reach over and grab Billy by the back of his sweatshirt. Billy stopped suddenly as Ben held him dangling in the air.

Billy gulped, "Thanks Ben!" as he was thinking about the fresh scrapes on his knees that had just been avoided.

"Just remember to slow down a bit when approaching a high curb," explained Ben.

"Nice move," whispered Jim.

"He'll figure how to do it without my help, it'll just take a lot longer!" Ben grinned to his friend.

Jim laughed. In a mocking voice Jim said, "Oh great Ben, could you teach me how to do a board slide?"

"You? Hey, I'm not a miracle worker."

48

At that moment Christyn called back to the guys. "There's no one home. I don't even hear Buster so they must both be out."

Buster was Frank's dog. Buster was a golden Labrador Retriever. Buster was a present when Frank retired. He was the smartest dog Jim had ever known. Frank and Buster would ride around in the Cadillac and Frank would take Buster out for ice cream all the time. Buster loved ice cream. All Frank had to say was "treat" and Buster would run and grab his lead and wait by the front door.

"I bet they are out getting ice cream right now," said Ben. You know how much they both love chocolate sundaes."

"Isn't chocolate bad for dogs?" Christyn asked.

"Yes but Frank always orders two chocolate sundaes but gets them to give Buster just a dish of plain vanilla ice cream. Frank gets the extra chocolate toppings put on his sundae.

"I thought Frank was looking a little beefier the last time I saw him at the church BBQ," said Scott.

Behind them a noise like a train horn erupted and each of them jumped a few inches off the ground. Into the driveway pulled a gleaming old car covered in shiny chrome. A large, balding man with a big grin on his face sat behind the wheel. Next to him, a beautiful yellow dog with his head poked out the passenger window was enjoying the bright sunshine and car ride.

"Hey Uncle Frank!" Jim greeted his favorite uncle.

"Well hello there, J.," Frank said with his booming voice. Frank had called him J. for as long as Jim could remember. Frank was always laughing and today was no exception.

Buster had already bounded out the window and had pounced on Billy. He was pretending that Buster was a vicious attack dog and Buster was playing the part by licking Billy's face.

"Help, help!" Billy laughed between licks. "A vicious attack dog has got me and I can't get him off me."

"Maybe you smell like ice cream?" said Christyn. As soon as Christyn said the words "ice cream" Buster hopped off Billy and raced back to Frank.

"Oh no you don't!" said Frank. "You aren't getting any ice cream yet my furry friend."

"What brings you to Peterson Avenue this fine day, J.? Just checking up on your old Uncle?" he said with a broad grin.

"No, Uncle Frank. We have something serious to discuss with you," Jim said, his eyes narrowing.

"Serious, you say. Hmmm…well this calls for us to go inside and talk. C'mon Buster, lead the way. Everyone, let's go inside and have a seat in the living room. Anyone feel like a Coke or something?"

Christyn glared at Scott. He could feel her eyes burning and piped up, "Do you have any lemonade?"

"I'm sure we can find you something cold to drink," said Uncle Frank.

Each of the kids picked up their board and headed up the stairs towards Frank's front door. Just before they entered the house, they placed their boards against the front of the house. Billy was the last one to come in and put his board against all the others. They promptly slid sideways and fell in a heap. Billy looked around to see if anyone noticed.

"Phew! No one saw," thought Billy.

Billy scrambled inside to join the others. When he got in the house he could see Uncle Frank pouring something into glasses in the kitchen. Christyn and Ben were sitting on the couch and Jim had pulled a dining room chair next to Uncle Frank's favorite recliner chair. Scott was over by the back wall looking at all the police medals and gun replicas.

"Are these real guns?" Scott asked.

Before Jim could answer, Uncle Frank came back into the room carrying a tray of lemonades.

"Those are gun replicas, Scott. They look just like the original gun in every way but they are actually made of wood. They can't fire any bullets."

"Why don't you have the real thing?" asked Scott.

"Scott, there are already too many guns available in this world and I didn't want to add more to the mix. As a policeman, I have seen many bad things that people have done when they got their hands on a gun. I don't want any more guns to get in the wrong hands," explained Frank.

Ben motioned to Jim to start the story.

Jim started, "Uncle Frank, we have come across something very interesting. Could you help us?"

Frank finished a long drink of his lemonade and put the cup down on the table. "Tell me what's on your mind and start from the beginning." He sounded just like a policeman.

Ben leaned forward on the couch, eager for Jim to get started.

"Today we found out that Mike's skate shop is not doing so good. Sales are way down and Mike is in danger of losing the store," Jim explained.

Uncle Frank turned to Ben and said, "That's terrible Ben. I thought Mike was doing well. The last time I went in there to buy a...birthday present for a certain nephew, there was a great crowd of kids spending money in there."

50

Ben continued the story. "He was doing pretty good and had been able to save almost $100,000 towards the new skate park he was planning to build. It was all the extra money he had and he paid that money to the developers to have the land prepared. The next phase for the skate park is to pour the concrete for the ramps. Mike was hoping for a good summer season to raise the rest of the money."

"Sounds like a great plan. So what's the problem?" said a puzzled Uncle Frank.

"Well, Mike was telling us this morning that for the past few weeks, kids have stopped buying boards at his shop. He has only sold a few boards when he would normally sell dozens," said Jim.

"Did someone else open up a new skateboarding shop nearby?" asked Uncle Frank.

"No, Mike had checked and no competitor had opened up," replied Ben.

"This is strange," said Uncle Frank.

"We found a clue though!" added Billy.

"A clue...tell me what it is," said Uncle Frank clearly interested in learning more.

Jim told Uncle Frank about Bradley Horton, the package that was handed off in the convenience store and their visit to Bradley's house.

"A counterfeit skateboard, huh?" remarked Uncle Frank. "Can I see it?"

Ben jumped up and made a beeline for the front door. He opened the screen door and saw the pile of boards that had mysteriously formed on the front step. "What the..." Ben exclaimed.

He was clearly annoyed at seeing his beloved Element board under all the other boards. Ben grabbed his board and the counterfeit World Industries board and headed back into the house. All eyes were on him.

"Here you go Uncle Frank," said Ben.

"You're going to have to explain to me how you know that this is a fake. I wouldn't know what to look for myself."

"No problem," said Ben. "The first thing to notice is the weight. Hold my board in one hand and the counterfeit board in the other. What do you notice?" queried Ben.

Uncle Frank did as he was instructed. He held the two boards out in front of him, one in each hand.

After some thought, Uncle Frank indicated that the counterfeit board was quite a bit lighter than the real board.

"That's right!" said Jim. "That was one of the first things we noticed. The counterfeit board is made of cheap components and we are pretty sure they are not as solid or strong as the original. They are probably going to break pretty quickly, maybe even after only a few uses."

"What did Bradley say about the guy who sold him the board?" asked Uncle Frank. "Had Bradley seen him around before?"

"No," said Christyn. "Bradley said the guy was a stranger selling boards from the back of his mini-van."

Scott added, "It was a blue mini-van parked at the side of L&J's convenience store."

"Did anyone get the license plate?" asked Frank sounding again like a former policeman.

"No, I don't think Bradley did," answered Jim. "He didn't say anything about getting the license plate although I didn't ask him directly. I'll call him later to find out."

"Well it sounds like we've got some bad stuff happening in our fine town and it's going to be up to us to put a stop to it. I'll call the guys at the station to see if they have any reports of suspicious blue mini-vans."

"In the meantime, it is getting close to dinner and I'm not going to feed all of you hungry kids. Why don't you all go home and we'll meet back here tomorrow at 9:00 a.m. Does that sound OK to everyone?" said Uncle Frank.

"Sure. Fine. OK. See you then," the five friends chimed in together. They got up to leave and Jim gathered all the cups onto the serving tray. As he took the tray into the kitchen he stopped his uncle who was on his way out to say good-bye.

"Do you think it is safe for us to try and find out who is providing counterfeit boards?" whispered Jim.

"Don't worry about that, J. I will be in contact with the local police. I know how busy they are these days. We'll do some detective work to give them some help. If at any time I think we need their assistance, I'll call them immediately."

Jim trusted his uncle and felt confident in his plan.

"I'm going to leave the counterfeit board here, OK?" said Jim. "I don't want to carry it all the way home and then bring it back in the morning."

"Sure. That sounds fine, J. It'll be safe with me. I'm not going to try too many tricks," chuckled Frank.

Jim laughed at the thought of Uncle Frank trying to 50–50 a rail.

"Would you guys like a ride home?" asked Uncle Frank.

"That would be awesome!" said Ben. "My mom has not been happy with me these days for being late for dinner so often."

"Go hop in the car everyone and put on a seatbelt. Buster, you stay here and hold the fort. There's no room in the car for this trip."

Buster was not happy and tried to scoot out the front door as Uncle Frank went to shut the front door.

"Nice try Buster. You stay and guard the house. I won't be long," said Frank as he shut and locked the door.

Buster barked a "Woof" that sounded like he was annoyed and ran to the living room. He climbed up on the couch and rested his paws on the front window ledge. Slowly he moved his head back and forth making a series of wet nose prints across the window.

Uncle Frank said to himself, "That dog does not like to be left out of things!"

"Maybe you'll have to teach him a new trick, Uncle Frank, how to wash windows!" laughed Billy.

As they drove down the driveway and turned towards the homes of the kids, Buster watched them leave and gave out a little whimper, as if he thought, "I could have gone. That little kid could have easily fit in the trunk."

The Calm Before the Storm

Uncle Frank first drove to Christyn's house in less than 10 minutes. During the ride Christyn was wondering how she got stuck in the back with Scott and Billy. At least she was in the middle and could separate the two.

As they were driving down Folsom Road, the worst sewer odor Christyn ever smelt began wafting in the car. She looked around to see if there was some sort of rotting mound of garbage. All she could see was the smiling face of Scott.

"I told you it would be spectacular!" announced Scott.

"Oh gross!" said Billy. "I can't breathe. What died in you?"

Scott, clearly delighted in his talent, tried to deflect the blame to Christyn.

"Jim, could you please get Uncle Frank to roll down a window. It seems poor Christyn is not feeling quite herself," said Scott.

Christyn was too interested in finding fresh air to worry about Scott's comments.

Billy kept taking deep breaths through his nose. "Mmmm…I remember this smell from before. Doesn't it smell like the time we ate all that black licorice while sleeping overnight in the camper?"

"Oh yeah!" pondered Scott. "I remember that night, my sleeping bag had to air out for a week before my mom let me put it in the house."

Finally Christyn spotted her house as they drove up her street. Uncle Frank pulled over and stopped right in front of Christyn's driveway. Christyn's grandmother's car was not in the driveway so she figured her grandmother had left.

Christyn had to climb over Scott to get out the back door of the car. She was in a hurry and in doing so she stepped square on his foot and he let out a yelp.

"Sorry," said Christyn, not sounding too sorry and perhaps even sounding sarcastic. "I guess I should be more careful where I step."

"Thanks for the ride, Uncle Frank."

"No problem!" said Uncle Frank. "You take care of that tummy," he said as he rolled down yet another window in the car and drove off.

"Grrr!" said Christyn to herself as she watched the car with a laughing Scott and Billy disappear.

Next to get dropped off was Scott. He lived just a short drive away from Christyn. When they pulled up to Scott's house, his mom was sitting on the rocking chair on their front porch. She waved at Uncle Frank as Scott got out.

"Thanks Uncle Frank," yelled Scott as he trotted up the stairs. He kissed his mom on the cheek and asked where Meagan was. Meagan was Scott's younger sister. Meagan was three years old and was adopted.

Scott's mom and dad had wanted more than one child but Scott's dad who was a Fire Captain was very busy with work for several years after Scott was born. When the parents decided to have a brother or sister for Scott, they found out that Scott's mom couldn't have any more babies.

Right away they decided they would try to adopt a local baby and after 11 months of visits and paperwork, they brought Meagan home. They were so happy to have another baby in the house and Scott really liked having a baby sister to hold.

It was less than two months after bringing Meagan home that the Crylex Factory fire happened. The fire was out of control by the time the first two fire stations responded. Scott's dad's fire company was the third to respond and when they arrived on scene half the factory was fully involved. There was thick black smoke pouring from the roof and flames were shooting out the broken windows.

Scott's dad was asked to coordinate the efforts of the firefighters who were going into the building. He was trying to set up a command post by the front entrance. The entire front of the building which was made of bricks, separated from the rest of the burning structure and toppled forward onto the command post. Six firefighters were badly injured including Scott's dad. He was rushed to hospital but never regained consciousness. He died two days later from the severe injuries he received from the falling bricks.

Ever since that happened, Scott had assumed the role of father in their household. He looked after his mother and sister and did his best to help out around the house in whatever way they needed.

He loved to come home and see them both. Meagan never really knew her adopted father but Scott was going to make sure she learned all about how great he was.

"She's having a nap right now. Why don't you sit down here with me and chat before we go in to prepare dinner?"

54

"OK, Mom. Have I got an interesting story to tell you!" said Scott with big wide eyes.

Uncle Frank dropped Jim and Billy off last because their house was the furthest away. Ben jumped out too.

"I'll be fine from here," said Ben. "I appreciate the ride Uncle Frank. See you tomorrow. Bye guys!"

"Bye Ben and thanks Uncle Frank," said Billy and Jim.

"Tell Felix I will stop by another time to visit," said Uncle Frank as he pulled away.

"OK, I'll tell Dad.... Uh oh! Dad." Jim and Billy looked over at their house and they could just make out something that looked like a big dent in the siding next to the screen door.

Out came Felix gingerly holding the screen door. "Hello boys," he said in a low, ominous voice. "I've been waiting all day for you to come home. Why don't you walk over here? I would like you to meet a friend of mine...Mr. John Deere." 55

Jim sighed to Billy. "You grab the rake and garbage bags and I'll get the mower started. Hey Dad. What's for dinner?"

Later that night as Jim and Billy were eating dinner with their parents, they told them the whole story and how they were going to continue the case tomorrow morning.

"Is that OK if we head over to meet the others at Uncle Frank's house tomorrow?" asked Jim.

"I don't see why not, dear. I see you worked hard to get the lawn done. You even raked up the clippings and trimmed all the hedges. I've never seen you do such a thorough job," commented Jim's mom. "There must be seven garbage bags full of grass piled up."

Jim grumbled, "There are eight bags but who's counting?"

Jim and Billy looked over at their father who had a sly grin on his face. "Yes," said Felix, "I think the boys have learned, I mean earned a break. Maybe we can fix that screen door as well tomorrow."

At Scott's house, dinner was over as well. Scott was helping his mom dry the dishes. "Mom, why don't you use the dishwasher more?" asked Scott.

"Washing dishes is something that we have to do every night Scott. It's one of those jobs that you can do while talking. Your dad and I would do the dishes together. We got a chance to spend some time talking about anything we wanted."

"Why do we even have a dishwasher?" Scott said confused.

"When we brought Meagan home, we were concerned the extra child would use up any free time we had, including doing the dishes together. We thought that a dishwasher would help us out by giving us more time to be together after she went to bed."

"I don't remember you using it much," responded Scott.

"You're right, dear. It wasn't long after that your Father was killed. Ever since then I have insisted that you and I do the dishes by hand. I like hearing about your day and I don't plan on turning this thing on any time soon."

"That's OK with me too, Mom. I like talking with you too."

Scott missed his dad a lot. He could hear his mom crying some nights and knew that it was still very hard on her too. He had made a vow to himself in the weeks following his dad's death, that he would always be there to support his mom. He intended to keep that promise.

Scott dried the last of the glasses and put the wet towel over the handle of the stove. "I'm going to take Meagan out for a short ride. Do you need anything from the store?" asked Scott.

"No sweetie, I'm fine. Make sure to do up her helmet tight."

Scott could have predicted she would say that. Scott made his way into the next room where Meagan was busy on the floor stacking blocks into the shape of a house.

"Who wants to go on the bike with me?" said Scott.

Meagan's face lit up. "Me do!" she shouted loudly.

"Well then, let's get going. C'mon little one, you need a jacket," Scott said in a caring tone.

Scott's mom, Tanya Wilson, watched the two of them leave. She knew that Scott took great care of Meagan and that Meagan loved to be with her big brother.

"Don't be long," she called out as Scott placed Meagan in the small trailer attached to Scott's mountain bike.

"We'll be no more than a half hour," said Scott.

And with that he hopped onto the bike and pedaled off down the street with Meagan in tow behind him. Meagan always pretended she was in a boat and was singing "Row, Row, Row Your Boat" as best she could.

Scott headed towards Jim's house. He wasn't going to stop unless he saw his friend outside. Meagan liked to visit Jim and Billy. They always picked her up and tickled her. As Scott approached the Brandt house he could see the front porch light was not on which meant that no one was outside. He did notice a ton of garbage bags by the curb. "Someone's been busy!" he thought out loud.

"Busy, busy, busy!" came a bubbling voice from the back of the bike.

"Shall I go faster, Meagan?" laughed Scott.

"Yeah! Faster, faster! 'Cott." Sometimes Meagan didn't quite pronounce names right.

Scott pedaled a bit faster and made vroom vroom sounds. Meagan squealed with delight.

"Let's go to the end of the block and then we'll turn around and head for home!" bellowed Scott.

"Maybe I'll make my famous Banana Split sundaes for us," said Scott.

"Home, home, home!" announced Meagan.

* * * *

Mohammed had started his evening shift about an hour earlier and was counting inventory in the store and in the back room. He was having trouble with something and kept having to come in and out of the stock room.

"Anything wrong, Mohammed?" asked Mr. Asad.

"I'm not sure, Father. I am counting the magazines and the numbers don't add up right. I think I am missing a bundle or something. Not to worry, I will find it. It is time that you go home to Mother. She will have your dinner waiting soon."

Mr. Asad knew that he could go home and leave the store in his youngest son's capable hands. He didn't like leaving his son alone at night but knew that the cameras and the bright lights were effective in keeping away bad people. Besides, there was very little crime in Exton. Still he wished that Mubarak was around more to help out. He often thought that Mubarak could learn a lot from Mohammed about being responsible.

"Good night Mohammed. Call me on the cell phone if you need anything."

"Good night, Father. I will," said Mohammed.

After his father left, Mohammed went back to counting the magazines. He did it twice more and was still short 50 comics.

"That is strange," thought Mohammed. "Fifty comics is exactly the number that comes in a bundle from the distributor. I wonder if one of the bundles was misplaced. I will have to phone them in the morning to confirm."

The bell on the door jangled and in walked a customer.

"Good evening, ma'am," said Mohammed in the same pleasant voice he used with everyone.

The woman was scanning the store. "Can you tell me where your ranch dressing is?" she said without looking at Mohammed.

"At the end of aisle three, ma'am. Go to the next aisle and all the way to the end. We have two varieties of ranch dressing to choose from."

The woman followed the instructions and found the bottle she was looking for. She paid for the item and walked out the door without saying too much. Mohammed knew it was going to be like that all night. His shift wouldn't end until 6:00 a.m. and every few minutes someone new would enter the shop looking for one or two things.

He liked helping people find things they were looking for. If he could only find the missing bundle of comics, he would be happier. "First it was two boxes of chocolate bars that went missing last month and now a bundle of comics. How strange."

Just then the bell jingled again as Mubarak opened the door to the store. Mohammed looked up from his magazines and smiled at his brother.

"Hello brother. Are you here to help me out tonight?"

"Is Father here?" asked Mubarak looking around quickly.

"No brother, he has gone for the evening," answered Mohammed.

"I cannot stay tonight brother. I have…uh…business to take care of. Did you make sure to deposit the money at the bank tonight before Father left?" Mubarak knew full well that no deposit had been made. Mubarak had made sure of that by secretly taking the empty deposit pouch from its place behind the counter that afternoon and placing it in his car while his father wasn't looking. Before Mohammed could answer the question, Mubarak asked for a drink. "Mohammed, can you pass me a Dr. Pepper please?"

"Sure, brother," replied Mohammed. Mohammed walked to the back of the store to the drink display case.

As Mohammed walked back, Mubarak slipped the deposit pouch from inside his jacket and put it back in its spot behind the counter. Mohammed came back and handed his brother the ice-cold beverage.

"Thanks Mohammed. Now about that deposit, did you make it yet?"

"No. Father said the deposit pouch was missing and he probably left it at home. He said I could make it tomorrow morning when Mother brings it in."

Mubarak reached behind the counter and pulled out the deposit bag. "Here it is, brother!" Mubarak announced.

"Hmm…Father said he had checked there," said Mohammed.

"Maybe we will have to get Father a new set of glasses," Mubarak laughed nervously. "Why don't I stay here and watch the store while you go and finish making the deposit. I would feel much better if you didn't have this cash with you all night."

Mohammed knew that Mubarak was right. It was always best to make the deposit before the evening shift began.

"I will walk over to the bank quickly. I will only be gone about five minutes. Will that be OK with you?" asked Mohammed.

"That will be fine," replied Mubarak. "I'll be here to watch the store."

Mohammed gathered the money that his father had already counted and bundled and placed it in the deposit pouch. He wrote down the total amount on a piece of paper and slipped that into the pouch. He sealed the pouch and put the small padlock on to ensure the zipper could not be opened.

"I will be back shortly," said Mohammed and quickly left the store.

Mubarak watched his brother disappear across the road and down the street towards the bank. When his brother was out of sight, he rushed over to the stock room and searched left and right for a particular box. He spotted the box he was looking for and reached inside it. He pulled out a bundle of comics and placed them in one of the garbage bags lying on the small table in the stock room.

When he heard the jangle of the front door bell, he cautiously cracked open the stock room door and looked out. It was a customer, not his brother. He sighed with relief and came out holding the garbage bag.

"Where do you keep the ranch dressing?" said the man.

"I am sorry sir, we do not carry ranch dressing," lied Mubarak. He knew they carried ranch dressing but he wanted this guy out of the store so Mubarak could stash the garbage back and comics in his car.

"But my wife said she was just in here and bought a bottle. We just need another one to replace the one she broke getting out of the car."

Mubarak, sensing that his brother would be coming back any second, decided to change the way he was dealing with this customer.

"Oh, ranch dressing!" exclaimed Mubarak. Mubarak rushed down aisle three and grabbed the first bottle he saw. He brought it back to the man and directed him towards the door.

"Here you go sir, sorry to hear that the first bottle broke. It was probably defective and please accept this free replacement."

The man looked confused but pleased he did not have to pay for the second bottle of dressing. "Th…thanks!" said the man.

"Have a good night sir," said Mubarak as the man walked out to the parking lot.

Mubarak could see his brother had just finished making the deposit. The bank had an outdoor secure storage area for all deposits made after bank hours. Mohammed started to walk back towards the convenience store.

Mubarak raced back to the counter and reached over and grabbed the garbage bag. In his haste to run out of the store, Mubarak grabbed the wrong end of the bag and a few dozen comic magazines flew up and down aisle

59

one. Mubarak was really sweating now. He quickly opened the bag and began picking up magazines from the floor and stuffing them into the bag. He kept looking towards the parking lot to see if Mohammed was approaching.

Finally he got the magazines in the bag and he raced to the front door. Mohammed was too close. He would see Mubarak putting the package in his car. There was only one thing left to do.

Mubarak raced to the back of the store and opened the rear door that lead to the garbage dumpster. He flung the package towards the dumpster and it hit the side of the bin with a loud bang that echoed quite loud in the quiet of the back alley. There was no one around at that time so it didn't matter.

He shut the door at the back of the store and turned around. There stood Mohammed at the front of the store.

"Uh hello Mohammed. I didn't hear you come in," Mubarak blurted.

"Are you OK? You look like you are sweating," said Mohammed. "Do you feel sick?"

Mubarak did feel sick inside himself. He wondered if all this stealing was worth the few bucks he made. At least it gave him some extra money to spend with his friends. "I am fine. I must go now. I will see you tomorrow," Mubarak said quickly.

With a shaky hand, he picked up his car keys and headed out the front door. He was almost out the door when Mohammed called his name.

"Mubarak! Aren't you forgetting something?

Mubarak was sweating even more. He turned around slowly not sure what his brother was going to say.

"You forgot your drink," said Mohammed and he held up the can for Mubarak to take. Mubarak came back, grabbed the can and left without another word.

Mohammed settled in for the evening. He had enjoyed the walk and the fresh air. "I sure hope my brother is feeling better tomorrow," he thought. "He is acting very strange these days."

Mubarak made sure to drive away from the store and go down one block before circling back to the convenience store he had just left. He turned into the parking lot of the dry cleaner that was next to the convenience store and hopped out of his car. He vaulted over the low white fence separating the dry cleaning store from the convenience store lot. He peeked around the corner and could see no one was visible. He sprinted over to the dumpster and while looking left and right for anyone watching, grabbed the package he had thrown there earlier. He tucked the package under his jacket and raced back to his car. He tossed the package into the trunk and then quickly jumped in the car and sped off.

Mohammed watched him from the back of the store. "Very strange."

Setting the Trap

The next day at 9:00 a.m. all the friends were assembled at Uncle Frank's house. Ben had gone over to Jim's house at 8:30 a.m. Ben, Jim and Billy had left on their boards together. Along the way they met up with Christyn who was buying a bagel and cream cheese at the Harvest Bakery on Pine Street and had just come outside to eat it.

When they got to Uncle Frank's house, Scott's board was already propped up against the front beside the door. They climbed the small set of stairs and knocked on the door. A voice from inside invited them in.

Upon entering they could clearly smell bacon and eggs cooking and noticed Scott sitting at the table eating a heaping pile of bacon.

"Well it's nice to see you eating something other than Twinkies!" said Christyn as she bit into her bagel.

Billy and Jim had already eaten their breakfast but were still licking their lips. The smell of maple-flavored bacon was not only driving them nuts but Buster was almost beside himself. He was dancing around the kitchen like his tail was on fire.

From his plate, Uncle Frank selected a strip of bacon that had cooled down. He rolled it up like a little carpet and asked Buster to sit in front of him. Everyone stopped to watch the trick. Most of them had seen this one before but had to watch again.

Uncle Frank placed the rolled up bacon on the top of Buster's nose. "STAY," he commanded Buster in a firm voice. You could see Buster quivering but he didn't eat the bacon. Uncle Frank waited a few more seconds to show that he could control the dog. To Buster it seemed like an eternity.

Finally Uncle Frank snapped, "Eat!" and in a flash of motion Buster flicked the bacon up in the air about two inches, opened his mouth and snapped his jaws shut around the piece of meat. It was so fast that it was really just a blur. The bacon went down to Buster's stomach without so much as one chew.

Everyone clapped for Buster.

Buster barked several times as if to say, "Thank-you, thank-you. I would like to thank all my adoring fans for gathering to witness such greatness. Later, I'll show you all how I can turn one of Frank's slippers into an appetizer!"

Uncle Frank looked at each the kids. "Even though Buster is just a dog, that trick required him to have a lot of discipline and patience. Those are also good qualities for budding detectives. Keep that in mind as we solve this case."

The kids were genuinely excited. With Uncle Frank in charge, they knew they would find the answer to Mike's problem.

Billy was excited. "Jim, Jim, tell them about your phone calls last night."

"What phone calls?" said Ben.

Uncle Frank put his dishes on the counter and turned to face Jim.

Jim stood up and addressed the group. "Last night I made a couple of phone calls. The first one was to Bradley Horton. I asked him about any visitors he might have had just before we got there. Bradley said that he did have a visitor just before we arrived but he said it had nothing to do with the skateboard and he didn't want to discuss that any further," Jim explained.

"That sounds odd," said Ben. "Bradley still seems to be keeping some secrets from us even though he knows better. Anything else from Bradley?"

"He said he had to go," said Jim. "I got nothing more."

"We'll have to talk to him in person, maybe at his house again," said Scott with a wink to Christyn.

Uncle Frank smiled, remembering the story from what Jim told him yesterday.

Uncle Frank added, "You said you made a couple of calls, what was the other call?"

"Remember when Bradley was telling his story about buying the board, he mentioned that Ryan Thornwell had also purchased a board. I called Ryan and I told him I heard that he had just purchased a board at a good price and could I get one too. Ryan told me that the board was no good and that he thinks he wasted his money," said Jim.

"What happened with the board?" asked Christyn.

"The same story as we found out, after just a couple of uses he noticed the deck starting to chip and the wheels do not spin well at all. He was pretty upset at paying $60 for something that started to fall apart almost immediately," Jim continued.

"$60!" exclaimed Ben. "People sure are getting taken for a lot of money!"

Uncle Frank said, "After you add up all those individual sales, this guy sounds like he is making a killing off you kids."

"We have to catch him in the act!" said Billy.

"I think we need to set a trap," said Ben firmly.

"Let's put a plan together right now," instructed Uncle Frank. "Jim, grab some paper and two pens from my desk. Ben, get me the phone book please. It's under the phone in the kitchen."

* * * *

Mubarak had slept in as usual after a late night with friends. When he woke up at 9:13 a.m., he realized he was going to have to hurry or he would be late for his 10:00 a.m. meeting.

His mom and dad were already gone to the store and he could hear Mohammed snoring from his room. He would have just gotten off his shift a few hours ago. "Mohammed is a fool," Mubarak thought. "He works too hard and never takes time for himself."

Mubarak got dressed quickly and grabbed a banana and orange juice from the fridge. "This isn't the brand of juice I like!" Mubarak said, clearly annoyed. "I will have to speak to Mother about this. She knows better!"

Mubarak grabbed his light jacket and car keys and headed out to the driveway. He went around to the back of the car and opened the trunk. He checked to ensure his package was still where he had stashed it for the night. It was. He closed the trunk and slid into the front seat. He started the car with a roar and backed down the driveway. He loved the sound this car made when he stepped on the gas.

"I hope Mohammed is a heavy sleeper!" he laughed, not really caring if he woke his brother. He turned south and headed towards the local high school parking lot. He would be there just in time to keep his appointment.

Mohammed was not snoring after all. His watch alarm had awoken him at 8:00 a.m. and he had been pretending to sleep ever since. He had been waiting for his brother to get up. He wanted to find out what his brother was doing with those mysterious packages. He hoped by following Mubarak this morning he would learn more. He waited until Mubarak had driven down the street a ways and then he put his helmet on and started up his Peugeot 103 moped. It was all he had to keep up with his brother.

"As long as Mubarak stays within the city limits, I should be able to stay with him," thought Mohammed.

As it happens, Mohammed would not have far to go at all. Mohammed had no trouble keeping Mubarak's blue car in sight without getting too close. Mubarak had only gone a few blocks and then turned into Pine Hills High School. Mohammed pulled over a block away and watched the car.

There was no one around and Mohammed wondered if Mubarak had noticed his brother following him.

It was three minutes to 10:00 a.m. and Mubarak did not see his contact yet. He fumbled around in his glove compartment looking for a CD. Just then a knock at the car window caused Mubarak to yell and spill his orange juice on his crotch.

"Darn it!" yelled Mubarak looking in the direction of the knocking.

Cody Friesen knocked on the window again. "I've got the money," Cody whispered. "Have you got the stuff?"

Mubarak couldn't hear a word he said. He opened the door. "Just a second," said Mubarak as he stood up and brushed the orange juice off his pants. The stain was not in a good place at all.

64

Cody couldn't help but laugh. "I hope that was just orange juice, Mubarak! I didn't mean to scare you."

Mubarak did not want to look weak in front of this kid. "You didn't scare me," he lied. "The bottle slipped from my hand." Mubarak walked over to the trunk and opened the lid. He reached in and pulled out the garbage bag.

Mohammed could see Mubarak open the trunk and pull something out. It looked like the package he had seen Mubarak slip under his coat last night when he was beside the dumpster. It was hard to tell from this distance but he could not get closer without being seen.

Mohammed saw Mubarak give the package to the other person. He was pretty sure it was Cody Friesen. He also saw Cody give something small to Mubarak that must have been money because it looked like Mubarak was counting it carefully before stuffing it into his shirt pocket.

Then Mubarak said something to Cody, shut the trunk and got in the car. Before Mubarak could leave the high school parking lot, Mohammed turned his moped around and drove away. He did not want to be there if Mubarak came back towards where he was. Mohammed pulled into a nearby alley and waited for his brother to disappear.

Sure enough, Mubarak drove by with his music blaring.

"So that's where my CD went!" said Mohammed to himself. He pulled his moped back onto the street and drove over to the high school parking lot. He could see Cody walking across the soccer pitch behind the school. Mohammed made a quick decision and drove his moped onto the soccer pitch to catch up with Cody.

Cody was very surprised to see someone riding a moped across the soccer pitch yelling something. When he realized the person was yelling, "Cody!" He became tense. He wasn't sure what was going on but he started to feel nervous.

As Mohammed approached Cody, he looked scared. Mohammed knew that he had to get some information from Cody. From the look of fear on his face, Mohammed knew that if he pressed hard right now, this kid would crack easily.

"Cody, we need to talk," said Mohammed in a firm and controlled voice.

Cody knew Mohammed from the store but didn't know him all that well. He did know this was the first time he had ever heard Mohammed use that kind of voice. Cody felt the package under his jacket. It was hidden but he felt like it was sticking out in plain view. "Maybe Mohammed doesn't know about the package," thought Cody nervously. "What am I scared for? I paid for this," he tried to justify in his head.

"What did my brother just give to you?" demanded Mohammed in the same serious tone.

"Wh…what are you talking about?" countered Cody trying to pretend like he didn't understand the question.

"Cody, I am not stupid. You have something under your jacket that my brother gave to you before he drove off. You gave him something in return that looked like money. If you don't show me right now, I will call your parents," said Mohammed pulling out his cell phone for Cody to see.

That was enough for Cody. "You don't have to call my parents," he stammered. "I've done nothing wrong. Mubarak sold me these comic books. He said they were his and he would give them to me at a great price," said Cody stuttering. He pulled out the package from under his coat and handed it to Mohammed. It was the garbage bag from the night before. It was wrapped up into a small package.

Mohammed opened the bag and took a quick look inside. He saw about two-dozen comics. "So that's where the missing comics have been going!" thought Mohammed. He closed the bag and glared at Cody.

"These do not belong to Mubarak, I will have to take them back to the store," Mohammed said.

"Mubarak said I could not tell you about the comics, Mohammed. Please don't get me in trouble," pleaded Cody.

Mohammed was disgusted. "You should be lucky that I don't call your parents right now!"

He stuffed the comics in his moped's sidesaddle bag and put on his helmet. Cody didn't look comfortable and started to walk away across the field. Mohammed jumped on his moped and headed back to the store. He was going to talk to his father.

On his way back to the store, Mohammed was thinking about what his brother was doing and how upset his father was going to be when he found out. He was mad at Mubarak but also worried about his father's reaction. He felt he had to tell the story. It was the right thing to do.

More Trouble for Mike

Uncle Frank said, "The first thing we have to do is let Mike know what we have found and that we are going to make a plan."

"I can call him right now and explain," volunteered Ben.

"Good, you do that while we lay out the rest of our plan on the kitchen table."

Ben went into the living room with the cordless phone and dialed Boardzone. Julie answered.

"Hi Julie, it's Ben. Is Mike there?" he asked.

"As a matter of fact, he isn't here. He has gone to meet with one of our suppliers this morning. They sent us a letter indicating they had concerns because we weren't ordering sufficient boards from them. They said they were going to discontinue supplying us unless our orders picked up this month."

"That's terrible!" exclaimed Ben.

"It sure is," said Julie. If that happens with one supplier, it could happen with others and then we would have to close for sure. Mike was going to meet with them face-to-face to see what he could work out."

"When will he be back?" asked Ben.

"After that he has to go to the site of the new skate park," said Julie.

"Why?" Ben asked. "I thought the site was just four acres of cleared land and poured concrete. They haven't started building the ramps, stands and pro shop yet have they?"

"No, no…" replied Julie. "The City asked Mike to come to the site as they had a zoning conflict to talk to him about."

"Poor Mike, this has not been his week!" Ben said in a consoling voice.

"No, Ben. It hasn't. Is there any message?" asked Julie.

Ben really wanted to talk to Mike in person but wasn't sure when that was going to happen. He also felt that Mike could use some good news as soon as possible. "Julie, tell Mike that the five of us including Jim's

Uncle Frank are figuring out what is going on with the lack of sales. We have found out that there are cheap counterfeit boards surfacing around town and that may be the main reason Boardzone is suffering. Tell him we will call again later when we have more news around our plan."

"Ben, that is very interesting news. Thank you for sharing it. I will tell Mike as soon as he gets back. You be careful and listen to what Frank says." Julie responded, sounding just like his mother.

"Will do!" said Ben. "Bye for now."

Ben hung up the phone and returned to the kitchen. He saw the group huddled around a few pieces of paper that contained notes and a drawing.

Uncle Frank turned around first.

"Did you talk to Mike?" he asked.

"No. But I did pass on the message to Julie," Ben replied.

"Good," Jim said.

"There may be another problem or two," Ben informed the group.

"What now!" Christyn said, a bit exasperated.

"One of Mike's suppliers is threatening to cut him off if he doesn't buy more stock and the City has some sort of zoning problem with the new skate park."

Uncle Frank gave a low whistle, "When it rains, it pours."

"We have to hurry," said Jim.

"What kind of plan have you come up with so far?" Ben said looking at the paper on the kitchen table.

Christyn spoke up. "I'll explain the plan so far." She cleared her throat and picked up the piece of paper that Uncle Frank had been writing on when Ben had come back into the room.

"Our plan is simple. We have to make contact with the person selling the counterfeit boards. Once we do that we will find out who their supplier is and we will bring in the police to shut them down. With them out of the way, Mike will be back in business," Christyn said with satisfaction in her voice.

"Sounds like a plan. How are you going to make contact with the guy selling the fake boards?" asked Ben.

"That was what we were just discussing," said Uncle Frank. "We need two things. We first need to know where to find this guy and secondly we need someone to pose as a buyer."

Scott piped up, "We were debating if one of us should pose as the buyer. It might be dangerous."

"I'll do it," announced Ben. "If it helps my brother, count me in."

68

"And me too," said Jim.

Uncle Frank shook his head. "Ben and J., I appreciate you wanting to help but you both might be too recognizable. The person may know who you are and that you are related to Mike. If that happens you will never get close enough to make the buy.

"I think the only person who might make a good buyer is Billy," said Frank. "He has not been as visible around town and the guy selling boards seems to like to sell to younger kids. I guess he figures they will not realize the boards are fake because they are not as experienced."

Billy was beaming. He loved being a key player in any plan the group was working on. He could see himself wearing a black and white tuxedo with one of those microphones in his ear.

"Agent 005 to base, do you copy?" he began to daydream. "I have the suspect in sight and am going to attempt to make the deal."

"Be careful," said an imaginary voice, the suspect is highly danger- 69 ous and is armed with every weapon known to man."

"Don't worry, I have my own surprises for this chump," said Agent 005.

"Billy…Billy…BILLY!!!" shouted Jim. "Are you there?"

Billy popped back to reality and could see everyone staring at him. He felt his cheeks turn a bit red. He was hoping none of that was said out loud.

"Well…are you in?" asked Jim to Billy.

"Agent 005 is…I mean, I sure am!" said Billy.

Uncle Frank added "I will give Felix and Clarice a call to discuss this with them too."

"Aww, Uncle Frank. They will say No," whined Billy.

"Leave the explanation to me, Billy," Uncle Frank said.

Billy believed that Uncle Frank would be able to convince his parents to let him play the important role in this plan.

"OK, then. The next thing we have to figure out is where to find this guy," said Scott.

"Christyn, you had an idea before. What was it?" said Jim.

Christyn spoke up, "I was thinking that this guy has been seen twice near L&J's convenience store. He must be watching kids coming and going from the store. Maybe if we hang around the store for a while we might see him."

Uncle Frank said "I think that two of you should stakeout the store from a safe distance while the rest of us take care of some other details. I think that J. and Ben should take the first watch. I will give you a two-way radio to carry so that you can keep in constant contact with us while we do our jobs."

"Sounds fine, Uncle Frank," agreed Jim. "What are you Scott, Christyn and Billy going to do?"

"We have to go and talk to Clarice and Felix about Billy. Then we have to go find Mike and talk to him. I don't like the news about the zoning problem. This skate park plan has been in the works for over a year and to have a zoning problem now doesn't make sense," Frank said.

"What is a zoning problem?" asked Billy.

Uncle Frank answered, "Zoning is where the City allows people to build certain things in certain areas. If you want to build a house, the place has to be approved or 'zoned' for housing. If you want to build an office building or warehouse, then the area has to be 'zoned' for business use only. You can't build an office building in a housing area. They do that to keep traffic down and other things."

70

"Mike doesn't want to build a house at his skate park," said Billy not fully clear on why Mike would have a zoning problem.

"I know," said Uncle Frank "that is why it is strange for him to have any sort of problem with the City."

"I will drive you both over to a location where you can watch the store," offered Uncle Frank. "Remember, you can't go in the store and you can't leave the other person alone. You must stay together. It is the only safe way. I want one of you to check in every 10 minutes to let us know what is going on. If you see anything suspicious, immediately inform us and we will be there within minutes."

"C'mon Buster," called Uncle Frank. "Quit drooling on my chair and let's get in the car." Buster bolted off the chair and was at the front door with the other kids in a heartbeat.

Mohammed Does the Right Thing

Mohammed approached the convenience store and noticed a blue mini-van was parked at the side.

"I've seen that mini-van before," thought Mohammed.

Mohammed could see the driver in the front seat and he was speaking with Devin Snively who was standing beside the van. Devin was looking around like he was searching for someone.

Mohammed didn't have time to chat with Devin. He actually didn't want to talk to Devin as he wasn't the nicest person he had ever met. Mohammed was on a mission. He had to go in and explain the situation to his father.

Mohammed parked his moped in the front parking lot off to one side. He said hello to Mrs. Gingras who was using the pay phone on the outside of the convenience store.

"Hello," she said not remembering if that was Mubarak or Mohammed. "Nice day, isn't it?"

"Very nice indeed," said Mohammed not really paying attention to the woman.

When he opened the door he immediately saw his mother behind the front counter. She was ringing in a sale for a customer.

"That will be $4.58 including taxes. Do you want a bag?" she said.

The man gave her a five-dollar bill and indicated that he would like a small bag. He waited for his change and looked at one of those gossip style magazines called *International Tattler*.

He read the lead headline on the front page and wondered if it was truly possible for a headless man to have actually been teaching college in Idaho for the last seven years. The first thought that came to his mind was, "Wouldn't his students have said something?"

Fasal gave the man his 42 cents change, which he put in the pocket of his jeans. He took the small bag and exited the store.

Mohammed then saw his father coming out of the back stock room carrying a case of milk.

"Ah, Mohammed. What are you doing here?" asked his mother. "You should be resting."

"He worked all night you know," Fasel said to Mr. Asad.

"He's a hard worker. We are fine here, Mohammed. Why don't you go home and get some sleep."

"Father, I need to talk with you in private," he said in an urgent tone.

"It was not like Mohammed to talk this way," thought Mr. Asad. "Come son, let us go to the back room where we can have a discussion in private," he said aloud.

Fasal was not worried or curious. This was a private discussion between a father and his son and they would work it out.

72   Mohammed followed his father to the back room and after they both were in the small room, Mohammed turned on the main light and shut the door. From the small closed-circuit TV monitor that was setup in the room, they could see Fasal behind the counter waiting on customers. Mr. Asad liked to be able to see what was going on in the main store when he was working in the back. If he ever had to call the police, there was a phone in the back room.

"Tell me, what is on your mind?" asked Mr. Asad.

"Father I have to bring something unfortunate to your attention. It has to do with Mubarak," declared Mohammed.

"Is Mubarak alright?" Mr. Asad asked quickly thinking that his other son might be hurt.

"Yes, yes, Mubarak is fine," said Mohammed.

For a moment, Mr. Asad breathed a sigh of relief. That relief wouldn't last long.

Mohammed began to describe his story.

"I have seen Mubarak doing some strange things at the store," explained Mohammed.

"What kind of strange things?" asked his father.

"He was talking to some kids the other day about a 'deal' and I saw a package being exchanged. Then last night Mubarak came by the store to ask if I had made the evening deposit."

"I noticed the deposit slip when we came in this morning. I was wondering how you made the deposit working here alone. How did you make the deposit? We could not find the deposit pouch last night before we left," said Mr. Asad.

"I know Father, I came in when you were looking for it and when I looked with you, I could not find it either. Last night after you had gone, Mubarak came in and asked about the deposit. I told him it had not been made. Mysteriously, Mubarak announced the pouch had reappeared in its place. He then had me go and do the deposit while he watched the store. I think he wanted to be alone in the store."

"Why would you say that?" asked Mr. Asad.

"When I came back Mohammed was just shutting the door to the back garbage area. He was sweating and looked scared.

"Maybe he was just getting rid of some heavy garbage, Mohammed," said his father looking for an obvious explanation.

"Father, I am ashamed to admit this but I do not think that Mubarak would take out the garbage on his own. He will only do it when you ask him."

"I suppose you are right, Mohammed. I notice these things too," sighed his father. 73

"There is more, Father. Right after Mubarak left I went to the back door and opened it up to see if everything looked normal. Everything was quiet but then I saw Mubarak's car pull into the lot beside our dumpster. Mubarak got out, hopped the little fence, ran over to our dumpster, grabbed a small package and then returned to his car. He put it in the trunk and drove off."

"That is very strange. Have you talked to your brother about this?" said his father.

"No, but I did follow Mubarak after he got up this morning. That is why I am up so early. I wanted to see what was in the package and where Mubarak was going with it."

"What did you see?" his father said a bit impatiently.

"I followed Mubarak to the high school parking lot and he exchanged the package with a kid named Cody for some money," Mohammed described.

"Are you sure?"

"100% sure Father. I spoke with the kid right after Mubarak left and here is the package that was exchanged," said Mohammed as he produced the garbage bag full of comics.

Mr. Asad looked down at the package sitting on the table. He found the opening and looked inside. "Comic books?" said his father with surprise in his voice. "Where did they come from?"

"I think from the store Father. Yesterday evening when I was doing inventory I noticed some comic magazines were missing. We were short exactly 50. There are 25 comics in this package. I think the earlier package might have had the other 25 comics. Do you remember last month when we were short a case of chocolate bars? Did you ever find out what happened?" Mohammed quizzed his father.

"No, we thought they must have been left on the truck or something. We paid for them but they never seemed to arrive," said Mr. Asad.

"Which courier did we use to move that order?"

"We didn't have to – Mubarak volunteered to drive…." Mr. Asad's voice trailed off.

"I am going to have to talk to my oldest son," Mr. Asad said with a serious look on his face. "Fasal!" he bellowed. Mohammed cringed a bit. "Get Mubarak on the phone and tell him I need him to come to the store right away."

Mr. Asad turned to Mohammed.

"Mohammed, thank you for bringing this information to me. I will talk to your brother in private. I think it is best that you leave now. Go home and rest," he said warmly.

"OK Father. I will go," said Mohammed.

He left the back room, gave his mother a kiss on the cheek. She passed him a piece of his favorite black licorice as he left the store. When he went outside he noticed the blue mini-van was still there but Devin Snively was nowhere to be seen. Even the driver was not around.

"That man should not park on our property unless he is using the store," thought Mohammed. "I should go and speak to the man."

He walked to the corner of the store and could see the entire mini-van. There seemed to be no one around. He walked over to the driver's door and looked instead. There was a ton of empty fast food containers, almost all of them from Wendy's.

"What a mess. The person driving this van sure likes hamburgers!" thought Mohammed.

Mohammed walked around to the back of the van and peered in the window. He could see boxes of different shapes and sizes visible. Under some papers it looked like skateboards.

Just then a shout from behind Mohammed made him jump and turn around quickly.

"Whatta you lookin' at?" said a man who was crossing the street. He was carrying an iced cappuccino from the Java Stop across the street. L&J's convenience store sold coffee and slush drinks but did not sell the iced cappuccinos that seemed to be the newest craze.

Mohammed said that he worked at the convenience store and that the parking lot was only for the customers of their store.

The man quickly became very pleasant and apologized. He told

Mohammed that he would return to park there in the future only when he had business in the store. The man got into his van and left quietly.

Mohammed felt pleased with himself. "If people think they can use our lot to park their vehicle, they are wrong," he thought. Mohammed went to unlock his moped.

 Not five minutes later, Uncle Frank and the kids pulled up in front of the drugstore that was one block away from L&J's convenience store. They all looked over at the convenience store parking lot. There was only two cars in the lot currently and neither of them was a blue mini-van.

Ben and Jim got out of the big car. Buster immediately took over the front seat.

The boys walked over to the bench in front of the drugstore and sat down. There was an awning over the bench to keep the hot morning sun off their heads. Jim tried the two-way radio and it worked fine. Frank responded quickly from the car. Ben was adjusting the view through a pair of binoculars that Frank had loaned them for the surveillance.

"Remember what I told you!" said Uncle Frank.

"Got it!" they said.

"Check in every 10 minutes" Frank reminded them.

"Got it," they said.

"If you see anything strange," Frank said.

"We'll call you," they said.

"OK, I can see you got the message," said Frank.

"Yes Uncle!" said Jim.

Frank nodded and then he drove off.

Frank had only gone 500 yards when Ben pushed the button on the two-way radio and said "Hey Jim, if we see the blue van, let's tackle the guy and make a citizen's arrest!"

"I heard that!" replied Uncle Frank on the other end of the two-way radio. "Just watch the store you two and stay out of trouble."

The boys laughed and began their surveillance.

"Isn't that Mohammed on his moped?" Jim asked Ben.

"Yes. He's coming this way. Don't attract attention!" said Ben. "We need to watch the store, not talk."

It was too late. Mohammed had seen the two boys sitting on the bench by the drugstore. He pulled over.

"Hi Jim and Ben." Mohammed noticed the binoculars. "It looks like you are watching for something?" said Mohammed. "Is this part of your plan to help Mike?"

The boys looked at each other. "How did you know?" they said amazed.

"Billy told me," Mohammed said matter-of-factly.

"Billy!" Jim said. "How could he blab so quickly?!!"

"Can I ask what are you doing here?" said Mohammed.

The boys looked at each other and decided it was OK to let Mohammed in on their plan.

"There is a guy hanging around town selling counterfeit skateboards to kids. We don't know much about him but he's dangerous and we think he is driving a blue mini-van."

A strange look came over Mohammed's face.

"What is it, Mohammed?" asked Ben.

"Oh my goodness! I am so stupid. I just told him to leave the parking lot," confessed Mohammed.

"You what!" cried out Jim.

"I am sorry, Jim! I saw a blue van parked illegally and when I looked in the back I saw boxes and what looked like skateboards," cried out Mohammed.

"It's OK, Mohammed, you didn't know. Is there anything about this guy you can tell us," said Ben.

Mohammed tried to think. Mohammed was lost in thought but said out loud, "The man was average: dark hair, not too tall, friendly. Nothing special comes to mind."

"What was he wearing?" said Jim.

"He was wearing a dark blue short sleeve shirt and blue jeans. He was coming over from the Java Stop with an iced cappuccino," said Mohammed.

"Tell us more about the van?" asked Jim.

"Sure, I looked in the back and there were several different-sized boxes scattered everywhere. Under some paper I could see the tops of skateboards," said Mohammed.

"Was there anything else special about the van?" asked Ben.

"Hmm...no, not really. I did not get the license plate. Wait! There was something else. The front seat was really messy. It was full of hamburger wrappers from Wendy's," said Mohammed.

"Perfect! We have just found our next place to watch," the boys said excitedly. "Let's call it in to Uncle Frank."

"Who is Uncle Frank?" asked Mohammed.

Jim picked up the two-way radio and pressed the button. "Eagle One to Base, Eagle One to Base." Eagle One was the call sign they had selected since eagles have great eyesight and they were in surveillance mode. They were using call signs in case the counterfeiters were monitoring radio frequencies. After a few seconds, a voice crackled on the radio.

"This is Base, go ahead Eagle One," said Uncle Frank. In the background they could hear Billy yelling "Hi Jim, Hi Ben! How's it going? See any blue vans yet?" They could hear "Shhhh" sounds from Uncle Frank.

Jim and Ben winced. Billy was never going to make it as a spy! Next they heard Buster barking up a storm. Frank came on the radio again. "Sorry guys, we are having a small cat problem at our end. Anything to report?"

"Have we ever!" said Jim. He explained what had happened since Uncle Frank had left and told them Mohammed's story.

"We would like permission to head over two blocks to the Wendy's restaurant on Clover St," said Jim. "We will setup surveillance there. It is getting close to lunch time and we might get lucky."

"That sounds like a good plan. I will visit Felix and Clarice, look for Mike and then meet you back at the new surveillance point. We will come and find you. Talk to you again on the radio when you get in place."

"Over and out!" said Ben.

"Are you going to come with us Mohammed?" asked Jim.

"I would love to!" said Mohammed. "Let's go."

"What about your bike?" asked Jim.

"It will be OK parked here," said Mohammed.

The three of them made their way to Clover Street and set themselves up at a bus shelter across from the Wendy's restaurant. There was one blue mini-van in the parking lot.

"Mohammed, is that the van you saw?" asked Ben.

"I'm not sure, I need to get closer to check it out."

The boys wondered if that was a good idea or not.

"If Mohammed crosses the street over there and walks down the sidewalk he can get a pretty good view of the van. He doesn't have to even get that close," Ben said.

"Is that OK with you, Mohammed?" Jim asked.

"That is fine," Mohammed said and turned around. He walked down a ways before crossing the street. He then casually turned around and began walking back towards the restaurant.

"He's pretty smooth," remarked Jim.

Mohammed walked by the restaurant and parking lot and slowly looked the van over. He kept walking down the street and after about 200 yards, crossed the street and headed back to the bus shelter. "That's not it," said

Mohammed. "The van I saw was a darker blue. I also think that because there were so many wrappers in the van, it is possible that the man only uses the drive-thru."

"Good thinking Mohammed. I will be sure to keep my eye on the drive-thru," said Jim.

"I'll call in," said Jim. He pressed the button on the radio and spoke into the microphone. "Eagle One to Base, we are in position at the bus shelter across from target restaurant."

"Copy that Eagle One. We are at your house now."

"Mohammed has joined our surveillance team."

"Roger. Over and out," replied Uncle Frank.

The boys settled in to watch the restaurant and wait. Ben could smell the hamburgers and his stomach was making sounds to remind him he was hungry.

78

"Can you keep the noise down!" laughed Jim. "Spies are trying to concentrate here!"

Deep down, Jim was getting hungry too. He was thinking about how good a cheeseburger would taste right now.

Mubarak Learns a Lesson

Mubarak had been driving his car to the mall when his cell phone had rung. He was surprised to hear his Mother calling him. She never used his cell phone number and he was even surprised to know that she knew his number.

"Father wants you to come back to the store," she said flatly.

He hung up and wondered what his Father wanted to talk to him about. "Probably wants me to work today or something!" said Mubarak clearly annoyed. "I have friends to hang out with at the mall," he thought.

He turned around and headed back to the store.

As he was coming up the street to where the convenience store was located he noticed his brother's moped in front of the drugstore.

"That can't be Mohammed, he is home sleeping," Mubarak said, dismissing the thought.

He pulled into the parking lot and found a spot right in front. There was a sign that read "Handicapped Parking Only" in front of this spot.

"Ah good, my usual spot is available," Mubarak thought. As he got out of his car he checked himself in the mirror, admiring how handsome he was. He then swaggered into the store.

Mr. Asad had watched Mubarak pull in and was waiting for him to come through the door.

"Mubarak, can I talk to you please?" Mr. Asad in his best, calm voice and motioned for him to follow him to the back room.

"Sure Father," said Mubarak unaware of his father's anger.

Mr. Asad let Mubarak come in and then he shut the door. Mr. Asad came directly to the point. That was his way of dealing with most things.

"Mubarak, we are missing some of our inventory – comics and chocolate bars. Do you know what has happened to them?"

Mubarak knew that one day he might be asked about missing items and had practiced this a hundred times in his head. He was supposed to give a look of surprise and act like he was concerned but not sure how it could have happened.

That is not the way it worked out when his father asked the question. The question caught Mubarak off-guard and before he could regain his composure, his expression already gave everything away.

Mubarak tried to recover.

"I...I...am not sure what you mean Father," he stammered rather than replied.

Mr. Asad was convinced there was something going on. He could read people very well, especially his sons.

"Mubarak, you are my son and I love you. Sometimes we make mistakes and get off track. If you are willing to tell the truth, it will get better. If you persist in lies, your problems will only get worse," his father counseled.

Mubarak was getting a very sick feeling again in the pit of his stomach. He tried to look away from his father but Mr. Asad was having none of that.

"Look at me when I am talking to you!" Mr. Asad snapped.

Mubarak looked up.

"Tell me what you have been doing, Mubarak," his father said calmly. "Do not lie any longer."

Mubarak's mouth was very dry. He could barely clear his throat. His hand was shaking as he brushed a spec of fluff from his lap.

Mr. Asad was waiting quietly for his son to begin. He did not move a muscle and that made Mubarak feel even more uncomfortable.

Mubarak started to explain. "I'm the only one of my friends who doesn't have any money. Every time I go out, I don't have any money to spend. I'm tired of feeling like I can't enjoy myself. I started taking inventory from the store and selling it to the local kids at cheap prices. There was so much inventory that I didn't think you'd mind. I started a business so I could be happy. Don't you want me to be happy?"

Mr. Asad listened to the story and was truly disappointed with his son. "If you needed money, did it occur to you to come to me first?" asked Mr. Asad.

"You would just tell me to work more hours," answered Mubarak.

"Of course I would," said Mr. Asad in a firm tone.

"But then I would have no time to enjoy my friends," countered Mubarak.

"Mubarak, the Asad's are a hard working family. Running a convenience store is not an easy job. The hard work of your mother and myself have given you and your brother a good life so far. Do you agree?" he asked.

"Yes," said Mubarak quietly.

"We check inventory all the time. I figured the missing chocolate was the work of someone else. I have wrongly assumed the shipper was at fault. I now feel bad for that assumption."

"I am sorry Father, I did not mean to hurt anyone else," Mubarak said meekly.

"Well you did, Mubarak. You have hurt your family greatly. I am very disappointed with your actions. This is not the son that I raised. The thing that has hurt me most is that you felt you could not come to talk to me about your money predicament."

Mubarak was feeling very bad and sorry. When he looked up he saw his Mother standing in the doorway looking at him. She had a tear in her eye. That really hurt him.

"Is there anything else that you want to tell us right now?" asked Mr. Asad.

"No, Father. I am sorry to have dishonored the family," Mubarak said with remorse in his voice.

"Perhaps it is time you should go home and think about what you have done," said Mr. Asad.

"If I am still welcome at home," Mubarak said slowly.

"Mubarak, you are my son. Your mother and I love you. You will always be our son. You have made mistakes and it is our hope that you will learn from those mistakes. You will have to live with the knowledge that you have hurt us deeply with your actions."

Mubarak bowed his head.

"Before you go I want you to think about something," said Mr. Asad to Mubarak. "You have to decide if you want to live a life where your friends are most important and your actions support them or whether your family is most important and your actions put us first."

Mubarak kissed his mother on the cheek and left the store to go home to think. He knew the answer before he even got to his car.

The Fairgrounds

Frank, Scott, Christyn, Billy and Buster were just leaving Billy's house. They had been to talk to Felix about the counterfeit operation and how Billy would play a small but important role. Felix was not too keen at first but listened to the whole plan. He knew that Frank was a good ex-cop and a responsible adult and that he would make sure Billy was safe at all times.

The biggest problem was that Clarice was out getting groceries right now and could not be reached. Frank needed an answer right away and Felix made a decision to let Billy do it. He wondered what Clarice would say when she got home. It was important to help Mike and he knew that she would not object as long as Billy was taken care of. They left and headed for their next stop, Mike's store.

On the short drive there, Buster was in the front seat of the big car with his head out the window and tongue flapping in the breeze. His wagging tail kept whacking Christyn in the face.

"Buster, watch that tail," she said.

Buster didn't move a muscle. He poked her in the eye again with his tail.

When they pulled up in front of Boardzone Frank stayed in the car with Scott and Billy.

"Christyn, go in and see if Mike has returned. If not, ask Julie where he might be now," said Frank.

"OK!" said Christyn with a cheery voice. She undid her seatbelt and dashed into Mike's store.

Once inside she only saw Julie working away on some paperwork at one of her spotless counters.

"Hi Christyn," said Julie looking up from her work.

"Hi Julie," said Christyn. "Has Mike returned yet?"

"Not yet. He did phone to say he was on his way to the skate park site to meet with the city officials," replied Julie.

"Did he get the message about the counterfeiter and our plan?" asked Christyn.

"I passed it on to him and he was excited at the news."

"We're going to go to the skate park site to meet up with Mike. If he calls, tell him to stay there. We'll be there in a few minutes."

"Who's with you?"

"Jim's Uncle Frank, Scott and Billy," said Christyn.

"Where are Ben and Jim?" asked Julie.

"They are staking out a restaurant that the counterfeiter goes to hoping they will show up," said Christyn. "I have to get going. Bye."

When Christyn got back to the car, Frank was talking into the two-way radio to Ben. "So you haven't seen any blue vans come in yet?" said Frank.

"Nothing yet but we are going to stay here and continue to watch. Can you bring us something to eat when you come by?" said Jim in the background.

"I will take a salad!" said Mohammed, who was also hungry.

"Roger that," said Frank. "We'll all grab a bite to eat shortly."

Christyn explained where Mike was. Frank spoke into the radio again.

"Guys, we're on our way to the site of the new skate park to meet with Mike. We won't be long and then we will come to you and bring some lunch," said Uncle Frank.

"Excellent," said Jim. "Over and out."

Uncle Frank drove to the old fairgrounds. The fairgrounds site was a prime piece of land right in the middle of the city. It had been the home for the annual Summer and Winter Fairs for 57 years until the City decided that a bigger area was needed. The new site of the fairgrounds was further away on the edge of the city limits but had much more space. This left the four acres of land from the old fairgrounds available for a new owner. The price tag for the land was $250,000.

There were many groups interested in purchasing the land, including Mike. The City had held a lottery to offer the land fairly to all the potential buyers. Mike's name was drawn first and he had to put down a mandatory deposit of $100,000 right away and agree to come up with the remaining $150,000 by the middle of August.

The City was selling the land at a good price if the new owner agreed to be fully responsible for tearing down the old buildings. The cost of that demolition was about $100,000 and that was where the deposit was spent right after the contract was signed. The remaining cost of the land was only $150,000, which was a real bargain. Mike was still in the process of arranging that financing as he only had $100,000 in the bank for the deposit.

The rules of the contract stated that Mike had until the city council meeting on August 15 to arrange financing and complete the deal or the land would become available for one of the other bidders. If he did not arrange financing, then his original $100,000 that had already been spent would be lost.

Uncle Frank knew that the site was a perfect place for a skate park. It was centrally accessible for kids from the whole city and it was a good size. Four acres was a lot of room to house a skate park, stands and pro shop. Mike even wanted to setup a canteen and offer healthy snacks at reasonable prices. Mike was going to re-locate Boardzone into the new skate park site too, which would save him a bunch of rent money.

As Frank pulled his car into the parking lot he could see Mike standing next to another vehicle at the far end. He drove over to the spot where the two men were talking. He shut the vehicle off. Mike looked up at them and waved them over.

They all got out including Buster who immediately went off to find a tree and some privacy.

Frank said to the kids, "Quiet, please. Let Mike finish his conversation with the gentleman from the city."

Frank knew it was a city worker because the other vehicle parked had City of Exton markings on the door. It also said "Permits and Inspections" on the door.

"John, I don't understand what you are saying," said Mike clearly losing his patience. "I own this land and can do what I want with it."

The city worker spoke, "Technically you don't own the land until you finish paying the City the remaining money owed. But the bigger issue is that another group has filed a protest saying that they can make better use of the land and bring more tax revenue to the City. They also are saying they can raise the $150,000 by Aug 1."

Mike was trying to explain. "It doesn't matter if there is another group. There has always been someone trying to get this land from me. I have a signed contract with the City that states I have until August 15 to come up with the rest of the money. No one can come in before me."

The city official explained, "There is slight but important difference. The contract actually states that the final payment must be made no later than the August council meeting."

"Yes, that is right. The August council meeting is scheduled for Aug 15," said Mike.

"That is where the problem for you comes in. Someone is lobbying the city council to invoke a seldom-used part of the city constitution that states a city council meeting can be held up to two weeks early if more than 50% of the city councilors will not be in attendance on the originally scheduled date."

"John, there are 18 councilors in this city. It's not like nine or more of them are all going to be away on that day," said Mike.

John looked around like he was nervous.

"Mike, I've known you for years and I like you. That is why I am here today. Let's just say that I heard a rumor that some group has been offering to take the entire city council on a three-day trip to the Bahamas to visit a golfing resort. And the trip date is during the originally scheduled date of the August council meeting. The trip is free, the councilor gets to bring their spouse and in return all the group is asking for the date of the August meeting to be moved two weeks earlier."

"Two weeks earlier!" gasped Mike. "My financing won't be complete by that time. Are the group's actions even legal?"

"I'm afraid it is, Mike. It's not fair but it is legal. I hear that most of the city councilors approached so far have signed up for the trip," said John.

Frank had heard enough. He knew John and asked him a question.

"John, can we find out who this group is?"

"I only know they are a numbered company and are represented by the law firm of Finkleman and Burns," said John. "It was someone from the law firm, one of their agents, that presented each councilor with a letter outlining the trip and the request.

"What is a numbered company?" asked Christyn.

Uncle Frank whispered to Christyn, "It's the name a company uses when it is trying to hide its true identity."

"Does that mean it is a company that does bad things?" asked Billy.

"Not always," said Uncle Frank. "Some numbered companies are engaged in legitimate business. They have a number instead of a name because having a name is not important to them. Most companies want a name that customers can remember. A numbered company name is something like 675442 Philadelphia Ltd. Not exactly memorable is it?" said Uncle Frank.

"I see!" said Scott.

"I wonder who runs the numbered company offering those trips to the councilors?" said Scott.

"I wish we could find out!" remarked Christyn.

"Oh, we can," said Frank with a slight smile on his lips. "We can."

"Do you have the company number?" asked Frank.

John referred to some notes in a binder he was holding and responded back with the company information. Frank wrote it down and thanked him profusely.

At that moment Christyn noticed a large mother raccoon crossing the grass at the back of the fairgrounds. She was hurrying to a large tree that was probably where her home was. Christyn thought that raccoons looked like masked robbers.

Mike was beginning to realize that someone was trying to prevent him from taking ownership of this land. He was not happy at all.

"Frank, anything you can do to help me would be greatly appreciated," Mike said almost pleading.

"Let me do some checking with some 'friends' of mine," said Frank. "We'll see what we can find out."

They left Mike and John to finish off their conversation.

At this point Buster came racing up, panting like crazy with his tongue hanging out. Buster was dancing around like someone had stepped on his tail. The raccoon mother was growling as she climbed the tree. Buster stared at her, turned and raced to the car with his tail folded between his legs. He hopped through the front window and curled up on the floor. He wasn't taking any chances on getting a face full of angry raccoon claws.

"What's got into him?" asked Billy.

Uncle Frank got into the car. "What's up Buster? You look like you've seen a robber," chuckled Uncle Frank, knowing that Buster was a big chicken and had probably been surprised by a bunny or something.

"Poor Mike," thought Christyn. "I'm glad Uncle Frank is here to help."

"Let's go grab a burger you guys. We have to go visit a trio of Eagles on surveillance," said Uncle Frank.

"I almost forgot about them," said Billy.

"Can I call them on the two-way radio?" asked Scott. "I want to tell them about what we found."

"You can call them to see how they are doing and to let them know we are coming but don't explain the story yet. There could be lots of people tuned into the same frequency and I don't want word to spread we know what is going on."

Frank handed the two-way to Scott.

Scott pressed the button and said "Big Shot Scott from Base calling the Eagle Beak boys!"

Uncle Frank laughed with the others in the car.

The boys had been intently watching the restaurant and were all slightly surprised when there was a voice on the other end of the radio.

"Eagle Beak!" exclaimed Jim.

"He must be referring to your nose," announced Jim.

"Ha, ha, ha," mocked Scott.

"Base this is Eagle One. Did you get lost on the way to finding food?" said Jim.

"We are on our way with a story to tell you. Anything happening there?" said Scott.

"Nothing here, we…wait a second, a blue mini-van has just pulled into the drive-thru," Jim said in a low voice.

"Mohammed," said Ben, "is that the same mini-van?"

"It looks very similar Ben," said Mohammed confidently. "Yes! Yes, it is the same man I talked to earlier who is driving."

"Uncle Frank, what do we do?" said Jim.

"Sweet!" said Scott as he handed Uncle Frank the two-way radio.

"The first thing you do is to stay put. Watch the van and record what he does. Especially watch which direction he goes if he leaves before we get there. We are only about three minutes away," said Frank.

"Let's hope the drive-thru takes their time," said Mohammed.

The three watched the van wait its turn in line. Luckily there were two cars ahead of the van. The first car had three kids in the backseat so chances are they would be there for at least a minute or so.

They wanted to stare at the mini-van but they didn't want to be spotted because the driver might take off. Ben hid behind a sign in the bus shelter and used his binoculars to watch the van and the person driving.

"It looks like there is only one person in the van," said Ben. "Mohammed, take the binoculars and tell me if the man is the same."

Mohammed took the binoculars from Ben and looked through them.

"It is fuzzy and I cannot tell," said Mohammed.

"To make it more clear, turn the black dial on top slowly to the right," said Ben.

Mohammed began to turn the dial while still watching the van through the binoculars.

"Ah, that is better, I can make out the man…YES! That is the man!" exclaimed Mohammed.

Ben's heart began to beat very fast. He looked over at Jim.

Jim was saying a small prayer that the fast food service would continue to be slow.

The van driver began to order and then pay for his meal. He waited for the food to be brought to the order window. It seemed like an eternity. There was no sign of Uncle Frank's car.

The cashier came to the window with a bag and handed it to the driver. She went to close the window and the driver must have said something to her because she re-opened the window and responded. She disappeared back into the restaurant.

At that moment Uncle Frank pulled up in front of the bus stop.

"Are we glad to see you!" Ben said almost shouting.

"Calm down. Where is the blue van now?" Frank said.

"He's just finishing at the drive-thru," said Jim.

"Hop in the car quickly and we will follow him."

"Suh-weeeeet!" cheered Billy. "We get to follow a bad guy!"

Frank advised the group. "I want everyone to buckle in and I want quiet as we do this. Everyone understand?"

"Yes," they said in unison.

"I want to get close enough so that I can make out his license plate number. I will then call it into a friend on the police force."

The exit of the drive-thru would force the blue mini-van to leave the restaurant 100 yards west of where Frank was parked. Frank hoped the van would turn west away from their vehicle. This would make following the van easier. If the van turned east, they would be forced to do a U-turn in traffic and they might get spotted.

Ben continued to watch the driver at the drive-thru. The cashier re-appeared with a large drink and handed it to the driver. The driver then exited the restaurant and turned west.

Frank mumbled, "Perfect." The kids knew why.

It was never easy to follow someone without being noticed. It was easier if you had a couple of vehicles to assist in the surveillance and of course, it was always easier when your car was not so noticeable like Frank's big old Cadillac.

For these reasons Frank decided to keep at least 300 yards between his vehicle and the blue mini-van. The van continued down the same street and after eight blocks turned right onto Sicamour Road. It was also a busy street so it would not attract much attention if another car turned onto it after the blue van did.

"Can anyone make out the license plate?" Frank said, cursing his aging eyes.

The van went a quarter of a mile down Sicamour Road until it turned into the Westway Village mall. The mall was small and contained a bowling alley, a convenience store, a hairdresser, a subway sandwich store and a storage place. The U-Store It had gone out of business about a year earlier. It was one of those places where you could rent some space to store things you had no room for at home. Each storage area was large enough to allow you to park a car. There were 18 storage areas each separate and with their own door. Now the buildings were vacant and the office had its windows and front door covered by sheets of plywood. It looked like no one had been there in months.

Frank drove slowly past the entrance of the mall, not wanting to attract any attention.

The blue van pulled into the lot at the far end closest to the convenience store. The driver turned off the engine of the van but remained in the vehicle.

Frank continued to the second entrance to the mall and turned in there. He pulled into an empty stall about 150 yards away from the van. There was a silver Ford F-250 Super Duty pick-up truck in the stall next to them that blocked them nicely from the van. The pick-up would still allow them to watch the van without being seen easily by the van driver.

The van driver began eating what looked like a burger. "I bet it is a cheeseburger he is eating!" said Mohammed like he was clairvoyant.

"Was that the kind of wrappers that you saw in the van when you looked in the front window?" asked Jim.

"Yes," said Mohammed.

They watched the driver eat for several minutes.

"This is getting kind of boring," whined Billy. "It's never this boring on TV."

That thought made Frank remember back to the days where he was a detective. He couldn't remember how many nights he sat watching a house all night and nothing happened. Cold, alone and sleepy was typically all he felt on those stakeouts. Occasionally something did happen and it was interesting but most stakeouts were very difficult to remain alert.

"You're right Billy," Frank said. "They can be boring but let's stay sharp. We have a suspect in sight and we want to see what he is up to."

"I think I got most of his license plate," said Jim. "I have it written down. I will keep looking and make sure I get the full and correct plate number."

The driver ate for a little while longer and then got out of the van. He looked around and got back into his car. He pulled out of the parking spot he was in and drove down towards the unused storage place. Frank was going to start his car and follow but then he noticed that there was no way to leave the parking lot from where the blue van had gone so he waited to see what would happen next.

The van driver pulled up in front of one of the storage lockers. There was a big "1" and "6" painted in white on the red door. The door was similar to a garage door except there was a big padlock on the side.

The van driver got out of the van again and walked over to the door. He looked around casually and Frank knew this was a man up to no good. He was acting very suspicious and the fact he looked like he was going to open a door on a business that was all boarded up was even more suspicious.

"This guy is a real 'mystery man'," thought Frank. "What are you up to?" Frank said so softly that none of the kids heard.

The mystery man approached the side of the big door where the lock was situated. He pulled a set of keys from his pants pocket and unlocked the padlock. He pulled the lock away, grabbed the handle and threw open the door. The rusty door made metal on metal grinding sound as it went up.

"Obviously the owner of the business had not been keeping the place in good condition," thought Frank. "I bet that's why it went out of business."

The man disappeared into the storage area. Frank could not see inside the storage area from where they were parked. Frank was thinking they were going to have to get closer to see what was inside the storage area. At that moment the man came out of the storage area and walked to the back of the van. He opened the back door of the van and returned to the storage area. After a minute he appeared carrying a large box with several smaller boxes on top.

Frank asked "J., can you see what's in those boxes?"

Jim was using the binoculars and after a few seconds responded "I can make out some letters and numbers on the boxes only. They are cardboard and plain otherwise."

"Keep watching," advised Uncle Frank. "You never know what you will see next."

Jim adjusted the zoom feature on the binoculars and was able to get a very close image of the boxes as the man placed them into the van.

The man went back to the storage shed and came out carrying four or five complete skateboards. Even Frank could make out what they were. Through the binoculars, Jim could see the name "Element" on the top deck.

"He's carrying at least one Element complete," Jim said excitedly. "We've got him Uncle Frank. Call the police!"

"We don't have anything yet," cautioned Frank. "Keep watching and see what else he does."

"But he's loading counterfeit skateboards. Let's call the police and have him arrested," said Scott.

"Look guys, I am with you and think he is loading up counterfeit skateboards but if he is the bad guy and we come down on him and he is actually loading old skateboards that he owns, we might scare him away forever. We can't be sure he is guilty yet," explained Uncle Frank.

"So how are we going to make sure he is guilty?" asked Billy.

"Funny you should ask Billy, anyone need to buy a skateboard?" said Uncle Frank with a wry smile on his face.

The man looked like he was finished loading the van because he shut the rear door on the van. He returned to the storage area and pulled the door shut. It looked like he had to pull very hard to close the door. The man replaced and locked the padlock and then got back into his van.

He started the van, backed out and proceeded to leave the lot. Uncle Frank advised everyone to ensure their seatbelts were once again buckled up. Frank let the van get ahead of him and then Frank pulled into traffic well behind the van.

"Where are we going?" asked Billy.

Frank was concentrating on the van but said, "We're going wherever he goes."

They followed the van for a few blocks and then the van turned down Rochelle Drive, which was lead toward the local school. When the van got to the school it slowed right down. The van driver was obviously looking for something or someone.

There were quite a few kids playing on the school's soccer pitch and on a nearby play structure. The van driver pulled into the lot and parked right next to the play structure.

Frank again drove past the parking lot and pulled onto the driveway beside the school. This would allow them to be out of sight but still nearby. They would have to go on foot from here to get closer.

The kids and Frank piled out of the car. Frank told Buster to stay with him. Buster seemed to sense the command in Frank's voice because this time he did not try to wander off.

Frank said, "We're going to split into two groups. "Ben, J. and Mohammed will go in the first group. Take this radio and head around the building towards the back. Keep listening to the radio but keep it turned down. We may have to leave in a hurry if the van leaves."

"I will lead the rest of us with the second radio to the front of the building. I want everyone to walk normally like you are here to play. Let's not look like we are watching this guy. I want to see what he is doing," said Frank.

Frank turned to Billy. "Billy, I am going to give you $50 to buy a complete."

"Suh-weeeeet!" Billy shouted pumping his fist into the air.

"Billy! Pay attention to Uncle Frank," Jim demanded.

Billy calmed down immediately and asked Uncle Frank to continue.

"When I give you the OK signal, I want you to walk over to the van and let the man see you coming. If he asks you about buying a skateboard, say you are interested in seeing what he has. If he asks you what kind of board you were looking for, tell him an Element," said Frank.

"But I want a Birdhouse board!" protested Billy.

Ben jumped into the conversation. "Billy, he may not have a Birdhouse board but we know he has an Element. Just follow Uncle Frank's instructions."

Frank continued with his plan.

"Ask him how much and tell him you can only afford $50. If he wants to make a deal, tell him you have to go to your room to get the money but you can be back in 10 minutes. Tell him to wait. Then you return to the car, here. Do you think you can handle all that?"

"Yes" said Billy cautiously "I approach the van, make sure the guy sees me, wait for him to ask about buying a board, ask about an Element board and go back to the car to get $50." 93

"I will give you the $50 to buy the board. Then bring the board back here," said Frank.

"Got it," said Billy.

"Team One, head into position," ordered Frank.

Team One ran off behind the school.

'Team Two, let's go," said Frank and they began their walk along the front of the school towards the play structure.

As they approached the edge of the parking lot where the van was parked a message over the radio came in loud and clear.

"Team One in place and watching subject," said Ben.

Frank responded, "Roger that, Team Two in place."

Frank could see the man standing behind the van. The van door was open and two boys were talking to the man. One boy was holding up a skateboard that the man had just passed him.

"Now's your chance," said Frank to Billy.

Billy was a little nervous but he knew this was an important job. He was ready to do it to help his good friend Mike.

Billy swallowed hard, got a thumb's up from Scott and Christyn and headed over to the van. As he walked closer to the van he could see the boy with the skateboard giving the man some money. He couldn't make out how much but the kid looked happy.

The man was about 45 years old and was dressed in dirty jeans and a Harley Davidson t-shirt. He was smoking and as Billy got closer he could see the man was missing one of his front teeth. Each time the man talked, the missing front tooth was visible. He had long greasy gray-black hair tied into a ponytail and a big stomach sticking out below his shirt.

"This guy obviously needs to work out," thought Billy.

Billy pretended to be interested by getting close to the van but not too close. The man could see that Billy was interested. He was watching Billy as he continued to talk to the other kids.

Finally the man spoke up.

"Hey kid," he said to Billy "do you like skateboarding?"

"I…I sure do." Billy tried to sound normal.

"I've got a friend at the skateboard factory who asked me to sell some of his boards for him, cheap. He needs the money to build some new boards. Got any money?" asked the man.

94

"I sure do, got $50 bucks from my Grannie," said Billy starting to adlib a bit as he felt more confident.

"What kind of board do you want?" asked the man.

"I've been saving for an Element complete," said Billy, "but I don't have enough money."

"Well today's your lucky day kid," the man said sounding just like a used car salesman. "I've got a new Element complete for $50."

Billy knew this was all he needed to do for Uncle Frank but he wanted to see the board so it wouldn't look obvious.

"Can I see the board?" said Billy.

"Sure, kid. C'mere," said the man and waved him over to the van.

Billy approached the van cautiously. He would never have done this on his own but he felt safe knowing his friends and Uncle Frank were watching.

He pulled out the Element board and handed it to Billy. Billy took it in his hands. Billy knew right away this board was quite a bit lighter than a real complete.

"Oh wow." Billy feigned interest. "This is a choice board."

The man gave a toothless smile.

"Listen kid, I gotta get going soon. Today, one day only I can give you the board for $50. Whatta ya say?"

"Uh…" hesitated Billy "I really want the board but I don't have the money on me. Can you give me 10 minutes to run home and get it from my room?"

Billy looked at the guy almost pleading with his eyes.

The guy looked around as another kid came up to the van.

"Sure kid. Ten minutes but hurry up though. I can't wait all day," said the man as he turned to talk to the next kid.

Billy turned around and ran back to the front of the school. He did not see the others and hoped they hadn't left without him. When he ran back to the side of the school he could see the others all gathered by the car.

Billy was really out of breath from the short run and the excitement of the charade he had just played on the man.

"Hi…guys…I did…it!!" puffed Billy.

"Tell us!" exclaimed Ben.

"What did he say?" said Christyn.

"Give him a moment to catch his breath!" said Uncle Frank.

Billy took a moment. Christyn offered him a drink from her bottle of water that he accepted gratefully. Billy thought for a moment that Christyn was actually pretty nice.

"Don't bother returning the bottle," said Christyn. "After you've back-washed all your disgusting cooties, I don't want it."

"Ah!" Billy thought, "there's the Christyn I remember."

"Uncle Frank, I need the $50," Billy said finally catching his breath. "The guy is offering me a complete Element board for $50."

"Do you think it is a counterfeit?" asked Uncle Frank.

"I held it in my hands and it looked real but was too light compared to the ones in Mike's shop," said Billy.

"Sounds like we got us a counterfeit board," said Scott.

Uncle Frank pulled out his wallet and took out two twenties and a ten. He rolled up the bills and gave it to Billy.

"Take this money and in a few minutes run back and say you want to buy the Element. Make sure he gives you the board and then you give him all the money. Before you go, try to remember his license plate number."

"Can you handle that cootie breath?" Christyn smirked.

"Yes sir!" and Billy saluted Christyn.

They waited about two minutes and then Frank sent Billy back. As Billy left Frank told everyone to stay by the car with one radio and Frank would watch Billy. Frank would carry the second radio.

Billy ran back around the front of the school and could see the van still there. There were no kids around it and the man was just putting out his cigarette.

"Hey kid. That was quick," the man said in surprise.

"I don't live far away," Billy mumbled.

"Got the money?" the man asked.

"Yes, can I see the board again," Billy asked.

"Sure kid, it's yours after all," said the man as he handed the board to Billy.

Billy held the board in one hand and dug around in his front pocket to get the money. He stalled for time pretending to look for the money but was really looking at the license plate.

"TH4582YT" said Billy over and over to himself.

Billy gave the money to the man and ran off clutching the counterfeit board with both hands.

As he turned around to leave Billy heard the man laugh out loud and say, "Pleasure doin' business with you partner."

All the way back to the car Billy kept repeating the license plate number over and over again.

When he got back to the car he quickly yelled for someone to write it down. The next thing he did was hand the counterfeit board to Scott who immediately put the board in the backseat.

"Let's all get in the car," suggested Frank. "We'll talk there."

All the kids hopped into the car. Buster was happy to have everyone back paying attention to him.

"Yup," said Scott with confidence in his voice. "This is indeed a counterfeit board. You can tell by the weight and the color on the graphics. Just like the other board we saw from Bradley."

Checking Out the Warehouse

"Let's see where this guy is going, shall we?" Frank started the car and pulled up to the edge of the street. The parking lot where the blue van was parked only had one exit and he had not appeared yet. About a minute later, the blue van came out of the parking lot and turned onto the street towards their car. The van drove past Frank's car and Frank pulled into traffic behind him at a safe distance. Frank did not want to be noticed by the driver.

The driver of the blue van drove carefully down Pine Boulevard and then turned west on Racicot Street. The van driver drove more slowly now and Frank thought he might have been noticed. As Frank watched the driver of the van it appeared like he was looking for something. The van driver was scanning the street from left to right as he drove.

Finally the blue van signaled and pulled over into the parking lot of Watson's Qwik Stop. The van driver went into the store and came out a couple of minutes later carrying a pack of cigarettes. He opened the back door of his van, lit up a cigarette and sat down on the rear bumper of his van. It seemed like he was waiting for someone who was late because he kept checking his watch.

"What is he doing?" asked Christyn.

"I'm not sure," said Frank, "but I'm thinking he is planning something to do with the counterfeit boards."

Buster was getting hot sitting in this car and was really looking forward to some ice cream or a drink of water. He stuck his nose right in Frank's right ear and began to pant and blow hot breath on Frank.

"Whoa Buster. I think it's time we got you some of those mint dog biscuits. When was the last time we brushed your teeth?" said Frank.

"You're getting hot, aren't you fella! I'm going to pull into this drive-thru while we wait and watch the blue van. Anyone up for a burger?"

Buster wagged his tail wildly at the word "burger".

"How 'bout a nice cup of water for you Buster?" said Frank.

Buster made a sighing sound. His ears dropped and put his nose between his paws.

The kids passed their orders to Frank. While Frank waited for the food to be prepared, the kids kept their eye on the blue van. After a few minutes the food was ready and Frank pulled into the parking lot of the restaurant. It was across the street and down a bit from the Qwik Stop so they could eat and still watch the blue van easily.

Everyone was hungry and the food tasted good. Buster had enjoyed his water and even had a few french fries from Billy when Billy wasn't looking.

"Look, someone is talking to the van driver," said Christyn.

A teenage boy had approached the van driver and struck up a conversation. The van driver reached into the van and pulled out two boards. The boy looked over both boards and gave the driver some money. The kid left with one board.

98 About 10 minutes later another group of kids arrived on bicycles and began to talk to the driver. Two of the kids ended up buying a board each. As they were leaving, a blue Mustang pulled up to the van. The driver of the sports car didn't even get out of the car. The van driver listened to the person in the car for a few seconds and then retrieved a skateboard from his van. He passed the board through the car window and grabbed some cash from the driver. The Mustang took off in a spray of gravel and dirt.

"This guy does pretty brisk business doesn't he?" exclaimed Uncle Frank.

"Unbelievable!" said Ben.

"No wonder Mike is having trouble selling boards. This guy is taking away all his business," lamented Jim.

They watched the van for about 30 minutes in total and then the van driver was on the move again. Uncle Frank began to follow the van again.

"I think I am going to get a little help," said Uncle Frank.

He used his cell phone to call someone.

"Hello. Is Ron there?" Frank said into the cell phone.

Frank waited for a few seconds.

"Hi Ron. Frank Brandt here."

Frank and the other person chatted for a few moments and then Frank asked for a favor.

"Ron, I need you to run a plate for me...sure...Pennsylvania TH4582YT."

Where ever Ron was he must have had access to a computer because Frank did not have to wait long for the answer.

Uncle Frank asked Christyn to write down the information about the registered owner of the van.

"Cliff Stinson, yes, I've got it. 476 Rengate Way Apt #4, Exton.

"Thanks Ron. Oh, one other thing. I know…I know…I'll bring you a dozen Krispy Kreme doughnuts in the morning…I need you to find anything you can on a numbered company."

Frank listened for a few seconds and then gave the numbered company information to Ron.

"Thanks Ron. You're a lifesaver. Later, I'll fill you in on what is going on. It looks like we're going to spend some work time together. I'll come by in the morning and we can discuss it. Good-bye."

While Uncle Frank put his cell phone away, the kids in the car waited anxiously for him to fill them in.

"Well" said Frank, "my buddy Ron Sampson has come through big for us. He has found the registered owner of the van and that person's address. He is also looking into the numbered company for us and should know more tomorrow."

Christyn looked at the paper and read the name of the van's registered owner out loud. "Cliff Stinson, that is a name I have never heard before," said Christyn.

"Me neither," said Frank. "People like him move around a lot so he is probably new to Exton."

"What do we do next, Uncle Frank?" asked Jim, clearly curious about the next steps.

"We continue to follow the van and see where our Mr. Stinson takes us," said Frank as he stared out the front windshield.

The van made a series of turns until it was on the west side of Exton in the warehouse district. This was the area of town where there was mostly large business buildings. The buildings were all basically the same, 30,000–50,000 square feet one-story warehouses with large loading docks for semi-trucks to load and unload goods.

Every few blocks there was at least one large warehouse that was several stories tall. The van pulled into one of these larger warehouses and the name on the front of the building said "Lee International Trading Co. – Wholesale Florist and Supplies. There were only a few cars in the large parking lot. The van backed up into a spot near a large loading door.

"This warehouse seems different than the others," thought Frank. Frank continued to survey the building. "Now what is it that is so different?" he wondered.

"Frank," said Scott, "why does this warehouse have barbed wire all along the top of the fence?"

"That's it!" exclaimed Frank. "I thought there was something strange about this place and look at the windows."

Uncle Frank didn't usually get excited but he was now. All the kids looked at the windows of the building.

"They are all covered in bars and wire mesh. This place is heavily protected. Look at the corners of the roof – do you see the surveillance cameras? Someone is probably watching every vehicle that comes in and out of the lot."

"Why would a wholesale florist have so much security?" asked Jim.

"I'm guessing they aren't just dealing in flowers and vases here J.," growled Uncle Frank.

They had pulled over across the street from the warehouse and had been watching to see what the van driver would do. The van driver had gotten out of the van and had entered the side door next to the large loading door.

"It's too bad we can't see what's going on inside," said Christyn.

Frank was about to agree when he noticed the large loading door open.

"Hey guys, look. Something is happening by the van," said Frank.

The van driver walked out of the building through the large open door and went around and opened up the back door of the van. Two other men walked out into the daylight and stood in front of the van. They looked impatient as they waited for the van driver. The van driver approached them and began talking to them. After a minute of talking, the van driver reached into his coat pocket and pulled out an envelope. He gave the envelope to the larger of the two men and the man pulled what was clearly a large amount of cash from the envelope. The large man started counting the cash.

When the man was finished counting the cash he said something quickly to the other man and that man nodded his head. The large man shouted something to someone inside the warehouse and a few seconds later a third man in blue overalls came out of the warehouse wheeling a pallet full of skateboards. A pallet is a wooden platform that someone loads merchandise on. A device called a pallet jack picks up the wooden platform and allows you to wheel it to where ever the merchandise has to be moved. It is just an easy way to move heavy or a large amount of objects. In this case, many skateboards at once.

"Look at all those counterfeit skateboards!" whistled Jim.

"Holy cow!" said Billy. "I have never seen so many skateboards at one time."

Jim was really annoyed at what he saw. These men were dealing in counterfeit skateboards and because of that Mike was close to losing his shop and his dream of opening a new skate park.

"Uncle Frank, what can we do to stop this," pleaded Jim. "If this guy sells all those counterfeit skateboards, Mike will never make any money."

At that point the van driver began loading the skateboards into the back of the truck while the other men went back inside the warehouse.

"J., I need to closer look at the building. I have to see what is going on inside," said Frank. "You kids have to stay in the car. It could be very dangerous and I don't want any of you to get hurt."

"Are you sure we can't help in any way?" said Ben.

"I will take one of the two-way radios and if I need your help, I will let you know," said Frank.

"OK!" said Jim "I'll man the radio."

Buster looked concerned. He wasn't worried about Frank but he could sure use another drink of water. As Frank left the car, Buster barked anxiously.

Frank got out of the car and tucked the two-way radio into his coat pocket. He wished he were still carrying his police-issue 9mm. He liked the security of having a reliable pistol close by. "Once a cop, always a cop," he muttered to himself.

Frank crossed the street and walked along the front of the building. He knew that if he entered into the lot through the front gate he would be in full view of the cameras that were watching the lot. He decided to do some checking of his own first. He walked to one end of the building and had a look around back. As he approached the back corner of the fence, he noticed there was a gate in the fence that was padlocked shut. "This looks like it used to be a back entrance," thought Frank.

The padlock was old and rusted and didn't look like it was in top condition any longer. Frank looked the back of the building over and to his delight did not see any cameras watching the back. The owners of the building must have thought that anyone coming to the building would have to come in through the front entrance. Frank decided to make his own entrance.

Looking around there was garbage and debris strewn everywhere on the ground. Clearly the owner of this building was spending all their money taking care of the building and not the outside of this property. Frank found a small length of heavy metal pipe. It looked like it came off of some big vehicle.

He picked it up and walked over to the gate. He looked around and no one was in sight. He raised the bar and brought it down very hard precisely on the old lock. The lock shattered in three pieces like it was made of clay.

Most of the lock fell to the ground. Frank quickly removed the remaining pieces of the broken lock and opened the door in the fence.

Frank felt a rush of excitement that he had not felt in a long time. What he was doing was not right but he needed to find out what was going on inside the building.

The kids could barely make out what Frank was doing but they did see him quickly open the back gate and slip inside the compound.

"He's in!" squealed Billy.

"Shall we call him on the two-way to see how he is doing?" asked Scott.

"No way!" said Ben. "If someone is close by, they may hear our voice and spot Frank. We will wait for his instructions."

Frank had slipped inside the compound and immediately made his way over to the side of the building. Frank was not as young and fit as he once was so the word "sprinting" is generous to describe how he moved.

102

He did not want to be seen by anyone looking out a back window of the warehouse. When he got to the edge of the building, he waited there for three minutes. He waited to see if anyone came rushing out to meet him and he needed to catch his breath a little. The excitement and the running had his heart racing. He knew he had to calm down before his next move.

Not far away from where Frank was standing there was a conversation going on inside the building. The three men were discussing the deal they had just made with Cliff Stinson.

"Cliff is our best customer these days. He seems to be able to sell as many skateboards as we can give him," said the smaller man.

The larger man just grunted. Obviously he was not much of a talker. The other man who had wheeled out the pallet full of counterfeit goods was busy moving other pallets of skateboards from a large container. The warehouse was huge inside. On the floor in front of them there were large shipping containers stacked. Each container could easily hold a large pick-up truck.

There were 18 containers stacked inside the warehouse and the first three containers held 20 pallets of skateboard decks, wheels, bearings and trucks.

The smaller man was named Vincent Lee. He had come to the United States from China as a young man and four years ago had taken over his father's wholesale florist business. Vincent had found there was not a lot of money to be made in selling wholesale floral supplies so he had started looking for other goods to trade. He had found the perfect scam. He had contacts in China and they could provide him with access to any type of goods he wanted.

He had a regular shipping schedule setup and the United States Customs Service treated Lee International Trading Co. as a legitimate company. They rarely got inspected anymore. The government was always trying to find drugs in shipments. Vincent knew that the Customs agents only had the capacity to check 1 out of every 100 containers that passed through U.S. ports. With this knowledge and the fact that he had no interest in drugs, Vincent felt very sure that he could import just about anything else without much worry.

He had decided that importing counterfeit items that were in high demand by teenagers was the most lucrative for him. He had found sources for counterfeit skateboards, counterfeit CDs and clothing that looked real but was not.

"I buy these items for about a $1.00 a piece and I can sell them for $20.00 to $30.00 each. Not a bad day's work!" he said to himself smiling. He liked easy money. He had never wanted to work as hard as his father. His father had worked six days a week for 12 hours a day and had died of a heart attack one Sunday while counting inventory. Vincent never wanted to die like that. His father never stopped once to enjoy what he had accumulated.

Vincent did though. In about two years after the death of his father, Vincent had enjoyed himself so much that he realized he was going to be out of money soon. It was then that Vincent had decided he needed to begin trading in other things beside floral supplies.

Vincent looked over the floor of the warehouse and thought about all the merchandise that was in the containers. The containers had just arrived two days earlier. Vincent had been waiting for this shipment. He had $100,000 of his money tied up in this shipment and after all the goods were sold, Vincent expected to make $1,250,000. He had buyers lined up for the counterfeit skateboards. He had other buyers ready to take the cases of CDs. There was even a semi-truck arriving in the morning that was going to take all of the counterfeit clothes. The clothes were headed for Florida, Georgia and Texas. This was going to be a good week for Vincent Lee. At last he was going to be able to buy that Porsche Boxster S that he had test driven a few weeks earlier. He was thinking about that car when there was a shout from the second floor catwalk. It was Sing Li. He worked in the building and was in charge of monitoring the security video. Sing Li was running high along the second floor catwalk that ran along the length of the building.

"Someone is hiding at the back of the building!" shouted Sing Li.

Vincent motioned for the large man to investigate. The man hurried off in the same direction as Sing Li had been running.

Vincent did not like surprises and was feeling a bit concerned at the news of a possible intruder.

Uncle Frank had been trying to look in a window but could not reach high enough to see in. He had been busy trying to pull some boxes towards a window and had not noticed he was in plain view of a different security camera watching the back of the building. Frank was in the middle of standing on the boxes and rubbing the dirt away from the window when he heard a sound behind him that made his blood freeze solid.

Uncle Frank Needs Help

From behind him Frank heard the familiar sound of a shell being pumped into the chamber of a shotgun.

"I don't know who you are, but you had better turn around slowly with your hands raised high in the air," said Sing Li. Sing Li had the shotgun raised and was aiming at Uncle Frank. He had a menacing look in his eyes.

Frank turned around slowly and raised his hands. "Doesn't this just figure!" Frank complained to himself. "Some ex-cop I am!"

"Come with me," ordered Sing Li and with his shotgun motioned Frank to move toward the back entrance. Also standing at the entrance now was the larger man Frank had seen earlier.

The kids could not see of this from where Frank had parked the car.

"How do you think he is doing?" asked Christyn.

"I'm sure he is fine," said Jim.

Uncle Frank was not fine. In fact he was in big trouble. The first man was enormous. He was at least 6 feet 5 inches and weighed over 300 lbs. The man was bald and when he opened his mouth he was missing all of his front teeth. The man was wearing a t-shirt and jeans and his arms were like tree trunks.

"This doesn't look good," thought Frank. "I have to think of something."

"Excuse me gentlemen," said Frank. "I was looking for the Watson Brothers Import/Export Company, I don't think this is the building. I'm sorry to inconvenience you, I will just be on my way."

Frank tried to turn and walk the other way but Sing Li prevented him from leaving.

"If you don't want to feel the power of this shotgun, you will come with us," demanded Sing Li.

Frank clearly had no choice and walked inside the building with his hands high in the air.

Jim was impatiently waiting for Frank to check in. Jim knew that Frank had been gone for over 20 minutes now and he said he would check in every 10 minutes. He hoped nothing had gone wrong.

"What could go wrong?" wondered Jim.

Back in the warehouse Frank did not like the situation he found himself in. Sing Li had the shotgun trained on Frank as his boss was looking over Frank trying to figure out who Frank was.

"Who are you?" demanded the large man.

Frank glared at him. "I'm Frank Brandt with the Exton Police. You have made a very big mistake detaining me at gunpoint. Very soon this building will be surrounded." Frank lied.

Sing Li looked at his boss and then looked around the massive warehouse. Sing Li began to laugh out loud.

106

"I don't think so. I don't think anyone is coming. You look more like an old man than a cop."

Frank was already mad at being caught but this guy with the shotgun was really getting on his nerves. Frank was thinking that he had to do two things. The first thing he had to do was figure out a plan to gain the upper hand on these guys. The second thing he planned to do was to take this annoying guy outside and kick his butt later.

As Frank was thinking about his options he knew that he did not like the current situation he had put himself into. Frank was not sure whom he was dealing with, he did not have any backup, he was not armed and he was outnumbered. He was thinking this situation couldn't get worse when it did.

"Uncle Frank," said a voice from Frank's pocket. The men around Frank looked at Frank like he was a ventriloquist.

"What was that?" barked Sing Li.

"Uncle Frank…are you OK?" said the voice again. Frank was not able to reach into his pocket and turn down the radio.

Frank looked at the men. He couldn't help but telegraph a helpless expression on his face. He was worried that the kids might somehow try to get involved and they would be put in danger because of Frank getting caught.

The smaller man looked at Frank and said, "So, you have backup after all. It sounds like you've got a kid waiting for you. Is he waiting outside on his bicycle?"

Sing Li laughed. The large man reached into Frank's pocket and took out the two-way radio.

The smaller man whispered something to Sing Li and Sing Li trotted off towards the back door.

"Sit down on that chair there," said the large man pointing to a metal folding chair near by.

Frank walked the few feet to the chair and sat down. The large man took a roll of gray duct tape from a shelf and wrapped it around Frank several times so he was securely fastened to the chair. Frank knew that he could still stand up, sort of, with the chair attached if he had to but he certainly couldn't move anywhere fast. He really needed to tell the kids to call for help and he wasn't sure how to do it.

Back in the car Jim was really concerned now. It had been 30 minutes since Frank had left the car and when he had called Frank twice on the radio, there was no answer. Jim decided that he was going to walk down to where Frank had entered the fence to see what he could see.

"Guys," declared Jim "I'm going to have a quick look at the back of the building to see if I can see Uncle Frank. I'm worried that something has happened to him and he may need my help."

Christyn was clearly worried at the thought that Frank may be in trouble. She was also very concerned about seeing Jim leave the car and go to the same place where Frank seemed to have disappeared.

"Are you sure that is what Frank would want?" Christyn asked in a hesitant voice.

"Look Christyn, Frank has helped us so many times and now I have a chance to help him. I'm going to take a quick look and report back. I won't be more than five minutes.

"Be careful," said Billy.

"Yes, watch your back," said Scott.

"Do you want me to come with you?" asked Ben.

"No, I need you to stay here with the others in case I need help," said Jim.

"Will do," said Ben.

"I'm going to be right back, don't worry," Jim said with a brave smile.

He opened the car door and Buster started to follow him.

"Sorry Buster old pal. You have to wait in the car too," said Jim.

Buster could feel that something was not right and stared intently at the building where Frank was now being held.

Jim crossed the street quickly and walked away from the front of the building where the cameras were and headed along the perimeter fence towards the back. When he got to the back gate he could see where Frank had smashed the lock to gain entrance to the fenced compound.

Jim could see the back of the building clearly now and Frank was nowhere to be found.

Jim thought to himself "Either Frank is on the other side of the building or he found a way inside. What should I do now?" he pondered to himself. "It looks pretty quiet back there, I think I will take a quick look."

In the car, Ben was watching Jim walk up to the back gate and look around. He could hardly stand it anymore. He did not want to see two people he cared for disappear.

Then Christyn had a great idea. "Ben, why don't you call the police on your cell phone?"

Ben was not sure if he should. He was not sure what was the right thing to do. When he looked back to where Jim was just a few seconds earlier, he could see no one standing by the fence. "What had happened to Jim?" he wondered.

"Christyn, you may be right. I just don't want it to be a false alarm. If I call the police and there is no problem, I would feel stupid. I am not sure what to do," said Ben.

"Are you willing to take that chance?" asked Christyn.

Jim had slipped through the opening in the fence like Frank had done and once inside the compound, Jim had quickly run over to the back wall of the building. He did not want to be seen and he wanted to try to get a look inside a window of the building. He crept along the edge of the building working his way towards a large mechanical unit. It was a rectangular shape about five feet high and seven feet long. He thought it might be some sort of air-conditioning unit for the warehouse. Whatever it was it was big enough for him to hide behind. He was thankful for this big obstacle. His heart was already beating fast and he was shaking a little.

From where he was hiding behind the metal unit, he could peek around the corner and make out a door. The door had one of those push-button combination locks on it. It looked like a solid metal door. He was wondering what the combination was when the door handle started to move. His heart froze.

"What am I going to do?" he thought, panic racing through his brain.

The door opened and a man appeared. The man was carrying a shotgun and he looked around as he came out the door. Satisfied that nothing was there, he turned right and headed along the back of the building away from Jim.

Jim had had enough. He was going to make a hasty exit. He was already scared and seeing a man coming out with a shotgun was enough for him to know he should not be there.

Jim turned around as quietly as he could and looking over his shoulder, checked to see where the man was heading. He was walking in the other direction so Jim decided to sprint back towards the gate in the fence.

Jim crouched down and bolted for the fence. Unfortunately for Jim, his foot kicked an empty soda can as he began his run and the can noisily clattered across the parking lot. This immediately made the man with the shotgun turn around. He saw Jim in mid-stride and the large man began to run back in the direction of Jim.

Jim was sweating. He could hear someone shouting from behind him and knew that he was being chased. Jim had made it across the parking lot and was approaching the old gate. He was only a few meters from the fence when he began to slip on some gravel. He almost fell down on his knee but was able to recover his balance by grabbing the fence to keep him upright. This slip had caused a couple of seconds of delay and the man with the gun was almost upon him.

Jim raced through the gate and as he passed the gate door at full speed he grabbed it and in one smooth motion swung it backwards with all the strength he could muster. The old gate door whipped back to-wards the man running after Jim and it almost hit him full force in the face. In trying to protect his face from the swinging gate door, the man was forced to drop the gun to catch the door before it hit him. He skidded to a stop and ran back a few feet to grab the gun.

From the commotion behind him Jim knew that the door had had some success in slowing down the man Jim but didn't want to waste a second to see. He poured on the speed and raced down the sidewalk towards the car.

"I will be safe when I get to the car, I hope!" he thought.

Christyn was glad she had called the police and when she saw Jim running back through the fence door at full speed like he had seen a ghost, she knew they were going to need help. She was even more pleased the police were on their way when she saw a large man with a shotgun close behind Jim.

Christyn looked around, hoping the police would arrive any second. There was nothing in sight and she could not hear any sirens. "They had better take this seriously," she grumbled.

Scott told Christyn to open the door as Jim got close.

"Get ready to let him in!" yelled Scott.

"What then?" shouted Billy.

"We start leaning on the horn and hope that someone comes!" said Christyn.

"Great plan genius!" said Billy.

Jim could see the car door opening and knew that he had about three seconds to get in. Jim was still racing along the sidewalk. He took one last step in full flight and launched himself toward the open door. He flew through the opening and his head just cleared the roof. He crashed in a heap on Billy.

"Whump!" Jim used Billy as a cushion and knocked the wind out of both of them.

"Ooooof!" said Billy as he groaned under the tremendous pressure from Jim's weight and speed.

Christyn immediately slammed the door shut. When he heard the door crash shut, Scott flicked the automatic door locks shut.

The man with the gun crashed up against the car door with a large thud. The car shook and the kids were terrified. The man was mad and he was yelling at the kids to open the car door.

"Do not touch the door!" yelled Christyn.

"You don't have to worry about that!" responded Scott.

110   Billy was really scared and was holding very tight around Buster. Buster was growling and barking at the man. He sensed danger and was going to protect these kids no matter what.

Buster jumped at the window nearest to the man and scratched at it frantically, snarling and barking.

The man turned the gun around, raised it high in the air and brought it crashing down hard on the door. It made a tremendous "bang" and left a huge dent. He then raised the butt of the gun and whacked it hard against the side window closest to Christyn. It hit the glass with a loud "Craaack" noise. Breaks in the glass spread out in all directions. The glass did not shatter and make a hole.

Just then a magical sound began to fill the ears of the children. They could clearly hear sirens, many sirens getting increasingly louder. The man with the gun must have heard them too because he stopped trying to break the glass and quickly retreated toward the building he came from.

A few moments later the police arrived in full force. There were four cruiser cars. Two went in the front and two went around the back. Jim, Scott and Christyn all scrambled out of the car and headed for the front of the building.

"Billy, you stay here with Buster and wait for us to return," said Jim as they ran towards the parked police cars.

"No problemo with me!" said Billy relieved that he did not have to go anywhere near men with guns.

Inside the building, a smile came over Frank's face when he heard the sirens. "Those kids are smart!" he thought to himself in a satisfying way. "They will be good detectives one day after all." He hoped they were OK.

The two men watching Frank were not pleased. The smaller man began shouting orders in Chinese to the large man. The large man raced over to one of the cars parked in the warehouse and got in the front seat. The car roared to life and he gunned the engine as he put it in reverse. The car tires squealed as he raced backwards towards the smaller man. The car screeched to a halt beside the smaller man and he flung open the door and jumped in.

The large man jammed on the accelerator and the wheels began to smoke as they spun on the smooth concrete floor. Slowly the tires began to grip on the surface and the car quickly raced forward toward the big overhead door that was down at the moment.

"Drive through the door, don't stop!" yelled the Vincent Lee to the large man. They both cringed as the car approached the door at about 40 mph. The car smashed into the door and pieces flew everywhere as it exited the building.

Little did they know that Officer Bentley of the Exton Police Department had just pulled his brand new Chevrolet Impala cruiser car to a stop on the other side of the big overhead door. The car was a beauty with the latest computer equipment installed. The car only had 58 miles on it.

He was just getting out of the car when the door in front of him exploded in a shower of pieces. Officer Bentley dove back into the car at the incredible sound of the door blowing apart and then felt the impact of Vincent's car crashing into the new police car. Everything in the car flew in a separate direction. His hat ended up in the back seat and the windshield and hood was littered with debris.

When he looked up he could see another car had hit them squarely in the front and had totaled both cars.

"Oh boy, am I in trouble!" he thought. "I knew I shouldn't have taken the Chief's new car."

He jumped out of the car and checked to see the condition of the driver. The driver and the passenger had obviously not been wearing seat belts. Both had been thrown forward into the windshield and were both unconscious in the front seat.

Officer Bentley quickly radioed for an ambulance. "You had better bring a couple of units, we have multiple injuries."

Frank had turned away as the car hit the big door. He wanted to shield his eyes from the pieces that were flying everywhere. Before he had a chance to open his eyes, he then heard a tremendous bang as the two cars hit. The noise was deafening inside the warehouse.

Frank struggled to his feet with the chair still attached to him. He was happy to see the cavalry. He wiggled one hand free and started to work at the duct tape binding up his arms.

Slowly the pieces started to come apart and he was able to free up both hands and his arms.

The police flooded into the warehouse through the smashed door. At the same time, there was shouting from the back of the warehouse. Frank was busy looking all around at the confusion when Ron appeared.

"Looks like you need some help old timer!" joked Ron.

"It's about time you got in here. I thought I was going to have to put away the bad guys all by myself." Frank finally felt able to laugh a bit.

Ron helped to free the rest of the duct tape from Frank while Frank told him the whole story.

The police from the back lead Sing Li by them in handcuffs. Sing Li glared at Frank and Frank just glared back.

"Where are the kids?" Frank said to Ron.

"If you mean that group of kids outside who saved your hide, they are anxiously waiting to see you," said Ron.

"Thanks Ron, I am so glad to see you," Frank said as he gave a hearty handshake to Ron.

Ron and Frank walked over to one of the large containers. They opened the door and inside they saw boxes and boxes of complete skateboard packages. There must have been 750–1000 in one container alone.

"This stash is worth one to two million dollars Frank," estimated Ron.

Ron said "Frank, you and your troupe have helped us to take down Vincent Lee. We have suspected him for a long time but we could never tie him to any illegal activity. We now have a warehouse full of evidence. This will put him away for a long time. You guys all deserve a commendation. Well, at least those that didn't get caught," Ron winked at Frank and Frank looked a little sheepish.

"I must be getting old," replied Frank. "I had better get outside and see how the kids are doing."

The kids were watching the building and checking out everyone who went in or out. As soon as they saw Frank, they all started cheering and Jim ran towards Frank.

"Uncle Frank, Uncle Frank...over here!" Jim yelled very happy to see his uncle.

"J., am I glad to see you. Are you guys OK?" Frank said.

"We're fine but your car has seen better days," said Jim.

"I don't care about the car, as long as you guys are fine. Where's Buster?" asked Frank.

"Not to worry, Buster is with Billy. They're waiting at the car," said Scott.

Jim told the whole story of the man with the shotgun and Frank realized how lucky they had all been that day.

"Hey, we shut the counterfeiter down! Let's go tell Mike!" said Ben.

"Yes," said Frank, "let's tell him the good news.

As Frank walked up to his car, he checked out the dent and the smashed window.

"So what were you guys doing with my car while I was gone? Did you let Billy drive or something!" Frank laughed.

Buster was so happy to see Frank. Uncle Frank was rubbing Buster's ears and Buster was lapping up all the attention.

As Uncle Frank looked over his car he was thinking to himself. Deep down he felt very bad that the kids had gone through what they had. He had taken them into a dangerous situation and had left them to fend for himself. He swore to himself he would never do such a stupid thing again.

"Let's get some ice cream on the way to Mike's shop!" announced Frank.

Buster ran around in circles, barking happily.

After they went for ice cream, they drove straight over to Boardzone. They sat around Mike's shop. Mike was listening intently to the whole story.

"So tell me again," said Mike. "What were you thinking Jim when you went inside that building?"

"Well, I didn't exactly get inside the building but I sure wanted to know what happened to Uncle Frank," confessed Jim.

"I was tied up at that moment," said Frank. "Literally!"

"Well, I guess that means I'm going to start seeing some customers coming back through the doors," said Mike.

"It's about time, Mike," said Scott. "Are you going to hold the contest again?"

Christyn and Billy looked at Mike with hope in their eyes.

Mike surveyed the crowd anxiously awaiting his answer.

"Of course we will!" he announced.

The kids erupted in cheers.

"But I'm going to need some help," cautioned Mike. "Do you think I could round up some volunteers to put up posters around town?"

"We will!" the kids said in unison.

Mike began to think about all the details that were necessary to plan for the competition. He remembered from last year how big a job it really was.

"Julie," Mike said, "are you up to helping me with another competition?"

"I'd follow you anywhere, Mike," she said with a smile. "You obviously have a huge fan club that looks after you each time you get into trouble."

"I know," said Mike. "I am lucky they are looking out for me. I wish they could fix this City Hall problem I've got," he muttered in a very low voice, almost low enough that no one heard. Almost. Julie heard him.

She looked deep into Mike's eyes and said in her most confident voice, "Don't worry Mike. Things will turn out fine for us."

"Thanks Julie. I always count on you for support. Now let's get planning for this competition. Do you have the file of things we did from last year?"

114

Ron Lends a Hand

The next day Frank woke at 6:00 a.m. as usual. Buster wanted to go for his walk and Frank loved to be outside early before all the hustle and bustle of daily life interrupted his neighborhood. The walk was usually about an hour but this morning Frank spent more time enjoying the scenery. He'd had a close call the previous day and felt like enjoying the peace and quiet a little longer that morning. Buster didn't mind. He loved to search for squirrels and those elusive bunnies.

He'd been close to catching a squirrel once but the little rodent was able to dash up a tree and chatter at him from a branch.

They had arrived home from their walk about 30 minutes earlier. Frank was reading the *Exton Gazette* when the phone rang. Frank was startled by the sound of the phone because he was engrossed in the story of the counterfeiter takedown at the warehouse. They had the whole story down and interviews with all the kids. "They're famous in Exton now," he thought. It was still early and Frank wondered who would call them so soon in the morning. Frank picked up the phone.

"Frank here," said Frank in the same professional way he answered the phone as a police officer.

It was his friend Ron from the Exton Police Service.

"Frank, it's Ron. I wanted you to know that I was able to get a priority search on the numbered company you were looking at. My captain said that anything you want is OK with him."

After yesterday's capture of Vincent Lee, Frank was a hero in the police service. He liked how that made him feel. Even though he was completely duct-taped during the capture! Frank didn't think about that part too much.

"What have you got?" asked Frank.

"I ran some checks and the numbered company comes back registered to a group represented in trust by a local law firm," said Ron.

"That's weird," said Frank. "Normally you can get the name of the owner."

"Don't worry, we're checking into the law firm and we'll find out soon enough. It is supposed to be public knowledge," said Ron. "When we get done with Finkleman and Burns, they will have to provide us with the owner's name."

"Ron, Finkleman and Burns is also the law firm that is up to no good on something else I am working on."

"Something else you're working on! I thought you were retired. Maybe you need some help on that one too," Ron said

"If you're offering, I'm accepting." Laughed Frank.

Frank filled Ron in on the story about Mike and the skate park and how Finkleman and Burns were representing someone who was trying to change the date of the next city council meeting on Mike so that he would lose the skate park.

"Let's see what we can dig up on these guys," said Ron. Frank could hear the feverish clatter of fingers flying over a keyboard in the background. "I'm looking forward to taking them down."

Frank knew that once Ron found out that one of his friends was in trouble, he would not stop until the bad guy was behind bars. Ron was that type of cop. He was a quite a determined person.

Ron had been that way all his life. It really started when he was fifteen as a result of the accident. The accident changed his entire life. It was June and school had not let out for the summer yet. Ron and two of his friends had decided to skip school one beautiful sunny day and head over to the river to go fishing. They had spent the morning sitting in the sun on the train bridge that crossed the river. It was a great day for catching trout and spending time together with friends.

Around noon a freight train came rumbling along the track headed for the bridge and the boys knew they had to move out of the way. Ron was busy reeling in a fairly large fish and told the others he would be there in a second. They two boys left Ron and walked 100 yards down the narrow train bridge to get to the bank.

Ron hurried to reel his fish in but the fish was giving him more trouble than usual. "He must be at least a four-pounder!" yelled Ron to his friends. They were watching from a distance.

"You'd better hurry up, Ron!" said one of them.

Ron checked over his shoulder and saw the train bearing down on him. The engineer must have seen the boys walking on the track because the train gave off a long warning blast from the big air horn.

Ron realized he was out of time but he wanted to bring this fish in. It was almost close enough to pull up. He checked the train and decided that this was a lucky day for the fish. He pulled out his jackknife and cut the line. The fish was gone but Ron still had to get out of the way of the freight train.

The freight train was going faster than Ron expected and he now had to run the 100 yards to get to safety. There was not enough room on the tracks for Ron and the train at the same time.

Ron was running fast and was confident he was going to make it. His friends were yelling for him to hurry. Ron took one final look over his shoulder to see where the train was and when he did his foot caught one of the ties and he proceeded to stumble and fall head first onto the tracks. He feel to one side and his head struck the rail. He was instantly knocked out and his body rolled over the rail and lay dangerously close to falling off the rail and into the water about 10 feet below. While his body was clear of the tracks, his left leg lay over one rail.

The engineer could see all the events unfold ahead of him. He had slammed the emergency brake on but a freight train traveling 30 mph and carrying 58 tons of iron ore takes one mile to stop.

The engineer was sickened as his train passed over the spot where the boy lay. He immediately called for assistance from the train dispatcher. When the big train finally came to a halt, the crew of the train ran back to where the boy lay. It was not pretty. His leg had been cut off just below the knee.

Ron spent almost a year in therapy and many more months learning how to walk without crutches. He knew he'd made a big mistake and he had decided he was going to walk and even run again…like normal. He wasn't going to let this one mistake ruin his life.

Ron even decided to fulfill a dream. He had always wanted to be a police officer. From the first day he had tried to join the police service he had had to convince everyone he could do the job even though he had an artificial leg. The physical part of the job was hard with an artificial leg but there were even harder parts for Ron.

Ron was definitely not in the top of his class in terms of marks and had trouble passing the exams during police training. However Ron approached his studies like he did everything else. He knew he needed to put more effort into his courses and was the one who spent the most hours studying. He kept trying and did his best in whatever it was he attempted. He knew that if he did his best he should be proud no matter what the outcome.

Today was no different. Ron had a challenge in front of him and he was going to help Frank figure this one out.

"Who is the agent that Finkleman and Burns has named as the contact on the numbered company?" asked Frank.

"It says here the contact name is…" Frank waited as Ron looked for the name, "…a lawyer named Andrew Ferris."

"Frank, why don't you meet me downtown in 30 minutes and let's go pay this Andrew Ferris a little visit?" asked Ron.

"I'll be waiting out front. I'll be the one driving the dented convertible with the smashed side window," Frank joked.

"Classy!" said Ron. "Can't you retired guys afford to pay your car bills?"

"If I didn't have to spend all my time doing your police work," Frank kidded his friend.

"Ouch, you got me there!" responded Ron. He knew that Frank was joking. "I'll be waiting on the front steps of the station."

Ron and Frank both hung up their phones and got ready to move this investigation forward.

Buster ran over to the entrance hall, nose quivering, and stared straight at the front door.

"Not today Buster. You can't stay in the car: it's too hot out. I'll check on you later though."

Frank put out some water for Buster and then headed out of the house.

Buster ran to the front window and rubbed his nose all over the window again.

As Frank pulled up in front of the police service building he thought about Buster. Buster was not happy about being left at home. "The poor dog," he thought. "I've never seen him look so down about being left at home."

As Frank parked the car in the loading area in front of the police service building, Ron came trotting down the stairs.

"Hey buddy," Ron said, "move that car or I'm going to have to slap a big fine on you."

"I'll move it as soon as you get it your…"

"Easy," said Ron, "I'm coming."

They were always joking with each other.

Ron opened the door and jumped into the car. "Let's go," said Ron. "We're heading down to Third Avenue South and Broadway."

"Next stop, law scum central."

Third Avenue was where a majority of the law firms were based. As they drove they talked about Mike and his skate park dream.

"That Mike sounds like a real nice guy," said Ron.

"He is. Mike sure loves those kids. He really isn't in it for the money. He just wants those kids to be happy," said Frank.

"It sure would be nice to help him out," Ron said.

They drove downtown and parked in a large parking lot next to the office building where the law firm of Finkleman and Burns was located. They went into the front entrance of the tall building. They passed by the security desk and headed over to the electronic sign that gave an index of the companies in the building and where they could be found. Ron punched "F" on the display and began looking through the list of companies in the building that began with an F. The display indicated that Finkleman and Burns occupied both the 18th and 19th floors. The main reception was on 18th.

"Let's go on up and see Mr. Ferris," said Ron.

They walked over to the bank of elevators and punched the up button. They only had to wait a few seconds before they heard the familiar "ding" sound and the doors opened up.

The elevator was one of those high-speed units that whisked them up to the 18th floor so fast that Frank's ears popped on the way up.

"God I hate these things," Frank grumbled.

Ron shook his head with a laugh.

The gold doors opened and Frank was quite happy to get out of the elevator. Ron was still watching the TV monitor in the elevator.

"C'mon Ron," said Frank. "You can catch the news anytime."

"News? I'm looking at the stock market prices."

"You're a cop, Ron" snickered Frank "you don't have money to invest in the stock market."

"I do OK," said Ron.

They both walked forward to the main front desk. Across the back wall behind the reception desk were large gold letters spelling out Finkleman and Burns. The receptionist behind the desk had one of those headsets on that didn't require her to actually pick up a telephone.

As they approached she was busy answering one call after another. "Finkleman and Burns, how can I help you?"

Frank noted that she was pretty but sounded very bored. Frank and Ron both stopped at the desk and waited for the woman to finish answering her calls. After a long minute of waiting, the woman finally spoke to them.

"Is there something I can help you with, gentlemen?" she said in a voice that only pretended to care.

"We're here to see Andrew Ferris," said Ron.

"Do you have an appointment?" she said.

"No. We just want to ask him a few questions," said Frank.

"Well he is a very busy man, if you would like to make an appointment, I can schedule time to meet him next month," she said.

"Next month!" stammered Ron.

"Is there anything else I can do for you gentlemen?" she said in a tone suggesting they leave.

Since this was not official police business yet, Ron did not feel right in flashing his badge.

"Let's come back later," said Ron.

Frank was puzzled by what Ron was suggesting. He wanted to talk to this Ferris guy and didn't see how leaving would achieve their goal.

Ron looked around the room and said, "Come with me Frank. We have to go."

Ron turned and walked back to the elevator. Frank followed and was going to have a chat with his friend inside. The doors opened and Ron and Frank stepped in. Frank was going to say something when Ron did the unexpected. Ron pressed the Open door button even though there was no one there.

"Where are we going?" said Frank certainly puzzled now.

"The 18th floor is for the average lawyers Frank. Anyone who is busy until next month must be one of the high priced lawyers, and we know the highest paid lawyers all live on the—"

"Highest floor!" Frank interrupted.

"Right!" said Ron.

The door was trying to close but Ron held it open like he was waiting for someone. Sure enough, a woman carrying a large bundle of file folders approached the doors. Ron kept pressing the Open button to hold the door for her. Ron was hoping for this break.

"This is just what we needed," Ron whispered to Frank. Frank did not know what Ron was talking about.

The woman came on the elevator and was struggling to insert her security card into the reader without dropping the large stack of files.

"Let me help you with that," Ron said in his most pleasant voice.

"Oh, thank-you," said the lady. "I think I'm carrying too many things."

Ron swiped the card into the reader and asked the lady what floor. He knew what she was going to say and resisted the urge to punch the 19th floor button.

"19th floor please," she said still juggling the files.

Ron pressed the 19th floor button and slipped the card in between the top two files the woman was carrying.

"Thank-you very much," she said.

The doors opened on the 19th floor and the woman quickly exited and went down the hall.

Ron and Frank waited a couple of seconds and when the door started to close, Frank hit the Open button again.

Both men stepped out and began to walk down the same hallway that seemed to swallow the woman. She was nowhere to be seen.

"What are we going to do now?" whispered Frank.

"Just act like you belong here," Ron whispered back urgently. "Let's look for Andrew Ferris' office."

Both men started to walk with an air of confidence and Ron began to search left while Frank searched right. After a few twists and turns they ran into a man standing next to a photocopier.

"Excuse me," said Ron, "can you tell me where we can find Andrew Ferris?"

"Down the hall at the end on the left," said the man.

"Thanks," Ron said.

Ron and Frank walked away from the man and he continued to stare at the machine.

At the end of the hallway, just like the man said, was an office with a bronze name-plate that said "Andrew Ferris – Corporate Counsel". Both men stopped in front of Andrew Ferris' office door. They could hear a man inside the office, it sounded like he was on the phone.

"What's your grand plan?" asked Frank with a twinkle in his eye.

"We wait for him to get off the phone and then we pay him a visit. Our goal is to find out what his involvement is with the numbered company," said Ron.

They waited for a minute hoping that no one would walk by and ask them what they were doing. The man in the office seemed to stop talking so they figured he was off the phone.

Ron knocked once and walked right in. A young man was sitting behind a large desk with not much on it. He was still on the phone and was in the middle of a conversation when he saw Ron and Frank come in."

"Sure I love you baby, you are the only woman for me – Excuse me, can I help you? I have to go. Call you later Haley…" There was some yelling in the background. "Sorry I mean Heather."

"Who are you?" demanded Andrew Ferris.

"Andrew," said Ron in his most stern voice, "we are the police."

The color in Andrew's face drained immediately and he attempted to put the phone down without looking. The handset banged awkwardly against the edge of his desk as he fumbled to find the right spot.

"How…how can I help you?" The words stumbled from his mouth.

"We understand you are the agent representing a numbered company that is involved in an ongoing investigation," said Frank.

Ron got right up in Andrew's face and snapped, "Is that the truth?"

Andrew was taken a back by the good cop-bad cop routine. He was scared and both Ron and Frank could see it. They knew this guy was going to spill information like a leaky bucket. "I…I…I represent a few numbered companies, sir."

"Sir," thought Ron, "I haven't been called that in a while."

"Which company are you investigating?" stammered Andrew.

"10098 Exton Co.," Frank said in a voice that suggested he was disgusted to be saying the name.

It worked because Andrew didn't even try to defend himself or ask what the investigation was about. He simply agreed to assist them in any way he could. He was clearly hoping these policemen would leave him alone as quickly as possible.

"Yes, that is a company I represent. How can I help you?" said Andrew.

"We need to speak with the owner. We have…questions for him," said Frank adding a pause in his speech for effect.

"Is that all? Let me look that up right away," Andrew said as he got up and went over to a filing cabinet.

He opened one drawer and then another and leafed through dozens of file folders. He was beginning to look a little nervous until he found what he was looking for.

"Ah ha!" Andrew exclaimed triumphantly. He held the file up in the air like he had just caught a fly ball that won the seventh game of the World Series.

"Here we go," said Andrew. Not even bothering to return to his desk he opened the file and began to recite the information Ron and Frank were looking for.

"Owner is listed as…uh…here it is…Philmore Snively at 1203 Wellington Crescent."

"Philmore Snively," said Frank to himself. He looked over at Ron and they both gave each other that look that said "of course".

Frank and Ron had their information. They didn't want to press their luck any longer with Andrew. He was young and scared but he might sense something was wrong at any time.

"You have been most helpful and we will remember this in our report. Please understand Mr. Ferris, this is an ongoing investigation and we ask that you not divulge any of this information to anyone," said Ron.

Andrew began to nod almost immediately. He wasn't even aware that there was nothing to divulge except maybe two cops had been nosing around asking questions. It wasn't likely he was going to do that, he was just glad to see the two men leave.

Ron and Frank made their own way to the door and left. They followed the hallway to the elevator and it arrived almost at the same instant they pressed the down button. When they got on and the door shut, they gave each other a high-five.

"That was fun!" said Frank. "Haven't done that in a while."

"Snively, eh?" said Ron. "That doesn't surprise me in the least."

"Me neither," said Frank. "He was the guy that allowed his mining company to strip mine some land next to Westchester State Park and when they were done, he abandoned the site and allowed all the accumulated waste to pollute the local water supply."

"The most frustrating part of that situation was that later the press found out he was part owner of the company that was called in to clean up the mess," said Ron.

"At the expense of the taxpayer!" said Frank. "He gets rich cleaning up his own mess. What nerve."

"How do guys like that get away with crimes?" said Ron. He and Frank both knew the answer: money.

Those with money had the power to do lots of things the average person could not. Philmore Snively had money and could hire a large army of lawyers to protect his interests.

"Let's see what we can find on old Mr. Snively shall we?" said Frank.

"Sounds like another good plan," said Ron.

123

Ron and Frank Go Downtown

Mike and Julie had been busy designing new posters for the competition and the kids had fanned out across the city on their bikes to put them up. There was quite a buzz brewing among the kids of Exton.

Just like the last competition, Mike had donated $1,000 as first prize and that was drawing a lot of attention. Mike didn't have $1,000 to donate but there was a $10 registration fee and the money collected would more than cover the prize money once everyone was signed up.

They had the course mapped out like last year and Mike had arranged to have 35 volunteers to help out on the day doing everything from setting up registration areas to cooking hot-dogs and monitoring races.

There was only 10 days away for the competition and still lots of details to be worked out. Things were going well and Mike felt like something in his life was working right for a change. "Thank goodness Julie and the kids are here to help me," he thought.

Ron and Frank drove to the building where Philmore Snively worked. They went inside and took the elevator to the 27th floor. It was at the top of the building. This building had very expensive trimmings. There was rich wood on all of the walls. Frank was sure the wood was teak. It looked very expensive. There was beautiful art on all the walls and the furniture looked like it was all Victorian antiques.

There were two massive wooden doors to the right of the reception area and the plaque on the door indicated that this was the office of Philmore Snively.

The receptionist at the main greeting area was behind a large glass island. The receptionist watched them approach and politely asked them if they needed assistance.

Ron and Frank asked if Philmore Snively was in.

"Do you have an appointment?" she said as she began reviewing her computer screen. "Mr. Snively is supposed to be on a conference call to our Costa Rican office."

At that moment one of the big double wooden doors opened and Philmore Snively came out holding a piece of paper.

"Carol, I've signed this agreement and I need it faxed to Charles in our Paris office ASAP."

He stopped when he noticed Frank and Ron standing there. Ron took advantage of the situation.

"Mr. Snively?" asked Ron.

"Yes. What do you want?" said Snively very abruptly.

Ron knew that this was also not official police business and Philmore Snively was going to be a lot harder to fool than that young Andrew Ferris. Ron decided to approach Snively as an average citizen. "Mr. Snively, my name is Ron and this is my friend Frank. Could we have a private word with you? It will only take a few minutes."

Snively was put out by the request but he was curious about what they wanted.

"I'm a busy man." He looked at his watch and said to Carol "Hold all my calls for two minutes."

"This way!" he ordered gruffly. Snively ushered Ron and Frank through the massive wooden doors. Philmore Snively had expensive tastes. The office looked like it belonged in a museum. Inside the large office there was even more art, more beautiful and likely more expensive than the previous room. Assorted African tribal artifacts were placed all around his office on tops of desks, tables and in the corners. There were spears and evil-looking daggers hanging on the wall.

At one end was a gun collection on display. There were several highly polished rifles including one mother of a gun that looked like it could take out an elephant. As a matter of fact, there was the mounted head of a rhinoceros, a Bengal tiger and a wild boar staring down at them from the far wall. They had all been made to look as ferocious as possible.

"I bet those animals never had a chance with Snively and his team of killers. I wonder if Snively was even brave enough to take a shot himself," thought Frank.

"Obviously this guy likes to hunt," thought Ron to himself. "Those are expensive guns in that case."

Frank felt kind of creepy in the office.

"Ah," said Philmore Snively noticing Frank looking at the animal heads on the wall, "you are admiring my trophies?"

Frank thought the word "admiring" was not the right word, he was thinking "repulsive".

"Uh…yes…" said Frank, not wanting to start something before they could get what they came to do.

"Are you a hunter?" asked Snively.

"No," said Frank.

"See that Bengal tiger? I bagged her in Northwestern India. Surprised her while she was nursing her young in a cave. We smoked them out with a brush fire and I got her when she appeared at the mouth of a cave. Never did find the two little cubs after they took off…at least we think they got out."

It was all Frank could do to hold himself back from knocking this guy into next week. He knew he could not do that because it was wrong but he sure wanted to.

Ron knew what Frank was thinking by the look on Frank's face. Ron decided to change the subject before things got out of hand.

"Mr. Snively, we understand you are the owner of the numbered company called 10098 Exton Co.," said Ron.

"That may be true. I own a lot of companies. Who did you say you were?"

Ron ignored the last part of his question.

"10098 Exton Co. is the company that has been offering city councilors trips to the Bahamas. Can you explain why?" said Frank.

If Snively was shocked or worried by the accusation, neither Frank nor Ron could tell by his expression. He did not flinch a bit.

"This guy is a pro!" thought Ron to himself.

"I'm afraid I have no knowledge of what you are talking about. I didn't catch your names?" enquired Snively.

Ron and Frank had no intention of giving their names.

"Mr. Snively, one of your companies is offering city councilors all-expense-paid trips to the Bahamas. Do you expect us to believe you do not know about that?"

"Yes," responded Snively using a disgusted tone. "I'm afraid you both will have to leave. I have business that needs attention."

"I'm sure you do," said Frank. Frank and Ron turned and headed slowly for the door.

They both left and Snively stood alone in his office for a minute thinking. He then picked up the phone and quickly dialed a number.

"Get me Ferris, NOW!" yelled Philmore Snively.

Frank and Ron wasted no time getting their next plan together. They knew they were not likely to get much, if any, information from Snively but they wanted to rattle his cage a bit and make him nervous. When someone is nervous they tend to make mistakes and Ron and Frank were hoping to catch Snively making a mistake. It wasn't going to be easy though, Snively wasn't the type to make mistakes.

Ron was the first to speak about a new plan.

"Frank," Ron said in a quizzical voice, "what is the one thing that politicians don't want?"

"I dunno…a scandal I suppose," answered Frank.

"Correct," Ron agreed.

"Go on…" said Frank not sure where this was going.

"We need a way to stop Snively but he is not doing anything illegal. I think we are looking at the wrong end of the telescope," replied Ron.

128

Frank was still not getting it. He asked Ron to elaborate. "Well, if we can't touch Snively then why don't we have a chat with a few city councilors. Perhaps they can be persuaded."

Down at City Hall, Ron and Frank walked the south corridor with a list of names printed on a sheet of white paper. The paper detailed the names and office locations for each of the city councilors.

"E-118 is our next stop," said Ron. "It has to be up here on the left."

"Which councilor will we find there?" said Frank.

"Jenny Harper," said Ron. "She represents the Coleview district."

"Isn't she the one who was so vocal about keeping the funding in place to allow those soup kitchens to remain open?" said Frank.

"I sure hope so," said Ron.

They stopped outside the door, knocked loudly and then opened the door. Inside was a young woman busy typing on a computer. She looked up at the two men when they entered.

"Can I help you?" she said pleasantly.

"We'd like to see Miss Harper," said Ron.

The woman glanced over at the phone handset. Ron figured she must be checking to see if her boss was on the phone.

"Who should I say is here?" asked the woman.

Ron looked over at Frank and then at the woman.

"Just two constituents with some quick questions for the councilor," said Ron.

"Sure. Please go right in," said the woman as she buzzed the councilor and pointed to an inside door.

Ron and Frank walked over to the door and knocked.

From behind the door, there was a pause and then a voice said, "Come in."

Jenny Harper was sitting behind her messy desk. There were papers everywhere and stacks of files covered all flat surfaces and even the two guest chairs in front of her desk.

"Hello," she said standing up to greet them. "Sorry about the mess. I am just so busy."

She was a heavyset woman with messy hair. Her shirt was not tucked in and she still had part of her lunch on her cheek.

"Hello Miss Harper," said Ron. "I'm Ron and this is Frank. We're a couple of constituents."

"What can I do for you?" said Jenny Harper with a smile.

"We understand you are on your way to the Bahamas," said Ron.

Jenny Harper immediately lost her smile. "I'm sorry," she said, "who did you say you were?"

"Just a couple of concerned citizens," said Frank.

"Concerned about what?" she said hesitantly.

"Well, we were wondering if it is normal practice for an elected official to accept an all expense paid trip to an exotic location?" said Ron.

Jenny clearly looked uncomfortable. She shifted nervously from foot to foot. Ron and Frank waited in silence, trying to make her feel even more uncomfortable.

"This is a trip that I deserve," she responded very feebly.

"I deserve lots of things but I work for each of them," said Frank. He glared at Jenny.

"Well Frank, shall we head down to the *Exton Gazette* to talk to a reporter about some questionable travel?" said Ron.

"Let's go," said Frank.

"Wait! You don't have to talk to a reporter. It's not illegal or anything. This is a perfectly legitimate trip."

"If it's perfectly legal, then you won't mind if we bring it to the attention of the whole city. I'm sure all your constituents will be happy to learn you are taking advantage of a trip you so richly deserve."

Ron and Frank could almost hear the wheels grinding in Jenny's head.

"What do you want?" she said.

"We don't think it is a good idea that you went on that trip. We need you to be here to help the city and attend your regularly scheduled August council meeting."

"Is that all?" she said her voice sounding more confident.

"You bet and you won't hear from us again," said Frank.

"You know, I was having trouble finding a bathing suit anyway," said Jenny Harper.

"Have a good day," said Ron as they left the office.

Frank and Ron proceeded to each of the offices on the list and played out the same routine for each of the councilors that were available. By the end of the day they had been able to meet with and talk eight councilors out of taking the trip. The last councilor they met with Barney Fodera.

Mr. Fodera had actually never agreed to take the trip. He felt it was not a good thing to do. Someone had indicated to Frank that Mr. Fodera had accepted the trip but that was not the case. Mr. Fodera was happy that the trip was no longer going to happen. "I didn't like the idea of owing anyone any favours and a trip like that meant someone somewhere would want some type of favour," Mr. Fodera said.

Each of the other councilors acted in the same way as Jenny Harper. They were happy to take the trip as long as the public didn't find out about it. As soon as it might appear in the newspaper, none of them wanted to be seen taking an expensive trip in case the average citizen felt like it was a bribe or something. Taking a bribe would spell the end of their career in politics and no one wanted to lose their job over one trip.

"That will do it," said Frank. "We now have enough councilors that have decided to cancel their trip to the Bahamas that they will have to hold the council meeting on the regularly scheduled date."

"Shall we pay Mr. Snively a return visit tomorrow and let him in on the news?"

"Fine idea," said Frank and they walked across the street to where the car was parked.

Back at the Philmore Building, Philmore Snively was on the phone and he was not just mad, he was fuming. He had talked to Andrew Ferris at Finkleman and Burns and Ferris told Snively about the visit by the police. Philmore was not sure what that was all about but he knew that something was up. He was sure that the visit he had today was linked to the visit Ferris had received.

Then, an hour later, he received other phone calls from Andrew again because a few of the city councilors had contacted him. For a variety of reasons, they each had decided to not accept the Bahamas trip. Snively definitely knew there was a problem and he wanted to find out what was going on.

"Ferris!" he barked into the phone. "Tell me about the two men who came to see you. Who did they say they were? What did they look like? Did they give you a business card or anything?" said Snively in a rapid-fire series of questions.

This threw the young lawyer for a loop. He was already nervous about calling Mr. Snively to begin with and now he felt on the hot seat.

"Well!" demanded Snively. "Speak up, I'm waiting and my time is valuable."

* * * *

The next day, Ron and Frank met at 8:00 a.m. and had a quick breakfast at the diner across from the police station. They had eggs, bacon and coffee.

"We're going to need our energy today," said Ron.

When they were done they had driven over to the Snively building and parked in the underground lot because there were no parking spots available on the street.

As they were walking through the underground parking lot they passed by a black Ferrari F50 convertible.

"Wow, that is one fine automobile," said Ron, whistling.

"Did you catch the license plate?" said Frank. "SNIVELY1".

"That figures," said Ron.

They made their way to the parking elevator that would take them to the main lobby. Once in the main lobby, they transferred to the business elevator that whisked them back to the 27th floor.

They exited the elevator and approached the same receptionist who was still sitting behind the glass island.

"Welcome back gentlemen. Are you here to see Mr. Snively?"

"Yes, is he in?" said Ron.

The receptionist was unaware the Philmore Snively was not happy with Ron and Frank. She thought they must have planned a return visit with her boss. She buzzed him on the intercom. "Mr. Snively, sorry to bother you sir. The two gentlemen who were here yesterday have returned and would like to meet with you."

There was a pause as she listened. She then hung up and looked at Ron and Frank.

"Mr. Snively would be happy to see you," she said. "Please go right in."

Ron and Frank opened up the big door and headed into the office of Philmore Snively.

Snively was sitting behind his massive desk smoking a cigar when they came in. The smell of the cigar was pungent and made Frank want to cough. Ron actually liked the odd cigar and knew the smell of an expensive cigar when he smelled one.

"Gentlemen, it's funny that you would be in here yesterday asking about a company of mine and then I find out from my law firm that the police paid them a visit asking questions as part of an ongoing investigation of that company. Now you show up today. More questions?" he asked in a mocking tone.

"Philmore Snively, I am Ron Sampson, a detective with the Exton Police Service. We are investigating possible illegal actions occurring as a result of actions made by your company against city officials."

"Illegal activity! Sounds serious, please tell me more." Snively said almost laughing at Ron.

Frank indicated that he had to use the washroom and would be right back. Ron was surprised by that but continued on with his questioning of Snively.

"We talked to several city councilors yesterday—"

"So I heard!" retorted Snively, interrupting Ron.

Ron explained the whole story. "They were all offered a free trip to an expensive resort in the Bahamas and the only thing in return was that the date of the next city council meeting was to be bumped up by two weeks. Any idea why your company had such an interest?"

As Philmore Snively began to answer, the door opened and Frank slipped back into the room.

"That was a quick bathroom visit!" thought Ron.

Snively started to change his tune. "I've done some checking and the numbered company that you are referring to is a land development company that is hoping to show the city councilors a facility in the Bahamas that is similar to one we want to develop here in Exton."

"Oh really," said Ron. It was his turn to use a mocking tone. "Wouldn't it be cheaper just to show them some pictures?"

"Pictures work but a site visit is much better. You get to see and feel everything," countered Snively.

"That's a pretty expensive trip, I'm sure you expect to get something in return of equal or greater value. You are a businessman after all. What is the significance of needing the city council meeting moved earlier by two weeks?" said Frank. He already knew what kind of impact moving the date would have on Mike's dreams of the new skate park. He wanted to hear what Snively had to say.

"It was the next date that the councilors could agree on, I guess," said Snively.

Snively knew the trip was going to cost him over $55,000 dollars and he certainly expected to secure the land away from some local named Mike who owned the Boardzone skate shop. Snively was going to use the old fairgrounds land to build a new housing complex and he stood to make five million dollars in profit when all the new housing units were sold. That was reason enough for him to do just about anything.

Ron continued, "Well Mr. Snively it looks like your city councilors have had a change of heart and won't be taking you up on your trip after all. According to city council rules, the meeting will be held on the regularly scheduled date."

Snively was getting really mad and Ron felt that this was a good time to leave.

"Let's go, Frank, we're done here," said Ron.

"We'll see ourselves out," said Frank.

Snively looked out the window and ignored their exit.

Ron and Frank walked out and as they passed the receptionist Frank went over to her and said "Hello Margaret, did you get a chance to print off that information?"

"Yes" she said "I have it right here."

She handed him two pieces of paper and he thanked her. He folded the papers and put them into his jacket.

Ron wasn't sure what that was all about and he planned to ask Frank in the car.

They made their way down to the parkade level where they had left the car.

"Alright, spill the beans! What did you get from his secretary?" said Ron.

"Well, it occurred to me that if she thought we were friendly with Snively, I could ask her for some information and she just might provide it because she assumed Snively would be OK with giving it to me," said Frank.

"Fast thinking, Frank. What information?" asked Ron.

"Not sure what I would get but I asked her to print off the memo referring to the Bahamas trip for the city councilors. Apparently there are two memos," said Frank as he held up two pieces of paper.

They got into the car and Frank reviewed the two pages. He handed one to Ron and began to read the other himself. Ron started to read his memo.

A minute later Frank spoke. "My memo looks like the actual letter that the city councilors received. Not too much here that we don't know. As we guessed, the resort they were planning to go to sounds expensive."

"Oh boy, mine is much better. This is a private memo from Snively to his law firm demanding that they take whatever means necessary to ensure that over 50% of the city council is not present for the August 15 meeting. It also states that they are to prepare a cheque in the amount of $150,000 payable to the City on Aug 1 to take control of the old Fairgrounds land."

"Perfect!" said Frank.

"This is great evidence but technically Snively is still not doing anything illegal and actually it doesn't seem to matter now that the councilors have decided not to go on the trip," said Ron.

"It doesn't hurt to have this anyway," said Frank.

* * * *

Snively was on the phone again. "This is Philmore Snively, get me Carter!" he barked rudely into the phone.

The person on the phone knew who Philmore Snively was and expected rude behaviour. He put Snively through to Mayor Randall Carter.

"Philmore, what can I do for you?" said Mayor Carter in a jovial voice. Mayor Carter was a career politician. He was not a strong man but he was quite a survivor. He had been in politics for over 20 years and had been re-elected on six occasions, even after a messy incident involving a gambling problem.

"Carter, listen and listen carefully. I want you to move the August 15 city council meeting to Aug 1."

Carter was puzzled. "Why do you want that?"

"I have my reasons, five million of them to be exact," said Snively to himself. Out loud he said, "That is not your concern. You owe me a favour after I got you off the hook for that little financial problem you got yourself into a couple of years ago."

Mayor Carter knew exactly what Philmore Snively was talking about. Mayor Carter had allowed two new casinos into the City of Exton as a way to generate new money for the city. A lot of people were against the idea and Mayor Carter spent a lot of time in the casinos trying to promote them as a way to have fun. Unfortunately, Mayor Carter became addicted to the slot machines and pretty soon was taking money from the Mayor's office budget to spend on gambling.

Philmore Snively had found out about the problem and offered to pay back the missing money for Mayor Carter and get him some help for his gambling problem. Philmore said he would do those things just to be nice.

"I guess this is payback now," said Mayor Carter.

"Yes, it is." said Snively. "And unless you want a scandal to brew that will get you kicked out of office and into a Federal prison, you had better do as I say."

"I can move the meeting date. That shouldn't be too hard," he thought to himself and was relieved the task was simple.

"One other thing," said Philmore Snively, "I don't want anyone to find out that the date has changed until the day before – July 31."

"I can't do that! That's not too far away and people need time to prepare for the meeting," spluttered Carter.

"Let's see how this will look on the headlines: 'Mayor Caught Taking Money'. I have the financial records to prove that too," noted Snively.

Carter was sweating. "OK, OK, I'll make it happen."

"I knew you would see it my way." Snively hung up.

Mayor Carter sat back in his chair, shaking.

Philmore Snively was very pleased with himself. "Why bother with an elaborate plan when you can do the same thing with a simple plan. And it won't cost me a dime. On July 31 when the Mayor announces the city council meeting is now the following day, it will not give anyone any time to react and I can then make a counter-bid on the fairgrounds land."

Snively had pulled one of the guns from the rack and was pretending to fire at the tiger.

"Just like I won the battle with you, I will win the war against them too."

Preparing for the Competition

In between helping organize the skateboard competition, the kids had been practicing their skateboarding on the course. The City of Exton had closed traffic to Bishop's Hill again to allow for the race preparations. The race was scheduled for Sunday July 31. It was only a few days away.

Scott was determined to do better this year. He remembered his crash in the semis last year. He had made it through turn one and two and was just coming out of three when the rider next to him, lost his balance. The rider, Barrett Campbell, had been trying to get some extra speed and was really motoring when he started to wobble due to the high speed. His board shot to the left while he flew to the right, directly into the path of Scott. Scott had nowhere to go and crashed into the skidding boy. Both Scott and Barrett ended up in a heap and the rest of the racers left them far behind. Scott was not hurt and Barrett was lucky too, suffering only wicked road-rash on his left arm. Barrett was really sorry and kept telling Scott that he didn't mean to get in his way. Scott knew that Barrett had just been pushing too hard and it was his inexperience that cost them both a finish.

Christyn had a different experience but the result was the same and she too wanted another chance to prove she could beat out those boys. She knew that she could do tricks just as well as Ben and Jim and if it weren't for that patch of gravel about halfway down the course, she would have been in the finals for sure. She remembered Jim telling her about the gravel and it was something she should have made a note of when she was walking the course before the race. She knew Jim was right but she didn't want to give him the satisfaction of hearing her say it. This year she would be better prepared. Not only would her tricks be well polished but she would know the course like the back of her hand. She was bound and determined to end up in the winner's circle.

Scott asked Christyn about her plans for the race. "What are the tricks you are going to perform at the competition this year?"

Christyn knew that she could trust Scott with her plans. They were friends and she wasn't concerned at all that he knew what she was going to try at the competition. "This year I am going to do a nollie heel-flip, front-side flip and a 360-flip," said Christyn like it was no big deal.

"Wow!" exclaimed Scott. "Those are pretty hard tricks. I haven't seen you do a 360-flip in a while. Are you sure you are ready?"

Scott wasn't trying to be mean and Christyn knew it. Scott was just checking to make sure Christyn was doing a set of tricks that she could handle. He knew that she was good enough to make the semi-finals and he wanted her to complete her tricks to give her a chance to be in the final four. If she missed her tricks that would likely be enough to knock her out of the whole competition.

"I've been practicing at home and I can do all three tricks pretty consistently. What about your tricks?"

"To be honest Christyn, I am just going to stick to some easy tricks like a fakie, kick-flip and a fakie-180. I know I can do them all and I hope to have a fast time on the course to keep my point total high."

During the competition, each rider received a certain amount of points for each trick they completed successfully and a final amount of points based on their elapsed course time. The rider with the highest point total would win the race and move on to the semi-finals and then finals.

A rider had to finish the race to get their points but they did not have to complete all the tricks. Skipping tricks was OK but it meant you ended up with fewer points. The competition was generally so tight that if a rider missed two or three tricks then there was no way to get enough points to make the final. The best boarders always had good times on the course and the tricks made the difference. Especially harder tricks because they were worth more points than easy tricks.

Scott's plan was risky for that reason. Christyn's plan made sense as long as she could pull off the tricks.

Billy was listening to their conversation with great interest. This was his first year in the competition and he was quite eager to show off what he could do. He knew that his tricks were not as good as the others but he knew he was better than many of the people who were going to enter the competition. He was a little worried about competing against other boys and girls he did not know. That made him a bit nervous.

"I'm going to keep my tricks a secret!" announced Billy.

"You do that squirt!" laughed Christyn.

Billy hated when Christyn called him "squirt". Christyn knew it and followed up with her second favourite line for Billy. "If you need help putting on some training wheels for your board, just give me a call."

Billy glared back at Christyn who pushed off, executed a perfect 360-flip and waved good-bye to the two boys.

"Did you see that?" exclaimed Scott. "What a trick!"

"She's good, but I'm still going to win the competition," said Billy.

"That's the spirit," said Scott. "I bet you will win."

"Let's practice some of our moves, we don't have many days left before we have to be perfect," said Scott.

Both boys began to practice their tricks. Each was watching the other but pretending to concentrate on their tricks.

Jim and Ben showed up a few minutes after Christyn had left.

"Hey Scott, great moves. Keep your back foot closer to the edge of the board when you do your flip, the board will come around easier," said Jim. "Where is Christyn?"

"She had to go home," said Billy.

"I want everyone to sit down over here," said Ben pointing to the nearby lawn. "I have something you should all hear."

"What is it?" asked Scott.

"I got a call from a guy named Richard Daly. He is Vice-President Sales for Quiksilver. He wants to do something good for Mike to say thank-you for shutting down the counterfeit operation. He figures that operation was costing his company $500,000 per year. He also told me that the other major boarding companies are happy about what we did."

"What does he want to do for Mike?" asked Scott.

"He didn't say but he said he would call back and let me know when they were ready," said Ben.

"Shall we tell Mike?" said Billy.

"Let's wait until we know more," said Ben, "kind of like a surprise."

"Now, who wants to go to Bishop's Hill to practice their downhill racing techniques?" said Jim.

"We do!" yelled Scott and Billy.

The boys all hopped on their boards and headed towards Bishop's Hill as fast as they could go, each eager to show who was fastest.

* * * *

Julie knew that Mike was still worried about the land deal. Losing the skate park would be a huge blow to their future plans. He had poured a lot of money and energy into buying the land and designing the park. He knew that the young people of Exton would really benefit from having a high-quality and safe place to board. All of this worrying had made it hard for Mike to concentrate on the competition. Julie wanted the competition to be a big success and decided she was going to do something else to help.

Julie called on Mike's friend Clay Osgood. Clay was now a famous skateboarder involved in most of the major professional skateboard competitions across the U.S. each year. Having a well-known name like him show up at Mike's competition would really boost attendance.

Julie made the call. "Hello Clay," said Julie. "How are you doing?"

Clay knew exactly who was on the phone without asking. "Julie Jones! What a nice surprise. Are you still hooked up with that Mike character?"

Julie laughed. "I sure am and he's the reason why I am calling."

"Is there a problem?" asked Clay with concern in his voice.

"No problem but I do need your help," replied Julie.

"You name it, I'll do what I can."

Julie explained the story about the skate park, the competition that was only a few days away and her idea. Clay listened and was enthusiastic about the whole plan.

"I can help. As a matter of fact, a few of us will be flying to Pittsburgh for another competition and we can be there for your entire competition day."

"Who is traveling with you?" asked Julie.

"Burnquist, Hawk, Muska and a few others. I know they would love to come and support Mike."

Julie could not believe her ears. "Wow!" she exclaimed. "This is going to be the most amazing show that Exton has ever seen."

"Well, don't thank me yet, I'll talk to a few people and get back to you. I'll call you at the shop later."

Clay came through just as he said he would. All the other professionals agreed to come and they were going to set up a half-pipe at the bottom of Bishop's Hill and put on a demonstration for the crowd.

When Julie got the word, she immediately designed a new poster to include the new information about the special guests. She emailed the design to the printer and asked for a rush order of 500 posters. They said they could have it ready by the end of the day. She called the kids to come over as they had more work to do.

Julie explained the whole story and they were all bubbling with excitement. "Burnquist, Hawk and Muska!" Jim was yelling as he was pumping the air with his fist.

Julie told them to come back first thing in the morning. "Can you be here at 8:00 a.m.? We have posters to put up all around town."

"What does Mike think of the news?" said Jim.

"He doesn't know yet," said Julie, "but when he sees the poster I know he will be impressed and feel much better."

The Day of the Competition

A few days past and the competition day finally arrived. Scott was confident. He had his moves down and he put new bearings in his wheels to ensure his speed was as high as possible. He showed his wheels to Billy.

"Hey, Billy, take a look at this," said Scott as he spun each wheel one at a time. Billy watched the wheels spin fast and silently. He was impressed. His wheels always had a faint rubbing noise. He kicked himself for not buying those Black Ice bearings when he saw them at Mike's shop the other day.

Christyn was a little nervous. She was still having trouble landing all her tricks and was debating with herself whether she should drop her 360-flip and stick to something easier.

"I have to do it," she said to herself. "These guys will be just as fast as me, if not faster so my tricks have to be better. I know none of them is going to do hard tricks."

Jim and Ben were excited but trying to stay cool. They both had their eye on the $1,000 prize.

"Hey, bud!" said Jim. "If either of us wins, let's say we split the money 50/50."

"Not a bad idea!" answered Ben. "Kind of doubles our chances."

They high-fived and then Jim asked Ben about his strategy.

Ben answered in typical Ben fashion. "I plan to win my races and then place first in the final. How 'bout you?"

Jim laughed "Deal or no deal, you aren't beating me in the final again this year. I'll be there with you and we aren't going to let Devin win are we."

Scott called the others together so they could go look for Mike and help out. Mike and Julie had finished setting up the course the day before and were just walking through the course making sure all was in order. The professionals had arrived early and were already drawing a big crowd of admirers. As they were helping to construct the half-pipe lots of people in the crowd were asking for autographs and pictures. The professionals were being really great and stopped often to sign scraps of paper or have a picture taken with some young boy or girl.

To keep the crowds well-fed there was an army of vendors and tents setup to provide everything from hot-dogs and hamburgers to chips, soda and popcorn. There was a guy selling corn dogs and another lady selling fudge and cotton candy. The smell of all the food mixing together made your mouth water.

Julie and Mike were going to be judges again in the same positions and they even had Mohammed and Mubarak helping this year. They were surprised to see Mubarak volunteering. Mike had never seen Mubarak so pleasant before. Julie even had to ask Mohammed if his brother was OK.

142

Mohammed said that Mubarak was turning over a new leaf and helping others was something he wanted to do more often. When the opportunity to pitch in at the competition came up, he wanted to join his brother. Mohammed and Mubarak were the judges at the bottom of the course and they would be responsible to ensure each contestant crossed the line and had a time recorded.

Devin Snively was admiring his board. He had picked it up a few weeks earlier and had only used it two times before so he could keep it in perfect condition for the competition. He liked the feel of this new board. "Not only do I have a professional board that the others don't have but I also got a great deal on it," Devin said smugly to himself. Devin did not realize the board was a counterfeit special from Vincent Lee.

Uncle Frank had volunteered to be the announcer and his booming voice was heard over the speakers Mike had setup at the top, middle and bottom of the course. "Welcome boarders to the 2nd Annual Boardzone Skate Competition. We have a record 92 entrants this year. We will be starting the first heat in fifteen minutes. Will all boarders assigned to the first heat please make their way to the starting point. We start in fifteen minutes sharp. Subsequent heats will start five minutes after the finish of the previous heat. When your heat is announced please make your way to the starting point as quickly as possible."

Mike was happy with 92 entrants; that meant that he had $920 of the prize money covered by the registration fees alone. This was going to be a good day.

Christyn and Billy had drawn Heat 3. Scott was Heat 7. Jim was in Heat 18 and Ben was in Heat 20. Devin had drawn Heat 15.

Each race had four boarders start on a raised platform. The boarders would push off once and head down the ramp and pick up speed quickly. They would go down the course about 100 yards and make a hard right turn, almost 90 degrees. They then had to proceed about 50 yards further down the course to go past the first judges booth where they could do their first trick. The idea was to land the trick successfully without losing much of your built up speed.

The skater would then continue another 100 yards before they had to make a hard winding left turn back almost 90 degrees. This turn is particularly tight and only two of the four boarders can go around the corner at the same time. Many crashes had occurred there last year and more were expected this year. Lots of spectators had positioned themselves right at that corner to watch the race.

The next stage of the course is long and boarders pickup a great deal of speed over the 200 yards before heading into the third turn. This turn is not as sharp as the skater gets close to the bottom of Bishop's Hill. This is a good thing because by then the skater's are going pretty fast. After the turn, there is a flat part where the skater can lose some of their speed and this is where Julie is positioned as the second judge.

As a judge, Julie was looking for a completed trick from each skater. The skater does not have to tell the judge ahead of time what trick they are planning but each trick has a point value and a completed trick gets all the points assigned to that trick. If a skater attempts a trick but does not land it, they can still get some points for the attempt. If they don't land it and crash in the process, they do not get any points.

The final leg of the course is a gradual downhill section that runs by the third judge and then 100 yards past that is the finish line. Mohammed and Mubarak were in the last judge's booth.

Mubarak was asking his brother a lot of questions about how to do the judging. Mohammed was pleased to have his brother there with him. Mubarak was finally showing signs of the caring person he used to be when they were younger. It was fun to have him around again.

Uncle Frank's voice came booming over the speakers again and he announced the start of Heat 1. The four boarders climbed onto the platform and lined up. Each competitor was looking around nervously at the crowd that had gathered. A few people in the crowd were yelling the name of their favourite racer. Finally the starter raised his arm and the skateboarders prepared to push off.

In Lane 1 Raymond Fillion was adjusting his helmet. Ray was nine years old and was an average skateboarder. He was wearing a new black helmet that appeared to be too big for his head. He kind of looked like a giant egg with legs. If it weren't for the Shorty's and Quiksilver logos on the side of the helmet, you might mistake him for a breakfast snack.

Janelle Culligan was in Lane 2. This was Janelle's first competition and she was nervous. Janelle loved to skateboard and when she saw the posters announcing the competition she told her mom that she wanted to compete. Her mom was happy that she was interested but Janelle confided to her that she was scared to race in front of so many others. Her mom encouraged her to enter the competition saying that she only had to please herself, not anyone else. Janelle planned to wear her lucky multi-colored socks for good luck. Janelle wasn't sure how well she was going to do but that didn't really matter. She set a goal to race hard, do her tricks and just finish the race. She would be happy with whatever time she received.

Lane 3 and 4 were filled with the Montgomery twins, Darryl and Earl. Their dad Merl was watching from the crowd. You could hear him yelling instructions to the boys.

"Watch the other boarders on the ramp! Don't let them push into you! Make sure to get out front so you can lead into the first turn."

The boys just waved to their dad. They were thoroughly embarrassed. Darryl looked at Earl and said, "I think he's talking to you."

Earl said with a smile, "So much for keeping our strategy a secret!"

144   All the racers watched the starter intently. After too long a delay there was a loud crack from the starter's pistol. The first four boarders at the 2nd Annual Boardzone Competition were off and running. They flew down the ramp and into the first straight four abreast. That was going to be fine until they had to make the first turn. This turn could only handle a maximum of two boarders side-by-side at any one time due to the width of the course at that point.

None of the boarders was going to give an inch. Ray decided he had to make a move. He began pushing with his foot and boosting his speed. He shot ahead of the others by about two board lengths.

Earl and Darryl both saw Ray begin to move ahead and they instinctively went down into a low aerodynamic crouch. This allowed them to gain more speed and they began to close the distance on Ray and pull away from Janelle at the same time. Darryl and Earl both wanted to win but they would also be happy if one of them came out on top.

In their crouch the twins glided by Ray and made it into the first turn together. They both leaned into the sharp corner and came out the other side. Earl had been on the inside and was slightly ahead of Darryl coming out of the turn.

Janelle followed Ray into the turn. She could see she was losing ground to the other three and decided it was time for a few pushes to get some speed back. That was a mistake. She was already going pretty fast and when she tried to plant her foot to push she began to lose her balance. That was when the wobble started. Everyone knows when you are racing and you start to get a speed wobble, there isn't much hope unless you slow down.

Janelle knew that she had to regain her balance and tried to position both feet back on the board. It was no use, the board was now zigzagging from left to right by at least a foot. She knew she was going to have to bail. She was mad at herself but her biggest concern now was where to have a graceful crash. She could see a perfect opportunity coming up. There was a man handing out cups of water. He had that Santa Claus look without the red suit of course. As she approached him she leaped off the swerving board and yelled a warning. She ploughed right into his large stomach and both of them ended up on the ground. The man was covered in dirt and Janelle was covered in cups and water.

"Sorry!" she said apologizing profusely.

"No worries, little lady. That was quite a spill. Are you OK?"

"Uh…yes, I seem to have found a good landing cushion."

The man laughed and said, "And my wife always said this big gut of mine was not good for anything!"

The other racers didn't even notice that Janelle was no longer behind them. They were concentrating on keeping their speed up so they could be the first ones to make the second turn. Ray was still trailing the twins after passing the first judge's stand. Each had successfully done a trick but Earl had been able to land the hardest trick.

Darryl began to pull in front and decided he would stay in his crouch position while also going through the second turn. Earl and Ray could see Darryl's strategy and decided that was too risky for them. It was harder to keep your balance when turning in a crouch.

Darryl was able to pull it off and came out of the turn much faster than the others. With the extra burst of speed, he started to pull away. He made it past the third turn and completed his second trick as well. He was feeling confident but he knew that he had to concentrate. Last year he had crashed in the preliminary heat because he was not looking ahead and he wasn't going to make that mistake again.

Earl and Ray completed their second trick and were about 20 feet behind Darryl. As they approached the last leg of the course, Darryl was in total control of the race and his strategy to crouch low had worked. He finished his final trick and then stayed low right passed the finish line.

Ray and Earl did their final trick and crossed the finish line too. Darryl had beaten them by about three seconds.

Darryl's mom was waiting and hugged Darryl when he stopped. Darryl picked up his board and rushed over to his brother.

"Nice race Earl!" said Darryl.

"You were awesome in that second turn, Darryl!" exclaimed Earl. "I didn't think you would be able to hold the crouch and do the turn at the same time, but you did."

The twins looked around and saw Ray. They went over and high-fived him still feeling excellent about the race. Ray was a little disappointed about not winning the heat but felt that he had done his best. "Great race guys!" said Ray. "Nice moves, you deserved to win."

"Thanks!" replied Darryl. "C'mon Earl, let's go find Dad and see when the next round of races begins."

The boys trotted back up the course to the starting area. They could hear the "bang" of the gun announcing Heat 2 had begun.

Heat 2 was just as fast paced and each of the four boarders flew down the course at top speed and successfully did their tricks. They crossed the finish line all in a row with less than a second gap between each skater. The winner was Mike Farber, a Grade 7 student who lived just outside of Exton.

Christyn and Billy were waiting for their heat to start. They didn't know Mike Farber very well because he didn't go to the same school as they did. He had posted a very fast time and they both knew that times were going to be fast today because of the excellent racing conditions.

146

"Did you see Farber coming down the final stretch?" Billy said to Christyn. "He was going ballistic."

"He was pretty fast, but we can do better, Billy!" she said, "We come down that stretch all the time."

Billy was looking back at Bishop's Hill and a slight shiver went down his back. He wasn't sure if he was scared or excited but he knew he had goose bumps on his arms.

"C'mon Billy, let's get to the starting gate. It's time we showed everyone who the real boarders are in this town," Christyn said confidently.

As they made their way to the starting gate, Jim and Ben appeared from the crowd to wish them luck. "Keep that helmet strapped nice and tight Billy," said Jim. "Remember, you want to be on the inside of the first turn and the outside of the second turn. Those will give you the best lines. And don't worry about doing hard tricks. Complete the easy ones and keep your speed up. You'll do just fine."

"Thanks, Jim." Billy felt much better after getting the pep talk from Jim.

"What am I, chopped liver?" whined Christyn.

"And good luck to you, Christyn!" said Ben and Jim at the same time.

"Would you two stop doing that!" exclaimed Christyn.

Christyn and Billy found their way to the starting gate and climbed the stairs. Billy was in Lane 1, Travis Kwan was in Lane 2, Christyn was in Lane 3 and Jane Watson was in Lane 4.

It was good to see so many competitors entered this year, especially since there were a lot more girls racing. Christyn was encouraged to see so many female competitors. She was one of only a handful of female competitors last year but this year she had lots of company.

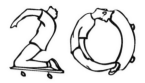

Billy Races Christyn

It was close to race time and each rider was checking to ensure his or her gear was in place and tightly fastened. It was mandatory that all boarders had to wear a helmet but it was optional to wear knee, elbow and hand pads. Billy wore a helmet, hand and kneepads. Christyn just wore a helmet. She did not like the feel of the extra gear and was confident that she would stay on her board for the whole race. Billy wore the knee and hand pads after a fall on Bishop's Hill a couple of months earlier. Ever since then, his mom and dad insisted that Billy wear the extra protection. They actually wanted him to wear elbow pads as well but Billy had convinced them that in a fall he would typically end up falling forward, but he also didn't like the restricted arm movement imposed by the bulky elbow pads. As the boarders lined up, Christyn caught Billy's eye and gave him a wink. He smiled back and looked down the ramp at the start of the course. His butterflies had returned but not too bad.

From the announcer's booth, Uncle Frank put his hand over the microphone and yelled "good luck" to Christyn and Billy.

The starter raised his arm and almost immediately he fired the gun. The boarders were each caught off guard and hesitated slightly. Billy used that opportunity to push ahead and was the first one down the ramp. He decided to risk a couple of quick pushes and that gave him a tiny bit of advantage on Christyn who was in second place right behind him.

Travis and Jane were in third and fourth place. Travis was close behind Christyn coming down the first straight and Jane was a little farther back from Travis. This was Jane's first race and she was just trying to stay close. She wanted to finish the race and wasn't too worried about her time. She wasn't going to try any risky moves. Being cautious was going to cost her time but if the others wiped out, she might end up in a good position after all. "Slow and steady wins the race," her father often told her.

Billy was feeling pretty good about being in the lead. He had just completed his first trick and was pushing hard to stay ahead of the others.

Christyn readied herself for her first trick, a nollie heel-flip. She had just the right amount of speed. As she passed by the judge's stand she flicked her board with her feet. The board came around and when she landed her feet were slightly too far back on the board. She had to steady herself for a split second by putting her foot down which cut into her speed.

Travis had allowed himself to get too close to Christyn and when Christyn slowed down quickly Travis realized he was closing in on Christyn too fast. Compounding his problem was he had done a simple two-deck ollie as his trick and had not lost any of his original speed. He had no choice but to brace himself as he was now going to hit the back of Christyn. He stuck out his arms and cushioned the impact as much as possible as he hit Christyn in the centre of her back.

Christyn was not expecting the push and the surprise from behind startled her. She fought to stay in control of her board. The push had caused her to almost lose her balance and fly off the front of her board.

148

As soon as Travis hit Christyn he knew he was disqualified. That actually didn't matter because he had already started to veer dramatically off to the left of the racecourse and had to jump off his board to avoid running into the crowd. His race was over.

Christyn knew that if she could regain her balance quickly she might actually be able to use the push from Travis to her advantage as it had given her a boost in speed. She fought the urge to fall over by leaning back as best she could and after what seemed like an eternity she slowly was able to regain control. As she looked ahead she was pretty sure she was starting to gain on Billy.

Jane had watched Travis bail in front of her and she had to be careful that she did not get caught up in the tangle of rider and board flying around ahead of her. In trying to avoid the mess she realized she was only going to have time to do a simple trick. She quickly did a kick-flip knowing that she could land it with little problem but it would not give her high points with the judge.

At this point Billy was still in the lead and had gotten into a tuck position. He was really burning up the course. Christyn was also now in a crouched low in a tuck position and hoped that her extra weight over Billy would give her more speed on the downward sloping course.

Jane was falling further behind Christyn. Jane was not going to try the tuck position. The best she could hope for now was another accident.

Christyn wasn't going to let that happen. She stood up, timed a couple of hard pushes and then got back into her tuck. She could see Billy slowing to do his second trick and she decided to do something completely new. She would not attempt a second trick at all. She decided to maintain her top speed and catch up to Billy.

Billy relaxed for just a second but that might have been his biggest mistake. He looked behind himself to see where Christyn was and he saw her back about 20 feet. He realized he had a good lead. Billy stood up and allowed himself to slow down so he could do his trick. Just as he was preparing to flip his board, Christyn blew past him and into the lead. Billy couldn't believe his eyes or his ears as Christyn flashed by shouting something.

"What the…" Billy was dumbfounded. "How did she get past me?"

Christyn was very pleased with herself. As she passed Billy she yelled "See you at the finish line slow poke!"

There was no rule about completing tricks, the only thing was that a completed trick was worth points and the more points you had the better your standing in the race. If you chose to skip one or more tricks, you just ended up with fewer points.

Now that Christyn was in the lead, she was going to pour on the speed. She decided that given the lead she now had, if she skipped the next trick she would likely be that much further ahead of Billy.

Billy realized the only way Christyn could have raced past her if she didn't slow down at the judge's station. That meant she didn't do a trick. He wondered if he should also skip the final trick. The problem was that he had successfully landed his two tricks so far and the points they were going to give him were as valuable as any lead. He decided to do the final trick and then concentrate on building his speed for the final leg of the race.

Christyn flew past the final judging area and was marked down as "Incomplete" for not attempting a trick. That meant she did not get any points at all. Given the fact that Christyn didn't even try to attempt a trick, Mohammed realized she was doing the speed strategy. That was a good idea as long as you had built up a sizeable lead from the person behind you. Christyn knew she had developed a big lead on Billy and was beginning to feel very confident. She could see the finish line and had dropped into a tuck to maximize her speed. Billy was also into a tuck now and thought he had closed the gap a little on Christyn. She was about 40 feet in front of Billy.

They crossed the finish line 2.4 seconds apart. It was now up to the calculation of the points total to see if Christyn would remain the leader. Her time was best so far and Billy's time was also better than the other racers who had raced so far that day. That fact made them both feel pretty good.

The judges calculated Christyn's point total based on her race time and the one trick she completed. The points assigned for her time were 245. Each trick had a maximum point total based on how hard the trick was to complete. The nollie heel-flip was a high degree of difficulty trick and was worth 30 points. Christyn had had a bit of trouble landing the trick and received 20 out of 30 points. Her total was 265 points.

Billy received 232 points based on his time. Each of his three tricks was not assigned a high degree of difficulty and had a maximum point value of 15. Billy had done all three fairly well and the judges had given pretty high point values. Would it be enough to pass Christyn?

The voice of Uncle Frank came over the PA again "Point total for Christyn Middlehurst in Heat 3 is 265 points. Billy was impressed. That was a high score and was going to be hard to beat. Christyn was feeling confident about her strategy. She held her breath as Uncle Frank read out the rest of the scores. "Next competitor is Billy Brandt. Billy finished the course and completed three tricks. Point total for Billy Brandt is 269 points." Uncle Frank's voice lingered over the last number to heighten the suspense.

Billy heard the number but could not believe his ears.

"Congratulations Billy!" said Christyn. "You beat me!"

"Point total for Jane Watson is 212. No point total was calculated for Travis Kwan. Winner of Heat 3 is Billy Brandt. Billy please report to the starting gate at the end of the heats to see what time you race again," said Uncle Frank's voice to the entire crowd.

Jim and Scott came running up to Billy and Christyn. "Nice heat guys!" said Scott. "You were really smoking down that course."

"Christyn, I thought you were a goner when Travis bailed and crashed into you," said Jim.

"So did I," said Christyn "I wasn't expecting the push and it was all I could to keep my balance without falling off the front. It was pretty hairy there for a few seconds."

"That was a pretty good strategy to skip your tricks to get the lead," said Billy. "I was shocked when you flew by me."

"I guess in the end I should have done more tricks but it was close. You won fair and square, Billy and we're going to cheer you on in the next set of heats."

Uncle Frank's voice came over the speaker system again announcing the start of the next heat. Scott knew that he had a few more heats to wait. He was scheduled to race in Heat 7. Jim and Ben were much later in the competition.

"Billy, why don't you and Christyn go grab a bottle of water and have a rest," said Scott. "You can watch me race."

"Perhaps I can give you some pointers on how to win!" laughed Billy.

Scott teased, "The big winner wants to share his worldly advice. OK, what's the most important thing I need to know?"

"Cross the finish line with more points than anyone else," Billy smirked.

Scott laughed. "Thanks champ! I'll see you in the semi-finals." Scott picked up his board and made his way to the starting point.

Billy and Christyn yelled "Good luck!" to him as he walked up the hill.

Racers Take a Break

Julie smiled at Mike and he gave her a big hug. The crowd was enormous. There were so many people coming to Bishop's Hill today there was no longer any parking available close by. Cars were parking up to a half a mile away. A local car dealer, Orion Motors, had come to the rescue by providing a dozen Silhouette mini-vans to shuttle people to and from the site. This saved a lot of walking for many people.

The first round of heats had just ended and Scott, Jim and Ben had been easy winners. In Jim's heat, he was so far ahead of the others that he had to wait for the last person to cross the finish line.

In Scott's heat, it was a little closer but his tricks were much better than the others and his point total was quite a bit higher.

Ben had the highest point total of all the kids. He had accumulated 301 points for his run. With a point total that high, Ben was going to be one of the favourites for the next round.

The next round of heats was going to start in 30 minutes, so the kids decided to grab a bite to eat.

"What does everyone feel like eating?" said Jim.

"The smell of those corn-dogs has been driving me crazy all day!" said Billy. "I'm going to have two of them and a chocolate milk."

"Corn-dogs! Yuck!" said Christyn. "Do you know what they put in those dogs?"

"Chihuahuas?" joked Jim.

"I'm going to have a big juicy cheeseburger," said Scott.

"Imagine my surprise!" said Christyn. "I'm going to have a salad from the Veggie King tent."

"Imagine our surprise!" said Jim.

"I have my eye on a big bag of French Fries and gravy. For dessert I'm going to get a bag of those tiny sugar coated donuts," said Jim.

"Yah, that's healthy," said Christyn.

"I'm going to wash it all down with a can of root beer."

The group decided to go off and grab their food and meet back at the spot near the band. They had reserved a spot by setting up the lawn chairs they had brought with them. They also had their towels laid out on the ground around the chairs. A short time later the friends finished getting their food and found their way back to their towels and chairs. Scott was first back and was busy wolfing down his cheeseburger. As Christyn approached her chair, which was next to Scott's chair, Scott had his head tilted way back and was guzzling a huge plastic bottle of Coca Cola. After what seemed to be an eternity, Scott finished his drink and was basically gasping for air. His eyes were almost popping out of his head.

"Serves you right!" announced Christyn.

"Brrrrrrraaaaaaaaaapppppppp!" Scott responded. "Ahhh, I feel much better now."

152

"Pig!" responded Christyn.

"If you think that was bad, wait around a while. Once that cheeseburger works its way through me, the real fireworks will begin," Scott said in a proud voice.

"Oh, great. Something to look forward to," sighed Christyn.

"Look forward to what?" asked Billy as he and Ben returned with their food. Each carried a large white Styrofoam container in one hand and a drink in the other.

"Trust me, nothing worth repeating in more ways than one."

Billy didn't understand. He just shrugged his shoulders and muttered "Girls!" to himself.

Ben and Billy had purchased corn dogs. Billy had slathered loads of mustard on each dog. Ben had always loved corn dogs and when he smelled them cooking nearby he realized that it had been ages since he last ate one. He was kind of staring into space looking at Billy's milk container. He thought about the last time he had chocolate milk and then remembered the food bank. He had almost gotten to the point where would no longer drink milk at all.

Over the past year, he had been volunteering Monday and Thursday nights at the Exton Food Bank. He had started out volunteering there as a way to get credit for a course he was taking in junior high school. The Human Economics course required that each student volunteer 30 hours of their own time to benefit the community. His dad had suggested the local food bank was a place always looking for volunteers. Ben had gone down to the food bank one Saturday morning and he was welcomed with open arms by the people who worked there.

George was his supervisor. George was not in charge of the food bank but he had been there for 19 years and basically ran the place. If you had a question or you wanted something, you would ask George. He was a very kind, quiet and hard-working man. Each time that Ben showed up for work, he always saw George. George would greet Ben and give him his daily assignment and all the while he would continue sorting food or packaging something up. George did not waste a second.

Normally Ben's job at the food bank was to clean out the main cooler. The main cooler was 10,000 square feet and was usually always one-half to three-quarters full of food donations from the local supermarkets, vegetable and dairy producers.

The food bank was for anyone who couldn't afford food for themselves or their families. The food donated to the food bank was still good but sometimes in the cooler things got dropped, spilled, broken and left a mess. Other times, items in the cooler would go past their due date and begin to smell. This required regular cleaning and Ben was the unofficial cooler-cleaner.

153

Ben had long since passed his 30 hours of required service and had become a regular on Tuesday and Thursday nights. He worked from 6:00 p.m. until they closed at 9:00 p.m. He liked the people at the food bank. Many of the people who volunteered there had been users of the food bank themselves and knew how valuable it was to help. Some were still users of the food bank.

"Being poor is not a crime," Ben had always thought, "and anyone who needs a helping hand to feed their family deserves a place to go to get that help." That was the real reason why Ben continued on. The work was not glamorous and actually it could get pretty disgusting.

To clean the cooler properly, you needed to wash down all surfaces with a mixture of bleach and water. To get access to all the surfaces, you had to move all the food out of the cooler temporarily. All the different types of milk, cheese, yogurt, juices, fruit and vegetables were stored in groups on pallets. The pallets had to be moved out of the cooler, one by one, using a pallet jack. That was a long job as there were typically 25 pallets loaded with food in the cooler at any given time. The job was made a little longer because each of the pallets of food had to be checked to ensure any spoiled food was removed and thrown in the garbage.

Once the pallets were all moved out, Ben had to hose down the walls and floor and then use a mop and the bleach solution and mop every square inch of surface inside the cooler.

When all the surfaces were cleaned, all the pallets had to be brought back into the cooler and arranged back into proper groups. The whole cleaning job was not allowed to take more than 60 minutes because the food on the pallets might begin to go bad if it was not kept refrigerated.

Ben had gotten so good that he rarely had to leave the food out for more than 45 minutes. The only time that he could remember where the food sat longer was the time he noticed that the water he was using to hose down the walls was no longer draining into the floor drains.

The water was starting to back up and cause a mini-flood inside the cooler. He wasn't sure how to unclog the pipe so he went to find George. George had seen this before and explained a quick way to clean out the pipes that ran under the main cooler.

He asked Ben to go find the portable spray gun and hose attachment. It was one of those high-pressure water spray units on wheels that most people used to clean their cars or boats. Ben wheeled it into the cooler and hooked up the power and water feeds.

There were two drains in the cooler and George figured that a blockage had occurred in between the two holes in the floor. George asked Ben to stick the nozzle of the spray gun into one of the holes and give it a blast. Ben did what he was told. George told him to not shoot the water full blast. Ben started to spray a bit but the water would hardly come out. He pulled on the trigger harder and the water shot out of the nozzle like a cannon.

The force of the blast of water made its way in seconds to the blockage but the blockage held firm. The excess water shot backwards and came spraying out of the hole, all over Ben and George. Dirty, smelly water that was full of spoiled milk and other dairy products is not a way you want to spend an evening.

The worst part was getting some of it in your mouth. Ben was sure he was going to die of some terrible disease. The taste of the water in the drain would never leave him. George had him go wash off with clean water while he continued to free the drain.

When Ben came back, after thoroughly soaping his face, he was relieved to see the flood was gone and George was rolling up the hose and electrical cords. That was a day, and a taste, he would never forget.

"Ben, Ben, Hello!" said Billy. Ben snapped back into the present. "Ben! How is your corndog?"

"Wh…oh, fine. Actually I haven't had a bite yet. Just a sec," said Ben as he dipped the end of the piping hot corndog into some mustard and bit off a large bite."

"Watch the stick inside the corndog!" exclaimed Billy.

"Trust me, I'm a professional," laughed Ben. "Oh man, this tastes good."

Christyn was content eating her salad as long as Scott didn't start farting.

154

Jim had selected and eaten his poutine. Poutine was a type of fast food from Quebec, but this year it had come to Exton: french fries, smothered in gravy and topped with cheese curds. It looked disgusting but Jim didn't seem to mind, he had it polished off in about five minutes.

He was busy popping his mini doughnuts into his mouth one at a time when he noticed Devin Snively walking by. Jim's eyes followed Devin as he made his way towards the food stands.

Ben could see Jim was watching something intently and he looked over to see what it was.

"Snively got you worked up?" said Ben to Jim.

"Yeah. I don't trust him. I see he won his heat too. I expect to see him in the finals again this year."

It was like Devin Snively had radar, at that precise moment he turned around and looked back towards the place where the kids were parked. He looked right at Jim, smirked and then walked away.

"Don't let him bug you Jim," advised Ben. "You've got to keep your focus only on the race. Pretend he isn't even there."

Round One Results

Mike was busy with Julie reviewing the attendance figures for the day. It was only 1:00 p.m. and already they had already doubled the number of people who had attended last year.

"Can you believe it Julie, there are still people showing up to get tickets and the day is already half over," Mike said excitedly.

"I know; I know," she exclaimed "I was just talking to State Trooper Jackson and he tells me it's a zoo on the highway, but he said that they are going to do their best to get everyone in."

"With all the ticket money we have taken in, we might be able to pay off the rest of the skate park land costs."

"Mike that would be awesome! Do you think we will get that much?"

Mike turned around. There were people as far as the eye could see. The line of people was five and six deep. Many were carrying lawn chairs and beach umbrellas to protect themselves from the blistering sun. "I don't know for sure, but I do know because of you we might just make it." He gave Julie a big hug and kiss.

* * * *

Meanwhile, the Mayor was drafting a memo to the city councilors informing them of the council meeting date change. He was worried about this memo. It was the day before the new meeting date and no one knew of the change yet. Worse, it was a Sunday and no one would be in the office to read the memo until tomorrow. When they came in the following morning they would only have one hour to prepare for the new meeting time.

He finished the memo and clicked the Send button. He hoped there would not be a riot tomorrow.

* * * *

There were 23 heat winners from the first round but only 16 of the winners would make it into the second round, based on their point total. The scores of all the winners from the first round were compared and the highest point totals were announced on a big white board next to the stage.

The board was getting a lot of attention from racers and spectators alike. All of the racers were asked to gather around the board at 3:00 p.m. They were going to make the announcement to define the order of the racers for the second round.

The first round of races had ended around 2:00 p.m. There had been a half-hour break to ensure everyone got a chance to eat. It was only 2:45 p.m. but already the area was packed with racers and spectators anxiously waiting to find out who had made it through to the second round and in which heat would they race.

Scott, Jim and Billy had gone ahead and were waiting in the crowd about 20 feet in front of the board. Christyn and Ben had stopped to talk with Julie and Mohammed about the race and had taken a few extra minutes to make their way to the board. The board was covered up with a large sheet of black plastic. This prevented anyone from seeing the results.

Christyn and Ben were working their way through the crowd trying not to knock over anyone. It was very slow going with all the people. "Do you see Scott or Jim?" asked Ben.

"Uh…no, wait…I see them. Over to the left about 20 yards." The two of them made their way to the others.

"What time do you have?" Christyn said to Billy as she tapped him on the shoulder.

Billy was startled by Christyn walking up behind him.

Christyn could see Billy jump. "Oh, sorry, squirt. I didn't notice you in the crowd." teased Julie.

"It's time you got yourself a watch," countered Billy not wanting to let Christyn get away with teasing him.

"It's 2:58pm," said Jim. "Would you two stop it?"

Uncle Frank's voice came booming over the public address system. "Hello everyone, welcome to the 2nd Annual Boardzone competition. We have completed the first round of racing and have 23 winners to announce. The racers with the 16 highest point totals will move on to compete in one of four heats in the second round." Uncle Frank read off the names of the 23 first-round winners but did not include their point total. He read the names of the winners in the order of their race. After each name was read the audience cheered wildly. When Ben, Jim, Scott and Billy heard their names, the rest of the kids went crazy. They were smiling and high-fiving. When Uncle Frank got to the last name, someone pulled the black sheet off the big board so that everyone could see the point total for each racer and who would make it into the second round.

There was an immediate buzz in the crowd. The top point total went to Ben Holt at 301 points. Next was Devin Snively at 296. Jim was third at 288. Scott was fourth at 284 and Billy had made it into the second round with a point total of 269. He had secured the last spot available.

Billy was beaming he was so happy. "I can't believe it, I made it into the next round!"

"Great job, Billy" said Jim. "I'm proud of you."

That was a big compliment from his brother and Billy felt wonderful.

Scott and Christyn approached Ben. "You did it, Ben! You got the highest point total."

"I did but that doesn't mean I win yet!" said Ben.

"No it doesn't, because I plan to win," said Jim.

"Me too!" Billy piped up. They all laughed.

Jim looked at the second-place finisher – Devin Snively.

* * * *

Across the crowd, about 150 yards away, Devin Snively was on his cell phone as soon as he saw the results on the board. "Hello?" it was hard to hear over the noise of the crowd. "Is this Ferguson?"

"Yes, Master Snively," said their butler.

"Let me speak to Mother," ordered Snively.

"Your Mother is not here, Master Snively. She has flown to Boston for the day to do some shopping."

"What about Father? Is he there?" asked Devin.

"Yes. Just a moment please," said the butler. Ferguson put Devin on hold while he brought the phone to Mr. Snively.

After a short wait, Devin heard a voice on the phone "Philmore Snively," announced Devin's father. It was the same way he answered all his phone calls even though he knew this call was from his son.

"Dad! Dad! Guess what?" Devin said elatedly.

"Devin, I'm a busy man with no time for guessing games. What do you want?" retorted the older Snively.

"I won my first race and I ended up with the second highest point total in the competition."

"What on earth are you talking about? What race?" said Mr. Snively, puzzled.

"The skateboarding competition!" shouted Devin a bit impatiently.

"The one I told you about yesterday."

"Are you still riding around on that silly board? You should be spending your time more wisely young man. Perhaps if you had a real job you would understand. I suggest you not be late for dinner tonight."

"Yes Father. Good-bye sir." Devin didn't even bother attempting to ask his father if he would come and watch him in the second round, he already knew the answer.

* * * *

The board outlined the scores of the first round winners and it also indicated in which heat and lane the next 16 racers were placed. The racers in Heat 1 were at the top right hand of the board. Jim saw it right away and so did Ben. They looked at each other and Jim just shrugged his shoulders.

"Don't worry," said Jim. "He'll give it his best shot. Who knows?"

160

Christyn and Scott weren't sure what Jim and Ben were talking about until they read the names of the racers in Heat 1. Both Ben and Billy were paired up in that race.

Billy was still busy reviewing the names of the winners when he noticed all his friends staring at him. "What?" said Billy.

Jim came over to Billy. "Billy, look at the top right hand side of the board in Heat 1. Billy looked up.

"Hey...there's my name...and look Ben's name is also.... oh." He paused. It had hit him. He was going to be racing against Ben in the next race. Billy had really wanted to win the competition but to race against Ben in the semi-final was a real setback. Ben was really good and Billy wasn't sure if he could beat him. He was hoping to only have to race Ben in the final but that was no longer a possibility. Billy turned around to look at everyone. He decided he was going to be funny and make the best of it.

"So Ben, don't be scared. Your competition may be tough but you've proven you are a better than average boarder."

Ben smiled and Billy began to laugh. "Don't count me out yet!" said Billy.

Scott was in Heat 2, Devin Snively was in Heat 3 and Jim was in Heat 4.

The booming voice of the announcer came over the PA system. Racers for Heat 1 should proceed to the starting gate. The race begins in five minutes.

Billy and Ben grabbed their boards and the others shouted encouragements to both of them.

"Good luck guys! We'll be watching you all the way down.

Billy the Ripper

Scott, Jim and Christyn had each decided to go and wait for the racers near the judging stations. Scott was going to take Judges Station 1 because he was racing in Heat 2 and needed to be near the top of the course to get to the starting gate on time. He followed Ben and Billy.

Jim took Judges Station 2 and Christyn made her way over to Judges Station 3, near the bottom of the course.

As Christyn was looking for a good spot to watch the race from she passed right by Mohammed and Mubarak sitting at the Judges Station.

"Hey Mohammed!" said Christyn. "Hi Mubarak."

"Hello Christyn," Mohammed greeted her in his normal cheery voice.

"Hello Christyn. How are you doing today?" asked Mubarak.

Christyn was taken aback by Mubarak's question. She had never heard him sound so pleasant before.

"Uh…fine…are you guys keeping cool in this heat?"

"We sure are. Mubarak has been kind enough to go and get us lots of ice-cold water and he brought this battery-powered fan for us. It is making all the difference."

"Glad to hear it. I'm just going to find a spot over there to watch Billy and Ben. They are both racing in the first race."

"Yes, I have a copy of the races and who is in each right here," Mohammed said and he held up a piece of paper.

"I'll talk to you later. I don't want to interrupt your judging," she said smiling and walked away.

Back at the top of the course, Billy and Ben were lining up in the starting gate. They did not know the other two boys they were racing against. Ben knew that the one boy named River was fairly new to skateboarding but had posted the 15th highest point total. Obviously he knew how to do tricks. The other boy was Skylar and had the 8th fastest time.

He was not only good at tricks but he was fast as well.

Skylar had the coolest helmet in the whole competition. He had a picture of a large green dragon with fire coming out of his mouth and nose airbrushed on to the front of the helmet. The dragon was breathing fire all over a silver knight who was trying to defend himself. The knight was swinging a large sword at the dragon and the dragon was towering over the knight. Below the picture was the Darkstar logo.

Ben had his choice of lanes and immediately selected Lane 1. He felt that Lane 1 would give him the best advantage going into the first turn if he could stay in front of the others. Being in Lane 1 meant that you did not have to cut over to get into the first turn properly.

Skylar had the next best point total and chose Lane 2. River was late getting to the starting line because of some equipment problem so Billy chose Lane 3. River had to take Lane 4 just before the race started.

162   Each racer was starting to feel the pressure. They knew they were racing against the winners of the first race so the talent had risen significantly. They also knew that Ben had the highest point total for the whole field of racers and they knew he was the racer to beat. They were all looking to gain an edge on him.

Ben was the calmest of the four racers. He had been in this situation before and he was the most confident about his abilities. Being calm meant that he would be able to think clearly throughout the race and that might give him the edge he needed to win.

The starter raised his arm and Ben looked over at Billy and their eyes locked. Ben mouthed silently, "Good luck."

Billy mouthed back, "Break a leg." Ben and Billy smiled.

"On your marks, get set…" The crack of the starter's pistol propelled the racers into motion. A loud noise and a puff of smoke momentarily covered some of the racers. By the time the smoke had cleared all the racers were well down the ramp and streaking towards the first turn.

Ben had a slight lead over Skylar but Ben had much stronger legs than any of the other racers and was already starting to build on the gap. River and Billy were neck and neck and Billy was maintaining perfect balance as he pushed himself down the course at full speed.

As they approached the first turn, Ben got down in a low crouch position and leaned backwards into the turn at an angle that should have resulted in a bail. The force of gravity kept him on the board and he shot out of the turn even faster than the others.

Billy knew this move and had learned it well from Ben. As he made his turn and tuck, Billy shot past Skylar to take second place for now.

River also made it through the first turn and started into a tuck position himself to gather more speed so he could try and catch the other racers.

Ben was approaching Judges Station 1 and as Ben passed by the spot where Scott was watching the race, Scott could see his friend had fierce determination in his eyes. Ben did not seem to notice Scott yelling from the side of the road.

"Go Ben, you've got a 20-yard lead!"

Ben flew by without acknowledging Scott. Scott watched Ben prepare for his first trick. Ben had decided he would repeat the same tricks he had done in the first race. He would start with a simple kick-flip. If he did that right, he would likely do two more at the other judging stations. All he wanted to do was cross the finish line first and complete three simple tricks.

As Ben approached the Judges Station he slowed down a bit and with the slightest movement Mike had ever seen, he flipped his board and landed a perfect kick-flip.

163

He pushed hard with his foot three times and got right back into his tuck position in order to keep his speed up going into the second turn.

Billy could see Ben's trick and decided that he was going to do a nollie heel-flip. That would get him more points than a simple kick-flip. All he had to do was land it. He had landed this move in practice many times but he had never done it going this fast before.

He decided to slow down to his normal speed first. He lined up for the trick and popped the board with his feet. The board flew around and landed perfectly. His feet dropped right back into position like they were magnets on steel.

He then continued to push himself down the course just like Ben did but Billy gave two extra pushes to maximize his speed. He was starting to feel like he was losing control so he jumped back on the board and got into a low tuck position. He wasn't sure but he thought he might even be gaining on Ben.

River was right on Skylar's tail. They were going to end up doing their tricks at the same time. Mike, who was judging, could handle watching two racers do tricks at the same time. During one race earlier in the day, three racers did their tricks at one time. The only problem with two or more racers doing tricks at the same time is that you risk the collision of the boards. This is exactly what happened to poor River and Skylar.

Skylar was lining up to do a 360-flip while River was planning a simple kick-flip. As River came along side Skylar, he was not watching how close he was to the other racer. Skylar attempted his trick at the same instant River attempted his trick. As the two boards were flipping around they brushed each other for the briefest amount of time. That was enough to change their speed and direction and both boards were not where their owners had expected them to be when their feet tried to land back on the board.

Both racers were in trouble. River's feet landed completely off the board and onto the pavement. Going at the speed he was going, it was like stopping from 20 mph to 0 mph in 0.1 second. His feet could not handle the rapid change in speed and he flew forward landing on his outstretched arms and hands. He was going to be picking gravel out of cuts for a while.

Skylar was also just about to experience some pain. His feet landed on the edge of his board and the motion of his body made the board shoot forward. Skylar flew up into the air and landed on his butt, skidding to a halt on the pavement after about five yards.

Skylar could feel the burning of road rash through his pants. "This is going to hurt!" he thought.

164   Billy and Ben had no idea of the accident behind them. They were busy concentrating on the race. Ben was concentrating on getting to the next Judges Station and Billy was concentrating on catching Ben.

The extra weight Ben had on Billy was helping Ben to gain speed and therefore distance on Billy but it made it harder for him to do his tricks. He had to slow down each time he wanted to do a trick. He thought about Christyn's plan to skip the tricks and go for a pure lead over the other racers but he knew that the others would likely do tricks and he wasn't sure if he could establish a large enough lead on any of them. He was also sure he could hear another racer not far behind and it was likely Billy.

He slowed down a bit and with one simple movement did a perfect kick-flip for Julie who was the judge at Judges Station 2. Julie watched the trick and marked a score down on her paper.

He felt better that he had now done two clean tricks. While the tricks were simple they were going to add to his point total. He had one more trick and then a burst of speed to the finish. He was feeling confident but he knew he had to continue to concentrate. He knew he could blow it if he didn't stay focused.

Billy had just finished his second trick, a heel-flip. He was in the process of zooming away from the Judges Station and was getting into his crouch. He was focusing very intently on Ben's back. In his mind Billy was pretending he was a big piece of metal and Ben was a giant magnet. He was willing himself to close the distance on Ben but he was running out of time.

Ben had taken a brief glance over his shoulder and could see the gap between himself and Billy. There was only about 25 yards separating them.

"Wow, Billy is sure keeping up with me. I should have known that little shrimp would keep up! I don't see the others, I wonder what happened to them."

Billy saw Ben's quick glance back. He said to himself, "That's right Ben, I'm on your tail and I'm coming for you right now."

He could see the gap closing on Ben. A smile came over his face. Billy thought, "One more good trick and I will have a solid chance of taking Ben out."

Ben had rounded the final turn and was heading toward the last Judges Station. He was weighing his trick options.

"With Billy this close, should I do a complex trick or stick with my standard trick?"

"I'm going standard. It's worked so far and I'm not going to change a good thing now."

As Ben passed Mohammed and Mubarak, he did his final kick-flip perfectly.

Billy was also thinking about his final trick. "I'm going to go for it and do another 360-flip. That will give me the maximum points and certainly better than the points Ben is getting for all those simple kick-flips."

He approached the judging area and got himself ready. He didn't feel quite right and thought his speed might be a bit too fast. He waited a couple of seconds and then popped his board around. Billy could remember every detail like it was in slow motion. The board began its spin and rotating flip at the same time. His feet just barely cleared the board as it whirled underneath him. The board came around and slapped itself onto the pavement, his feet landed back on the deck in the perfect position.

"Oh yes!" thought Billy. He immediately crouched and began his final drive to catch up to Ben. He was really moving as he approached the last leg of the course. This was as fast as he had ever gone and he was starting to get uncomfortable with the speed. He was thinking about the wreck he would have if he had to bail right now.

Ben was also in a tuck for the final leg of the course. He was only about 20 yards ahead of Billy. Ben knew that Billy would not just do a simple kick-flip and if he was still behind Ben then chances were good he had done three clean tricks. Ben knew that he had to make the gap between him and Billy as big as possible to win this race.

Ben got as low as he could go. Crouching down reduces the wind resistance and allows the racer to maximize their speed. The only drawback to crouching is that the racer has to have exceptionally good balance, especially if you are going to hold the crouch for an extended period of time.

Ben was an expert in the crouching or tuck position. He felt totally comfortable getting low and moving fast. He loved the thrill of the speed. He knew that Billy would never allow himself to go as fast as he could. Ben decided to use that knowledge to his own benefit by holding his tuck position all the way down the final leg and right past the finish line. He wasn't sure how he was going to stop after the finish line, but he figured he'd find a way.

Billy could see how low Ben was crouching. Billy wasn't going to match that technique. He knew that he couldn't hold a tuck position as low or as long as Ben.

Ben could see the finish line rapidly approaching. He wanted to look behind himself to see where Billy was. He resisted the urge. "I'm not going to blow this race now by checking to see where Billy is. Concentrate!" he told himself. He had to wipe the image of him accepting the $1,000 cheque from his mind. It was too early to celebrate yet.

Billy and Ben whizzed down the last part of the course and blasted by the finish line. They were moving very fast and each racer took special care to get out of their tuck position. As their bodies caught the wind, they began to slow down. When they both had slowed to a reasonable speed they jumped off their boards. Ben scooped up his board and made his way over to Billy.

"Awesome race, Billy! You have been practicing!"

"You too Ben!" replied Billy.

The two friends exchanged stories about the race. Ben was interested in Billy's tricks.

"I may have crossed the finish line first, Billy but you could still pass me in the points race."

"This sounds like déjà vu!" said Christyn who had arrived and was listening to the conversation.

"And it is just like our last race!" said Billy.

Jim and Christyn exchanged looks, laughing silently at Billy.

Shoelaces and Squirrels

The announcer's voice once again came booming over the PA system. This time it was not Uncle Frank.

"We will have the results of the last heat in a few moments. Will the racers in the next heat please proceed immediately to the starting gate."

"This is Scott's race!" exclaimed Billy. He was still quite excited about the outcome of his race. "Let's go grab a spot to watch it."

Before Billy could run off, Ben grabbed him by the arm and held him back for a moment.

"Billy, I just want you to know that no matter how the results turn out, you raced a heck of a good race and I hope you win."

Billy was feeling good already but this made him feel even better. He didn't know what to say but he felt like he should say something.

"Th…thanks Ben. Coming from you that means a lot." He looked over at Christyn who was listening to the whole conversation. "Certainly it means a lot more than if it came from someone…like Christyn!" He ducked away from Christyn who tried to give him a playful cuff to the head.

They all made their way over to the course and took up positions. Most people were waiting for the sound of the starter's pistol to fire. The starting gate was too far away to see but you could hear the starting pistol crack and within a couple of minutes you could see the racers making their way down the course.

Billy was sort of concentrating on the upcoming race but he was also listening hard for the announcer's voice. He was dying to hear the results of his race with Ben.

At the starting gate the racers lined up in their positions. Scott was in Lane 1 and Phil Toutges was in Lane 2. Phil was quite a bit older than most of the other racers. He was 17 years old and had been skateboarding for eight years. He was actually sponsored by NitroGlycerine Snowboards and spent most of his winter attending snowboarding competitions. He was always getting free equipment. He was amazing on a snowboard and was pretty good on a skateboard. His best moves on a skateboard were tricks, not true speed. Scott knew this and planned to try and gain as much distance on Phil as possible.

"Do simple but good tricks and keep your speed high," Scott said to himself. That should win it for you.

Phil had been practicing his tricks for weeks before the race and was confident that he could land the hard ones. When he looked down the steep starting gate at the course that lay ahead of him, he immediately thought that he should have spent more time practicing for the downhill part. It was scary to look down Bishop's Hill and think in a few moments he was going to be hurtling down the pavement shoulder to shoulder with three other boarders.

Jon Vance was in Lane 3. Jon was clearly the largest racer of the day. Jon was only 12 years old but was already 5' 11" and weighed 204 lbs. Jon was self-conscious about his size and had taken up skateboarding to show the others that he could do something that required balance.

Jon was basically lucky to be in the semi-finals and he knew it. He loved to skateboard but was not too eager to do the racing part. He didn't want to make a fool of himself in front of so many people but his friends said they would cheer him on if he entered, so he did.

He hadn't expected to win the first round and wouldn't have except for some incredible luck.

In the first race he was behind the other racers in his heat. As the others entered the third turn ahead of him, he saw them get tangled up and crash into each other in a big heap. Jon had just enough time to lean way out to the right to avoid them. In fact, he just cleared the outstretched leg of one racer who had once occupied Lane 4. Jon was sure that he was going to clip the racer's foot and had braced himself for the impact. But it never came.

When Jon realized that there was no bump that was going to knock him off his board, he opened his eyes and realized that there was no one between him and the finish line. He decided then and there to not do any more tricks and to just ride the board to the finish line as quickly and safely as he could. That's what he did and he ended up winning his heat.

In Lane 4 was Penny Maxwell. Penny was a real tomboy. She was one of the best female skateboarders in Exton and was in the semi-finals last year too. Penny was not a nice person but not a mean person either. She didn't talk much and was very competitive. Her dad was a real estate agent and he was usually trying to sell someone a new house. He was always on his cell phone taking calls from some new client. Penny's dad always told her, "if you want to be the best, you have to do your best".

That was Penny's motto. She lived her life by those words and didn't waste too much time on activities that didn't work towards one of her goals. Her goal on this day was to win the race.

Scott knew that Penny was good but he was confident that he was faster. He had seen Penny practicing some tricks a couple of weeks ago at the local high school. She had been trying to 50–50 the handrail but could never quite get enough height in her ollie to get up onto the rail. Scott knew he owned that rail and could 50–50 it whenever he wanted.

Penny was wearing her trademark overalls and blue helmet with the silver lightening bolts down the side. On one side it said "Maxwell Realty" and on the other side it had the BMW logo. The BMW M3 was Penny's dream car. She once went to a car show where they had an M3 on display. It was a convertible and Penny dreamed of owning it.

Scott knew this from listening to her. He decided to use that to his advantage. As they were lining up in the final few seconds before the race started, Scott began to speak. "Hey Jon. What has four wheels, makes a terrible racket and spews out black smoke?"

169

"I dunno...what?" Mike said, wondering what Scott was talking about.

"Every BMW that I ever saw," needled Scott.

Penny heard the comment and immediately whipped her head around. She looked at Scott. Actually she was glaring at Scott who was looking at the ground. As his eyes slowly came up to meet her stare, the starter's pistol banged and Scott mouthed the words, "See you later Penny!"

Penny was shocked for an instant. First she was mad about the car comment, then she was surprised at the sound of the gun and when Scott spoke to her she realized she had been taken. She had lost her concentration when it counted most. Scott had tricked her and she had fallen for it.

By the time Penny was moving Scott, Phil and Jon were already well down the starting ramp.

"Grrrrr...I'm going to get that Scott Wilson!" fumed Penny. She powered down the ramp and followed the others down the course.

Scott was very proud of himself. "One down, two to go!" he thought to himself. "Now let's see how I can beat Phil and Jon."

It wasn't going to be hard to take out Jon. In classic Jon style, he hadn't done up his shoes properly. It was hard for him to bend down to tie his shoes so he often didn't bother. Not a good thing to skip before a big skateboard race.

As he was building up speed and heading into the first turn, he was dragging a foot long shoelace behind his board. It was dragging and bumping along dangerously close to his wheels. The shoelace was keeping its distance from the spinning wheel but when he rounded the corner for the turn, the shoelace started to slap against the right rear wheel. If the shoelace caught, it would wrap itself around the wheel and axle and cause the wheel to stop spinning immediately. If that happened it would cause Jon to become the first kid in Exton to try and launch himself into outer space.

Jon was totally oblivious to the dangling shoelace. He was actually starting to feel really good about the race. He was keeping up with Scott and Phil and was just behind them as they both did their first trick in front of the judge in Station 1.

Jon lined up for his trick. He was going to stick to a simple kick-flip for the first trick to make sure he would get some points. As he approached the station, Mike the judge was watching intently looking for how well the trick would be done. Mike had his clipboard ready to record the scores.

170

Jon felt like he had the correct speed and when he was right in front of the judge he jumped and flicked his toe to spin the board around. The board did exactly what he wanted. However, it was not to be his day. As the board spun around on its axis the shoelace that was once dragging behind the board began to wrap around the back left wheel like a bandage on an Egyptian mummy. This caused the board to stop its spin and when gravity took over and brought Jon back down from his leap, the board was now upside down. Jon landed on the board hard and began to do the longest darkslide Mike the judge had ever seen.

The biggest problem with this darkslide, other than it was unplanned, was that Jon's foot was actually pinned to the back wheel and he couldn't jump off the board if he wanted to. The board was slowing down much faster than Jon's original speed and he could feel himself starting to fall forward. He had no control over this.

From where Christyn was watching the race she could see the whole event take place. She would never forget the look of confusion on Jon's face as the skateboard and his foot became permanently tangled which caused him to fly forward in a kind of windmill effect, legs and arms were flying everywhere. Head over heels he tumbled with skateboard whipping around at the same time.

Christyn was truly impressed with this bail. She wished she had brought her family's video camera. "I could have sent this in to Real TV!" she thought.

Jon on the other hand was not thinking about how juicy this bail would look on video at the moment. He was wondering how he had gotten into this mess. All he knew at this point was he was heading for the pavement and today was the day he had forgotten to bring his protective gloves.

Christyn and Mike both winced and covered their eyes for a second as Jon hit the ground. He used both his outstretched arms to protect his body but they immediately folded like a cheap card table under his tremendous weight.

Jon had at least had the presence of mind to do a roll, like a somersault, to break the fall. After that he skidded for a while and ended up in a heap with a cloud of dirt swirling around him.

Several people including Christyn ran onto the course to see if he was OK. This was good for Jon but bad for Penny who was coming up behind the pile of people now in her way.

"Watch out, watch out!" she cried.

The announcer's voice (Uncle Frank was still not doing the announcements) came over the speakers asking all non-essential people to clear the track.

Penny was trying to pick a lane where she could make it through without colliding with anyone. She was going at a very good clip and now there were people running back and forth across the track, right in her path!

She had to make a choice. This was where she needed to do her first trick but if she did, she was likely to end up colliding with someone. She decided to slalom around the people pretending they were like pylons. OK, moving pylons.

She whizzed by the first group and avoided them by leaning hard left. She then had to immediately lean backwards to the right to avoid a guy standing in the centre of the course talking into a radio.

As Penny whipped by him she was close enough to nudge his arm a bit and he was shocked to see someone appear and then disappear so fast. Penny hoped his surprise didn't translate into any colorful language into the radio.

The last group was dead ahead and this time it wasn't going to be as easy to avoid them. The group of people could see Penny coming and they were standing there not moving like a bunch of deer caught in the headlights of a car.

"Get outta the way!" cried Penny.

This yell caused them to move finally. Half of the group went to the left and luckily half of the group went to the right. Penny shot through the exact spot where the group used to be a couple of seconds earlier and now she was passed the people.

Penny never saw the squirrel. The little guy was busy carrying a mouthful of peanuts that some kid had spilled earlier in the day. The squirrel hadn't been happy to see so many people invade his territory that morning but he soon realized that all these people meant a lot of food was being dropped.

The squirrel had already picked up eight peanuts and was about to grab one more before heading to his tree when a toddler on a Big Wheel tricycle decided that she wanted a pet squirrel. She ran towards the busy squirrel and tried to grab his tail.

The squirrel was always keeping an eye out for danger and while this person chasing him was not that big, he still didn't want to have any part of having his tail grabbed.

The squirrel instinctively bolted in the opposite direction of the little girl and began to run as fast as his little legs would carry him. His path went directly across the racecourse.

Penny did a quick calculation in her head and realized there was going to be squirrel road kill in about three seconds if she didn't do something fast.

She veered hard to the right and found herself heading for a row of small bushes that ran along this part of the course. She realized her day was now done and she was just trying to save herself like Jon had done a short time earlier.

"Stupid squirrel!" she thought.

Penny began to drag her foot on the ground to slow down and in doing so she lost her balance, spun the board sideways and rolled into the bushes mowing down the first four. The bushes actually were quite soft and broke her fall very nicely.

When she came to a stop she realized right away that she was not hurt and she sat up. There were only a couple of people that had been sitting and watching the race at this particular point and one of them came over to ask if she was OK.

Penny got up and told the lady she was fine. She dusted the dirt from her pants and looked around.

The squirrel was sitting on a tree stump nearby. He was looking directly at her.

"Are you OK?" Penny said.

The squirrel looked at her for a couple more seconds and then scampered off to his tree nest. She had babies to feed and these peanuts were going to be their dinner for tonight.

Devin Eliminates the Competition

Only Scott and Phil were still in the current race. Both had passed the second judging station and were building up more speed. Phil was slightly ahead of Scott, having dropped into his streamline tuck position just a bit earlier than Scott. Scott had a bit of trouble landing his second trick and lost a bit of speed.

Scott actually didn't mind being in this position. Scott had completed a harder second trick than Phil and now he was drafting Phil. He was catching and pushing all the wind out of the way for Scott. The rushing air in Phil's wake was also pulling Scott closer to Phil. Scott wanted use this as an advantage to slingshot his way ahead of Phil just as they approached the finish line.

They both headed into the last part of the course. Each had done their final trick. Both had played it safe and did a simple heel-flip. Each racer was crouched as low as they could go to maximize their speed. Scott was tucked close in behind Phil. There was only about 100 yards left in the race and Scott decided to make his move.

He leaned quickly out to the left, still in his tuck position, and pulled up along side of Phil. They were heading neck and neck into the finish area.

Billy and Ben had watched Scott and Phil race by. They were really moving fast.

"Go Scott go!" shouted an excited Billy.

"You got him Scottie!" said Ben.

The voice of the announcer came over the PA system. "Results from the first race are as follows: Billy Brandt – 292 points, Ben Holt – 291 points, Skylar and River – did not finish and no point total was assigned."

"You did it Billy!" said Ben. "You did it."

"I did it!" whooped Billy. "Are you mad Ben?"

"I'm not mad at all Billy. I'm proud of you and I'm going to lead the cheering section for you in the finals."

Christyn came running up to Billy and Ben. "I just heard the news! Congratulations Billy. Isn't that awesome?"

"It sure is," answered Ben. "Billy really pulled it off. But I want a re-match sometime!!" Ben smiled.

"You got it!" replied Billy.

As they approached the finish line Scott and Phil had no idea of the results of the first race. They were so focused on winning their race each of them could not hear a thing.

Scott was gaining on Phil a bit. Phil had a bit more weight than Scott and that seemed to be slowing him down, kind of like an anchor for some reason. Scott was just trying to stay balanced and work every bit of speed he could out of the board.

"It's a good thing the course is free of pebbles and dirt!" thought Scott.

The race committee who put together the Boardzone Competition had assigned a bunch of volunteers to continually sweep the racecourse free of small rocks and dirt. The smoother the course the faster the racers could go. It was also safer for the racers as one rock could cause a wheel to seize and a racer would "pull a Jon".

It was a bit bumpy as the two racers approached the finish line and Scott felt like the sweepers hadn't done a good job. It must have been those small pebbles that were causing Phil to slow down because Scott moved ahead by two feet and crossed the finish line first.

As Scott crossed the line he stood up and started pumping his fist into the air, in classic Scott fashion. "I'm the man!" he began to yell. "Who's your daddy!"

Phil raced by in second place. In all the races so far, that had been the closest finish yet.

Phil was pretty happy with the race and wasn't sure how the judges would score the tricks. He felt he had done a good job on his tricks. He hadn't seen all the tricks from Scott so he wasn't sure how Scott was feeling.

The crowd was roaring at the finish line. They had never seen such a close and exciting finish. They were cheering wildly for both racers. Even though Scott had won the race, it was the point total that mattered and only the person with the highest point total in the race would get to go on to the final.

When Scott slowed down enough to jump off his board safely he looked around at the cheering crowd. It was an amazing sight. There was a sea of faces all yelling, cheering, whistling and clapping. There were dozens of smiling faces that Scott knew from the neighborhood and

174

hundreds of others that he didn't know at all. They were all making noise and it was very, very loud. It made the hair on Scott's arms stand on end and he got goose bumps.

All the gang joined Scott in the finish area. Jim and Ben were patting him on the back and congratulating Scott. Scott was all smiles and was thanking everyone. Christyn broke the news to Scott about Billy winning the first race.

"You did?" Scott said to Billy with mocked surprise. "How much did you have to pay the judges?"

"I did not!" stammered Billy.

"I'm just kidding you little shrimp! Great job."

"What happened Ben?" Scott whispered to Ben.

Ben took Scott aside and whispered back, "I don't believe it myself. He pulled off some hard tricks and kept his speed up. I had a good lead but his tricks gave him a one-point advantage over me."

"Oh, I thought you must have bailed or something!" he laughed.

"Ha, ha, ha! He really ran a great race, just like you."

Uncle Frank's voice came over the PA system. "Results from the second race are now in. Scott Wilson – 287 points, Phil Toutges – 289 points, Penny Maxwell did not finish and no point total assigned. Jon Vance, well let's just say he's alive and doing well with the ambulance attendants. Better luck next year Jon, we'll see if we can find you some Velcro straps for your shoes."

Everyone was chuckling at the comments, even Jon. He didn't mind. He was being taken care of by the most beautiful-looking girl he had ever seen. Her name was Sarah and she was an ambulance attendant from Exton.

"I hurt all over," said Jon with a wry smile as Sarah was feeling around his body looking for areas that hurt. "Oh, yes…I mean…that's right, my arm too."

Sarah was used to this sort of faking but she found Jon appealing and let him get away with his act. It definitely wasn't the best acting she had ever seen.

* * * *

Devin Snively was up near the starting gate. He was getting ready for his race. He was sitting on the ground looking over his new board. "This baby has been excellent so far.," he thought. Devin was carefully eye-balling every square inch of his board. He looked over the deck, trucks and wheels. He scraped away bits of dirt that had built up on some of the wheels and then spun each wheel to ensure that it could still roll smoothly.

175

He noticed that the back trucks were a little scratched. It actually looked like a crack had begun in the metal but he knew on a new board that it was just jagged marks caused by rocks or something. He was pleased with his board and he was confident of his ability to win. Not simply because he was good on a board but because during the race he planned to increase his chances of winning.

He looked around and no one was really watching him. There were many people in the area but most were looking towards the racecourse or walking to some position to get the best viewing point.

He reached into the duffle bag that he had brought with him and pulled out the package he had prepared the night before. It was a small sandwich baggie. Inside, instead of finding peanut butter and jelly, there was a small quantity of black goo. It was actually grease.

Devin's plan was simple. He was going to eliminate his competition just like he had done last year. The grease was his own idea and he thought it was brilliant. He had squirted about 3 oz of grease into a baggie and had taped the bag shut. He had then poked a tiny hole into the bag using a small pencil. To keep the grease from leaking out, he had placed a piece of duct tape over the hole.

The baggie was ready for him to give a quick squeeze and it would squirt out a small quantity of very slippery grease, grease that would make it nearly impossible to control a fast moving skateboard. He was certain he would have at least three squirts in that one baggie. Funny enough, there were three competitors in his next race.

Just then, the announcer addressed the crowd. "Will the racers in the next heat please proceed immediately to the starting gate."

Devin put his duffle bag under his lawn chair, grabbed his board and slipped the baggie into his shirt pocket. "Don't want to get caught with this!" he laughed to himself and headed over to the starting area.

* * * *

All over City Hall computers beeped to announce that new mail had arrived. Only one city councilor happened to be working that Sunday. She was in a rush to leave for the day. When the new mail arrived she debated on whether to read the message or not.

"Who would send me email on a Sunday?" she wondered. She opened up her Inbox and could see the new message was sent from Mayor Carter. "Now that's strange. He never works on the weekend." She proceeded to read the quick message. When she was done, she immediately picked up the phone.

The phone in the Mayor's private office began to ring. Two rings.

Three rings. The Mayor was sitting there with the curtains drawn shut and the room in semi-darkness.

"That was quick," he thought.

Four rings. Five rings. They aren't going to give up. He punched the speakerphone button. This button allowed him to answer the phone without having to pick up the receiver. He could talk and listen without ever having to touch the phone.

"Mayor Carter," he said feebly.

"Hello, Mayor Carter, it's Jenny Harper," she said sternly.

The Mayor knew exactly what she was calling about but still asked her how he could help her. Maybe he was mistaken.

That thought was shattered in about two seconds.

"Mr. Mayor, I just received your email stating the next city council meeting was tomorrow. You can't do that!" she whined into the phone.

At first the Mayor was not in the mood to fight. He wasn't happy about having to make this decision but didn't want to lose his job over a scandal. When he heard the sharp tone of the councilor, he began to get angry and some life popped back into him. "As a matter of fact, Miss Harper, I can do that. I am the Mayor in case you had forgotten. I don't have to justify anything to you. Good day."

He hung up the phone by pressing the speakerphone button before she could answer.

Jenny Harper could not believe her ears. "He's up to something," she thought. "First it was the free trip, then those two guys came around threatening to expose the trip and now the Mayor is changing the date with no notice. Something fishy is going on." She picked up her phone again and called the home number of another councilor.

"Fodera residence," said the voice answering the phone. It was Barney Fodera.

"Barney, it's Jenny Harper. I just got word from the Mayor that he is moving the council meeting to tomorrow."

"That's two weeks early. Wait a second, wasn't that whole trip scheme trying to get the council meeting to be held two weeks early?" said Barney.

"That's right!" Jenny said. "Do you think it's a coincidence?"

"I doubt it. I think our Mayor is up to something."

"That is exactly what I thought. What do you want to do?"

"Jenny, I don't know if there is much we can do. When I first heard about the trips and the new council meeting date, I looked up in the rules and the Mayor has the right to move the council meeting date."

"Why would he want to do that?" asked Jenny.

"I'm not sure but I bet we find out tomorrow at the meeting. You watch and see."

"OK, see you tomorrow then."

They both hung up wondering what was going to happen at the city council meeting in the morning.

* * * *

Devin was on the starting platform and had been given first choice of lanes as he had the best point total of the four racers in his current heat. He had surprised everyone by choosing Lane 2. Most racers if given the choice immediately chose Lane 1 because Lane 1 gave you the best advantage going into the first turn. Devin had other ideas in mind and wanted to be in between two of the other racers. His plan required him to be close, very close to his competition.

The other racers were adjusting their helmets and kneepads. Each was looking around and preparing for the race ahead. Almost all of them were thinking about running a good, clean race and trying their best. The only exception was Devin. He was looking for his first opportunity.

The starter looked at all the racers and they were ready. He raised his arm and fired the pistol. The racers all scrambled down the ramp trying to get out ahead. Devin knew his first opportunity was just around the corner, literally.

The racers all pushed as hard as their legs could go to get maximum speed built up. It didn't take them long to reach the first turn. Devin knew that this was going to be tight and he wanted to be in second place coming out of the turn. He leaned into the turn and cut off the two riders that were trying to get around him. One of the racers almost banged into Devin. As Devin came out of the first turn, he went back into his crouch position.

Devin then reached into his shirt pocket and took out the baggie. He flicked the duct tape out of the way and took a quick look behind him. Right on his tail was the third and fourth racers.

"Perfect!" thought Devin. He took a quick look around and only a few spectators were watching this section of the racecourse. With the baggie mostly hidden in his palm, Devin put his hand towards the back of his board so it was almost sticking out the end of his board. Devin made it look like he was using his hand for balance but he was really giving the baggie a good squeeze.

The grease shot out onto the pavement. It was almost invisible to the eye as it came out of the baggie. The grease landed on the course and was almost immediately run over by the next racer. The fourth racer did not hit the grease patch.

The racer who hit the grease had no idea how much trouble he was in. The first thing he knew was that his board was getting harder to control. Each time he moved the board it felt like it was slipping rather than rolling.

The grease had splattered on impact with the front wheels and had coated the back wheels as well. This resulted in the board losing its ability to go straight. The natural momentum was enough to keep the racer going straight but at the second turn when the racer attempted to lean, the board kept moving in the original direction and at full speed he zoomed right off the end of the course, hit the gravel shoulder and rolled down a small hill.

Devin was aware that the racer behind him was in trouble but when he looked back after the second turn and didn't see him any longer, Devin knew his plan was working.

The next part of his plan was an oldie but a goodie. He was going to use the old "slow, bump and run" to take care of the racer behind him.

There was still 100 yards before the first judge's station so Devin flipped the duct tape back over the hole in the baggie and put it back into his shirt pocket. Devin got into a tuck position to gain maximum speed.

The fourth racer saw Devin go into a tuck and even though they were awfully close to the judge's station, he decided to follow Devin's lead.

Devin sneaked a peek behind him and saw the last racer in a tuck as well. Devin smiled a wicked smile. "Perfect," he said with a menacing laugh. "Let's see you get out of this one."

Devin waited until he was almost at the judge's stand and then he quickly stood up and dragged his foot on the ground hard. In an instant he had cut his speed in half. This classic little move put the fourth racer into a very awkward position. Hit the rider in front of you or bail outright. The rider did not have a choice. He was going to bang into Devin, there was no way to prevent it. He was going too fast and Devin was right in his way.

Devin was totally prepared for the impact and planned to use it to his advantage. He was waiting for the hit and when it happened Devin used the impact to help propel him forward. The racer was basically just protecting himself at this point and might have been able to stay on his board had Devin not given him a violent push back during the hit.

To the average person in the crowd, it looked like Devin had been hit from behind by an out of control racer but had managed to survive. It also appeared the out of control racer had to bail due to the accident he caused.

Devin was thinking to himself and smiling, "Two down and one to go."

The racer ahead of Devin had developed a lead of about five yards. She had done her first trick well and was trying to go as fast as she could by staying away from any pebbles or mud patches on the course.

Devin had gone back into his crouch and was trying to gain on the other rider. He knew that he had missed doing a trick and was going to have to get well ahead of this rider or take her out like the others.

"If I'm going to take her out, I have to get ahead." Devin began to scheme. "To get ahead I know one sure way. Skip the next trick and race ahead when she slows down." Devin was really hatching a nasty trick. "I think this is going to work just fine," he snickered.

There were rules about contact in the competition. Bumping into another racer was definitely against the rules but only if it was done on purpose. Devin knew this and had become a master at gentle nudges and subtle bumps. This next one was going to be a masterpiece and right in front of a judge too. Devin loved the challenge.

He could see the racer approaching the judge's booth and watched her drag her foot slightly to slow down. This was the opportunity he was waiting for. He got back into his crouch and kept his speed up. He closed the five yards in a matter of a few seconds and as she was flipping her board around for a 360-flip, Devin zoomed by her.

Devin could have zoomed by with lots of room to spare but he cut it as close as he could. Sure enough, he timed it perfectly and hit her board as he passed. It looked completely innocent to the judge and to the audience. Only Devin knew it was part of his plan.

The racer who Devin had just interfered with tried her best to not fall. One second she was riding along with her board underneath her and the next there was nothing but pavement. Her legs hit the ground and she just started running trying to slow down.

She was able to do it. She stopped and looked up quickly. She was watching Devin disappear down the course. She had a strange feeling about what just happened. She didn't know Devin well but she thought it was kind of weird how quickly he caught up with her.

It was hard for Devin to hold back the grin he wanted to show. He was definitely proud of his work today. All he had to do now was coast into the finish line. He didn't even have to do a trick. He waited for a spot where no one was watching from the side and he pulled out the baggie from his pocket and dumped it. "Don't want to be caught with any evidence."

The baggie of grease fell behind him and now there was nothing to tie Devin to the earlier bails. He relaxed and rode carefully to the end. He crossed the line but there wasn't much cheering. None of the crowd had seen any of the earlier bails. All they knew is that there was only one racer left and it was not very exciting to see a single person cross the line all by themselves.

The relatively quiet crowd really annoyed Devin. "What's with these people? Don't they know greatness when they see it?"

Devin Gets a Warning

Ben and Scott were discussing the last race.

"How come when Devin is racing there is a guarantee of an accident?" Scott said.

"And not just one accident!" replied Ben.

"Do you remember last year when he pulled that duct tape trick?"

"In the end he got what he deserved, didn't he?" said Ben.

"But he causes so many problems along the way. Some really good boarders don't get a chance to win because he cheats," said Scott. He was annoyed. Scott didn't like cheaters and Devin was one of the biggest.

Ben was worried about Billy. "Billy will be in the final against Devin. I don't want Devin to pull any fast tricks on him."

"I say we have a little talk with Devin before the race to let him know we're watching," said Scott.

"Great idea. Let's go find Devin."

Jim had been listening. "I'm sorry I can't go with you. I have to make my way to the starting area for the final heat."

"Good luck Jim. You'll do fine. We'll be cheering you on."

The two boys marched off toward the area where Devin was last seen and Jim headed up the hill. While Scott and Ben were looking for Devin, Christyn and Billy had gone to grab a drink and some popcorn.

"How are you feeling about the finals Billy?" asked Christyn.

"Actually I'm feeling pretty good. I have to beat three other racers and I win $1,000. That is all I'm thinking about right now."

"Well, you beat me and you beat Ben. I think today is going to be your day," Christyn said, encouraging him.

"You know what? Even if I don't win the final, it was still my day."

"Aw that's so sweet," said Christyn "it makes me want to puke."

And then she stuffed some popcorn in his face.

"Hey, watch it racer-wanna-be! You better not damage the best boarder in Exton," he said laughing.

"We'll see in a while who the real best boarder in Exton is," she replied.

"Yes we will," said Billy. He was getting nervous.

Ben and Scott were busy looking for Devin but he was hard to spot in the crowd. "He has to be here somewhere. But he crowd is so big it will be hard to find anyone. At least this big crowd is good news for Mike and Julie," Scott said.

Mike and Julie were talking on the two-way radios. "Julie, you are not going to believe this. I just talked to Sam at the front gate and he told me the attendance figures are going to exceed 22,000. With our portion of the gate money and the food vendor sales, I project we will take in about $100,000."

182

"Mike, that is excellent news! I knew there were a lot of people but I never would have guessed 22,000. With $100,000 you will make a huge dent in the rest of the money you need for the skate park," Julie said sounding so happy.

"I know, I know! With two weeks to go to arrange the financing it is looking really good for us to finalize the skate park land sale." Mike was so excited he could not keep the enthusiasm from his voice.

"Get back to work, mister, the day isn't over yet!" teased Julie.

Scott and Ben spotted Devin in the crowd. He was standing near the second turn and waiting for the race to start.

"There he is, Scott," said Ben. "Over there by the tree."

"OK, I see him. You go to the left and I will go to the right. Let's meet up on either side of him so he can't walk away."

Scott moved toward Devin coming at the unsuspecting kid from the right. Ben moved in as well and circled around and came in from the left. "Hello Devin," Ben said casually.

Devin did not see Ben approach and was slightly surprised when he heard the greeting. He looked up and saw Ben. He knew Ben Holt and didn't much like him. He wasn't sure why Ben wanted to talk but he didn't feel like it and he turned to leave the other way.

"Hello Devin," said Scott very coolly. Devin stopped in his tracks. He sensed something was going on.

"Devin, how come every race you enter ends up with at least one of the racers, sometimes two, crashing mysteriously?" said Ben.

"I dunno…bad luck?" Devin countered just as calmly.

"Let's just say Scott and I don't believe in so much bad luck happening around you and we're going to watch you like a hawk!"

"We'll be all over you like wolves on a baked ham!" added Scott.

"I don't know what you're talking about but if it's a lesson in awesome skateboarding you're looking for, then go ahead and watch the best," Devin countered boldly.

"Oh, we will and his name is Billy Brandt."

Devin just glared back at Ben. "I don't think so." Devin turned around and walked away from the two boys.

"We're watching every move!" yelled out Scott.

Devin was close enough to hear but he didn't respond. He quickly disappeared into the crowd.

"At least he knows someone is on to him and he is being watched closely," said Ben. "Let's go see how Jim has done."

The boys ran back to the finish area just in time to hear the Uncle Frank announce the results of the last semi-final race. "Results from the final race of the semis are as follows: Carmen-Lynn Ashton – 304 points, Jim Brandt – 299 points, Thomas Collette – 287 points and Randy Sullivan did not finish."

Jim was really disappointed. He had raced well but his tricks hadn't been that great. The first trick he did almost didn't work and that shook his confidence. The other racers had all passed by the judging station together and it was hard to line up properly to do the trick. Jim found it hard to concentrate on the trick because he was also thinking about his speed and the others in his way. He didn't want to bump into any of them and bail.

Jim saw Carmen-Lynn near by. She was a really good boarder, but more importantly than that, she was beautiful. She had brown hair and the most incredible laugh. He used to sit next to her in Science class and he always found it hard to concentrate when she was around, especially when he heard her laugh from a distance. She was very popular with everyone because she was fun to be around. He got up the nerve and went over to congratulate her. "Carmen-Lynn!" he called over the noise of the crowd. At first she didn't hear him and he was going to walk away but he didn't want to miss this opportunity to talk to her. He called her name again.

This time she turned his way and waved. "Hey Jim, great race. I can't believe I got more points than you. I saw your second trick and it was amazing."

"I had trouble with my first trick but really you ran the best race and deserved to win. I saw your last trick and no one does a 360-flip like you do. It was sweet."

"Thanks Jim," she said with a smile.

Jim wasn't sure why but her smile made him feel much better. And more than just about the losing the race.

"Will you cheer me on in the finals?" she asked.

"Sure, as long as my brother thinks I'm cheering for him!" he laughed.

Carmen-Lynn laughed too. "That's right, Billy won his semi. Now you have a real dilemma on your hands. I know what you can do. You cheer on Billy during the race but come and meet me after it's over. How does that sound?"

Jim thought that was a great idea. "I will come and find you for sure."

"Great, see you then," she said as her dad and brother approached her to give her a big hug. Her dad was a tall man who was a local dentist. Carmen-Lynn's brother was a big guy. Not the kind of guy you wanted to tangle with and certainly not the type of guy you wanted to upset because you had treated his sister badly.

"Good luck in the final, Carmen-Lynn!" he called. Jim was about to go looking for the others when he spotted them making their way towards him. He walked about 25 yards to meet up with them.

"Hey Jim, we saw most of the race!" yelled Christyn. A band had begun playing again and the noise was quite loud. People were starting to dance and party. The band was going to play a set while the course was readied for the final race.

"You were awesome," said Billy "I think you should have won."

"Thanks Billy, I did my best and that's all that counts." He was thinking about Carmen-Lynn. "Besides, Carmen-Lynn ran a heck of a good race and I think she deserved to win. She was boarding like a pro. I've never seen such a beauti…I mean, excellent moves."

Ben, Scott, Christyn and Billy were just standing there staring at him. Each had their mouths wide open but was not saying anything.

Scott looked at Christyn. "I think we better get this boy to the doctor – he's sick, love sick."

"She ran a great race," stammered Jim. "I was admiring her form."

"I bet you were," said Ben. Jim began to blush and Ben decided he was going to let his friend off the hook. "Let's go find our stuff and relax for a bit before the final."

Jim was relieved. "Sounds like a great idea, anyone want to grab some food on the way?"

They all moved along with the crowd and headed towards the place where their lawn chairs were setup. As they passed the side of the stage they could see a huge line-up of people waiting to get autographs from the professional skateboarders. They were signing autograph books, programs, shirts and skateboards.

"I bet they are going to have sore hands tomorrow!" said Scott.

Grease is the Word

Harvey Flatts was a volunteer for the day. His son was one of the racers and he liked to get involved with his son's activities. He had been there to cheer him in his race. His son had not won his race but Harvey was amazed at how fast his son could go on the racecourse. He even got to see one of his tricks because he was standing near the second judging station when he passed.

Right now Harvey was responsible to clean an area of the racetrack on the lower section. He had a Jani-King Dirt Whacker 2000 with the extra wide attachment on it. It was a heavy-duty broom that was designed to sweep in this kind of condition. It picked up rocks and dirt with no problem from the pavement and pushed it into neat piles.

As he was cleaning Harvey came across a small plastic bag that someone had discarded. "It must have blown onto the track." Thought Harvey. He gave it a push with the broom. The problem with this type of broom is that it needed very hard bristles to be able to pick up the rocks and dirt. When you tried to pick up delicate things like a plastic bag, the bag usually got pierced by the bristles and stuck in the broom itself.

This is exactly what happened to Harvey. He noticed this and gave the broom another couple of quick pushes along the pavement to free the bag. All he noticed was a trail of black on the pavement.

"Hmm," he said to himself. "I guess that isn't going to work." Harvey turned the broom over and plucked the plastic bag from the end of the broom with his fingers.

He walked over to a garbage can that was close by and threw the bag in. He didn't pay any attention to the black gooey substance on the bag. He then returned to his job. He had to make sure there were no pebbles on the course for the final.

While the friends were gathered around munching on french fries and drinking soda, up walked Uncle Frank with Buster.

"Hey Uncle Frank!" said Jim.

"Hello J. Hi guys!" he said to the others. "Billy I am really proud of your racing today. You sure showed these guys a thing or two about being a competitor."

"Thanks Uncle Frank," said Billy, looking at his friends.

Buster was eying Christyn's chocolate sundae.

"We heard you announcing and then halfway through the race someone else took over. We thought you had left or something," said Scott.

"I had to leave for a short period. I went home to free this guy," said Frank pointing to Buster. "I couldn't leave him alone all day in the house and he wanted to come and see you in the final, Billy."

Billy was wrestling with Buster and gave him a big hug. Buster was happy to play with Billy but he still had his eye on the sundae.

"The final starts in about 15 minutes, so Billy you make sure to get to the starting area in plenty of time," said Uncle Frank as he was trying to keep Buster from chasing something.

"We will make sure he gets there on time and we'll also make sure he has the biggest cheering section!" said Christyn.

Buster saw his chance. He leaped forward quickly and the leash flew out of Uncle Frank's hand. Buster cleared the 10 feet between him and Christyn's sundae in the blink of an eye. His front paw knocked the plastic container from her hand and onto the grass dumping the remaining ice cream out.

In an instant Buster had wolfed down the ice cream and began to polish off the chocolate sauce.

"Buster!" yelled Uncle Frank and Christyn at the same time.

Buster looked up with chocolate and an innocent expression on his face.

"Bad dog, bad dog!" said Uncle Frank.

Buster wasn't sure why he was in trouble. It had been a perfect jump; he had connected with the container of ice cream; and had successfully eaten the contents, all in about four seconds.

"I'm sorry Christyn, let me buy you another sundae," said Uncle Frank.

Buster licked his chops, staring and Uncle Frank and Christyn.

"Don't worry about it, Uncle Frank. I'm OK, I had enough," replied Christyn.

"I don't know what got into Buster!" Uncle Frank said.

"Good luck in the race Billy," said Uncle Frank as he made his way back to the announcer's booth.

Buster looked back at Christyn as if to say thank-you.

"I swear to God that dog knows how to talk!" exclaimed Christyn. "Did you see that look he just gave me?"

"I think you're seeing things Christyn," laughed Scott. "He's just a dog with a thing for ice cream."

"Come on Billy, finish up your drink and we'll head up to the starting area," said Jim.

Scott leaned over to Ben and Jim. In a whispered voice he said, "Yah, let's get there a bit early so we can watch Devin too."

Ben had filled Jim in on their feeling about Devin and the conversation he and Scott had had with Devin. Jim thought that was a good idea. He didn't trust Devin either.

Devin was already at the top of the hill next to the starting gate. He was going over his board and making sure it was free of dirt and other problems. While he was cleaning his board, he was also thinking to himself. He wasn't happy.

"Darn those kids! If they are going to be watching me, I won't be able to pull any sneaky tricks in the final. I really want to win this year."

187

Devin should have been concentrating on his board a little more. He might have noticed how many deep scratches and cuts were appearing on his trucks. He should have noticed as well that his front right wheel had developed a bit of a wobble and that usually meant some sort of bearing problem. But Devin was too busy thinking about his schemes. Devin had prepared for the final in his own unique way. Instead of practicing his tricks like all the other riders, Devin had gone to the local hardware store and purchased some items to give him an edge – like a tube of super glue. Devin figured a quick shot of that in someone's bearings would make a nice little surprise as it dried. Now he wasn't going to be able to use it. He would be noticed for sure.

"I would have liked to have used this on that Billy Brat!" fumed Devin, mangling Billy's name on purpose.

The other thing that Devin liked to do to gain an advantage was bumping. That was also going to be hard to do because Mike always taped the final. He would play the video in his store constantly to remind people how exciting the event was. He knew that if he started bumping riders in the final he would be videotaped and he didn't want to risk being disqualified. He didn't like it but he was going to have to race this time using nothing but his skill.

Phil Toutges was also looking over his board. He had decided to tighten up his trucks a bit. They had felt a bit loose in his last race and he wanted to make sure he could maintain full control on his turns. He was looking for his truck wrench in his bag when Billy and the others stopped by.

"Hey, Phil!" said Scott. "You all ready for the final?"

"I think so. How about you, Billy?" said Phil.

"I'm a little nervous but I'm ready," replied Billy.

"Me too," whispered Phil. "I'm a little concerned about racing with Devin. I know I'm better than him but people seem to have a way of crashing when he's around."

"Don't worry about that this time, Phil. All of us are going to be watching Devin very closely. We let him know already."

"Excellent!" said Phil. "I'm just going to tighten up my trucks and I'll meet you on the starting line."

They all moved over to the starting line. Billy climbed up onto the starting ramp and did up his safety equipment. Jim was watching Billy when he felt a gentle tap on his shoulder. He turned around expecting to see Scott or Jim but it was Carmen-Lynn. She was smiling that same way.

"Wish me luck!" she said.

"You don't need luck, Carmen-Lynn, you have enough skill to win."

"Thanks Jim."

"Race hard, Carmen-Lynn. I'll see you at the bottom."

"I'm counting on it," said Carmen-Lynn. She climbed onto the starting ramp and was immediately followed by Devin. Phil came a minute later and got into position.

The final race order was set. The four racers to make the final were Billy Brandt with 292 points, Devin Snively with 270 points, Phil Toutges with 289 points and Carmen-Lynn Ashton with 304 points.

Since Carmen-Lynn had the highest point total she was given first Lane choice. Carmen-Lynn picked Lane 1. Billy had the next highest total and picked Lane 2. Phil picked Lane 3 and Devin was left to take Lane 4.

Devin's tricks in the last race were not completed like the others so his point total just wasn't as high. Devin felt that this was a real insult to him.

"I'm better than these wanna-bees and I'm going to use my new board to prove how good I am."

The racers all lined up in their order. Carmen-Lynn was adjusting her kneepad and Billy was looking over at Jim. He was leaning as close as he could to Billy, telling him to focus on the race and keep his tricks simple. Billy was glad he was in between Phil and Carmen-Lynn and not too close to Devin.

Phil on the other hand was not happy to be next to Devin. He looked over at Devin and said "There are a bunch of people watching you right now Snively. You had better stick to racing. Keep your hands to yourself."

Devin ignored the comment from Phil but inside he was thinking about what Scott and Ben had warned. "Does everyone know?" he wondered.

A huge crowd had gathered at the starting area and all along the race-course. From Billy's point of view, it seemed like all 22,000 were now looking at him. Even though he had been in the same position earlier in the day, there seemed to be twice as many faces packed into the starting area. People were yelling and cheering again and shouting things that he couldn't quite make out. But he could hear a dog barking. Billy smiled. "I bet I know who that is!"

Carmen-Lynn's brother was standing next to Jim. He noticed her brother and felt obligated to speak to him. "That Carmen-Lynn sure is talented to reach the final."

The big guy turned and looked at Jim, "So is your brother. Maybe there will be a tie and they both can win."

Jim was surprised that this guy knew who he was and was even more surprised by his answer. He was a nice guy after all. He wasn't sure why he had been intimidated by his size. They talked for a while waiting for the race to get underway.

189

The new announcer's voice came over the PA system. "Welcome everyone to the final of the 2nd Annual Boardzone Competition. We have a great final four ready to go. In Lane 1, please give a cheer for Carmen-Lynn Ashton."

The crowd went wild and the Ashton's lead the cheering with loud whoops and hollers. "Go Carmen-Lynn Go!" boomed the deep voice of her brother. He sounded like a cannon going off with each of his words. Carmen-Lynn was waving to the crowd and smiling. She caught Jim's eye and he winked back.

The announcer spoke again. "In Lane 2 put your hands together for our youngest racer, Billy Brandt." The crowd roared its appreciation. The announcer continued, "Billy came up big in the semi-final, knocking out last year's champion Ben Holt."

Ben had mixed feelings about being remembered as last year's champion at the same time as being identified as losing this year. "Oh well, it's all about Billy now, not about me."

"In Lane 3 give it up for Phil Toutges. Phil is not only turning pro in snowboarding but we now know he is a pretty good skateboarder as well."

There must have been a large number of snowboarders in the crowd because they went crazy.

The crowd loved it and the party atmosphere continued. It was getting to be early evening and it was still quite hot. The sun was starting to go down and there was just a bit of a breeze to sort of cool things down.

The racers were anxious to get going. The only time any of them felt cooled was when they were whooshing down the course with the wind in their faces.

"Rounding out the final four is Devin Snively." There was noticeably less cheering from the crowd. Devin didn't seem to care and was raising his arm in the air like he was already a winner.

Jim was already looking Devin over to see if he could see anything out of the ordinary.

The announcer said "Racers…are you ready?" They all looked over at the announcing booth and nodded.

The starter stepped up onto the platform, checked his pistol and then looked over at the race marshall. The race marshall was the person in charge of the course. He checked on his walkie-talkie one more time to ensure that all his cleaning crew was off the course. They had finished their work and the course was clear. The race marshall nodded to the starter. The video cameras began to roll.

The starter raised his pistol, waited two seconds and fired. The final of the 2nd Annual Boardzone Competition was underway.

190

Billy watched the race marshall give his nod and then watched the starter. He was going to try and get an advantage on Carmen-Lynn as quickly as he could. His plan was to anticipate the firing of the gun. He was going to watch the finger of the starter, not the starter himself. This was a trick that Scott had told him.

Carmen-Lynn was ready to go. She wanted to start the race. She had butterflies in her stomach and knew the best way to get rid of them was to start racing. She wasn't really watching the starter.

Phil was toying with Devin a bit by waving his arms in front of Devin's face. He was pretending to stretch when the starter was preparing to fire. Devin was annoyed by this distraction. Phil was quite proud of himself.

"Baaannnnggg!" went the gun.

Billy had been watching the starter's finger on the trigger and he noticed there was no movement for what seemed like an eternity. Then he saw it. The finger started to tense a bit and then move. "This was it!" thought Billy. "He's going to do it."

Without waiting any longer Billy proceeded to give his first big push at the exact moment the gun went off. He had a half step on every rider on the platform and the announcer did not call a false start. A false start occurs when a rider starts moving down the ramp before the gun goes off. In Billy's case, he timed it perfectly.

"YYYYesss!!!" thought Billy to himself. He flew down the ramp, lined his foot properly and then began pushing furiously with his other leg. He was really picking up speed. "Just a bit more and then I'm going low into the first turn."

Carmen-Lynn was shocked to see Billy shoot ahead in front of her. "How the heck did he do that?" she said kind of in a daze. She too was using her powerful legs to rocket her along the course. "He may be ahead but I'm going to catch him soon enough." She brought her speed up and then jumped into her low tuck position.

Phil and Devin were side-by-side as they roared down the ramp. Devin had to resist the urge to give Phil a little push. He knew that too many people were watching including the video cameras.

Phil had a bit of trouble coming off the bottom of the ramp and hesitated just slightly before starting to push himself with his foot. Devin had no trouble on the ramp and was able to get in two full pushes ahead of Phil. This gave him almost a five-yard lead on Phil.

"See you later, sucker!" shouted Devin to Phil.

Phil ignored the comment. He realized he no longer had to win to be happy: all he had to do was beat Snively and it would be a great day.

Billy was heading fast and low into the first turn. Carmen-Lynn was right behind him drafting. The cleaners had done an excellent job on the course and there wasn't a pebble or dirt patch to be seen. This meant that the final was going to be the fastest of the day.

Billy rounded the corner of the first turn and Carmen-Lynn was with him every inch of the way. Devin was behind them by about three yards. He was also leaning hard as he headed into the turn.

Phil had decided that he was going to make his move later. For now he was content to keep up with Devin and the others. He still felt he was close enough that he had time to catch up and take over the lead.

Carmen-Lynn had her plan in order. This race was going to be fast. It was likely that all racers were going to finish and they would be close to each other's time. That meant that the tricks would play a big role. She knew that she could do three kick-flips and get average points for sure or she could risk it and try harder tricks but she may not complete them and lose valuable points.

She had already decided to do the simple tricks and get the sure points. They were approaching the first judging station and she knew they were both going too fast. She was thinking about Billy's strategy. "Since he's going so fast, I wonder if he's going to try and skip the trick."

Billy had no intention of skipping any trick. He knew, like Carmen-Lynn, how important the points were in this race. The winner of the race was not likely to be that far ahead of the second place finisher so the trick points would count a lot.

Billy just wanted to maintain his lead going into the judging area and decided not to slow down until the absolute last second.

191

He lined himself up to be in the right position so when he finished his trick he would be first again. He carefully put his right foot down and dragged it a bit to slow down his speed.

Carmen-Lynn could see the foot drag from Billy and knew he was going to do a trick after all. She prepared herself for her kick-flip.

Billy had been practicing a high-speed kick-flip with Jim on the hill in front of their house. It wasn't the same as Bishop's Hill but it was still fast. Billy had seen professional boarders on TV do the high-speed kick-flip before and had wanted Jim to show him how to do it. Jim was able to do them but not always successfully. The hard thing about a high-speed kick-flip wasn't really the kick-flip at all. It was thinking about what would happen to the rider if the kick-flip didn't work. At high speed you were guaranteed a spectacular bail. Billy didn't want to bail at high speed.

Billy knew the high-speed kick-flip was also worth more points than a regular kick-flip.

192

Carmen-Lynn slowed down a lot more than Billy and a gap started to grow between the racers. She and Billy both did their tricks at the same time.

Devin could also see that Billy was not slowing down much and knew that he was going to try a high-speed trick. There was only one or two high-speed tricks and he was pretty sure that Billy would try the kick-flip over the heel-flip at high-speed because the heel-flip was a bit harder. It was also worth even more points than a high-speed kick-flip. "I can do one," thought Devin, "and I can beat that Billy Brat!"

Phil was not worried about Devin and his trick at all. Phil was focusing on his own plan. He was going to try a hard trick at regular trick speed. He figured he could pick up the speed he needed to stay with the rest of the crowd when he was on the course. He was going to use his point total from three hard tricks to put him over the top to win the race. Phil slowed down and prepared for a 360-flip.

Devin flashed by the judging area and for a second Mike thought he too was going to skip the trick. He had briefly thought the same about Billy but Billy had pulled off a high-speed kick-flip and Mike couldn't believe his eyes. Billy was certainly showing that he belonged in this final.

Devin flicked his feet and his board flew around and landed in one smooth motion. His feet landed back on the board and he immediately went into his tuck position. He didn't have to regain his speed by pushing so he used that time to gain further distance on Phil.

Phil had slowed enough and was ready to do his trick. He waited until he was directly across from Mike the judge and then he whirled his board around. He landed it and then began to push hard to catch up with the others who were starting to gain some distance on him.

Underneath Devin's board, his right front wheel was getting very hot. It was not turning smoothly and the rubbing was starting to affect his speed. Devin hadn't noticed it yet but his counterfeit skateboard was starting to fall apart.

There was a crack, not a scratch, in the trucks that had shown up from the pounding of the last race. Now the crack was starting to widen due to the high speed and hard use from the current race.

Devin thought he could feel some wobbling beneath him but was concentrating on heading into the next big turn. Taking a quick look backwards, he was wondering to himself how Phil had gained back so much of the distance between them. He did not realize he was slowing down.

Phil could see he was closing the gap on Devin and he got as low as he could go. There was only about a yard between the two riders and now he could hear some sort of whining noise that seemed like it was coming from Devin's board.

All the racers made it through the turns and passed the second judging station. Billy did another high-speed kick-flip and it turned out perfect. Carmen-Lynn had seen Billy's move and while she wanted to try the same, she had never done one before and knew that trying a trick for the first time in competition was a bad idea. She stuck to her plan and did the same trick again. It landed perfectly and she powered herself forward down the course trying to stay close to Billy.

Devin had stayed just ahead of Phil going into the judging area and had somehow landed another high-speed move, this time a kick-flip. Devin may have landed it but the board was definitely not holding together well. The force of the impact of landing at high speed put severe stress on all his wheels and the wheel with the bearing problems was so hot Devin would have burned his finger if he could have touched it.

Phil did his trick and pushed himself hard to catch up with Devin. Devin should have been further ahead but in no time at all Phil was right back on his tail. Phil stayed low and close to Devin. Phil was watching Devin's movements closely, trying to find a way to get around him when he saw the most extraordinary thing. Something popped off one of Devin's rear wheels. He didn't really see what it was because it had happened so quick but something small and round flew out.

Devin's wheel was literally falling apart. One of the bearings had worn down so much that it no longer stayed in its case and it flew out. This left a space and the rest of the bearings were going to follow suit if Devin didn't stop immediately. Devin was totally unaware of his pending problem. He was fixated on catching Carmen-Lynn and Billy and was trying to close the gap so he could take over first place.

Billy and Carmen-Lynn flashed past Harvey Flatts. He had finished his cleaning job and was watching the race still holding his broom. He was proud of the job he had done. In his mind, the area of the track in front of him was the cleanest on the course, because he had done it.

Two black lines lay in the path of the racers. They were very hard to see and certainly would not have been easy to avoid at high speed. These were the two grease marks left behind from where Devin's baggie was found by the cleaner.

Billy and Carmen-Lynn had whizzed by the black marks without touching them but Devin was not so lucky. His wheels contacted the black and all four wheels were instantly coated with very slippery grease. The skateboard was basically lifted off the ground on a cushion of grease and the effect was that Devin no longer had any steering capability. The board started to turn sideways a bit and the edges of his wheels started to dig into the pavement.

That was all the extra stress his wheels needed. With a loud pop both wheels on the left side of his board flew off and a shower of ball-bearings went everywhere. Devin went from feeling confident to feeling sheer panic as his board started to disintegrate underneath him. "Wh…what's going on? What's happening?" Devin said to himself, not fully understanding what was wrong. In an instant Devin knew what was going to happen next, just not why it was happening. As the wheels dug harder into the pavement, the truck could no longer take the strain and the crack finally sliced all the way through the truck. Pieces of wheel and truck were now scattering everywhere on the course.

Devin was no longer on his board having been launched a second earlier. He was heading for the side of the course and as people got out of the way, he could see the only thing in his way was a large trash can. With no way to control himself, Devin hurtled the 10 feet through the air and right into the wide open mouth of the trash can. Both he and the can continued to fly backwards and then, with Devin inside, the can rolled down the small hill, scattering bits of hotdog, popcorn and mustard everywhere.

When the can came to a rest. Several people ran up to offer assistance. One of the race volunteers helped the dazed racer out of the dented can. Devin sat on the ground and looked up at the large crowd that had gathered to witness what had to be the best bail of the day. Devin had ketchup, mustard and relish all over his face, hair and shirt. He had part of a corndog sticking out the side of his helmet.

"Are you OK?" asked a race official who had a first aid symbol on his shirt.

"Yah…I think I'm fine," said a dazed Devin.

"What happened?" said Devin to the official. "One second I was racing along just fine and the next thing I remember was heading out of control toward the crowd."

A sharp voice came from behind him. "This is what happened!" said Jim holding up Devin's wrecked skateboard so everyone could see it.

"Your counterfeit board fell apart on you Devin. You might have had a chance if you had bought a real board but you blew it," said Jim.

"What are you talking about?" Devin complained.

Jim brought the board over and dumped some of the pieces onto his lap. "Your board was counterfeit and made of crap. You may not have known about the board but you still got what was coming to you. All your cheating has finally caught up with you Devin. I'm glad that a real boarder is going to have a chance to win the competition fair and square." Jim dropped the rest of the board to the ground beside Devin and began to walk away. The board hit the ground and made a loud thump. Jim turned back briefly and said "And Devin, you might want to wipe the grease off your face."

Not only was Devin covered in hotdog leftovers, but the garbage can he fell into was the same one where Harvey had thrown the baggie full of grease. Devin had grease stains all over his favourite shirt.

"Arrrghhhh!!" yelled Devin. People around him thought he might be going crazy. They started to walk away and leave him alone sitting in the mess.

As the crowd walked back up the hill, a man with a walkie-talkie called in to the Race Centre. "This is Steve, did anyone catch that bail?" There was a pause and then a voice came back, "You bet Steve, got the whole thing on video. Mike will play that one in the shop everyday I'm betting!"

Back on the course, Phil could not believe his eyes as he watched Devin careen off to the side and launch himself into a garbage can. He had heard the popping sound and then found himself swerving back and forth to avoid hitting pieces of wheel and bouncing ball-bearings.

He knew that he would not be able to catch Carmen-Lynn and Billy any longer but he was happy knowing that Devin was out of the way.

Carmen-Lynn and Billy were not aware that Devin had bailed. They would enjoy the video of it later. For now they were both concentrating on the final stretch of the race. They had each done their last trick and were racing neck-and-neck into the last straightaway.

Billy knew that if he could keep the lead or stay within a couple of yards of Carmen-Lynn he would have a great chance of winning. His tricks had been flawless but he wasn't sure what kind of tricks Carmen-Lynn had done.

Carmen-Lynn knew a bit more. She knew that her chances of winning were still good. Billy had pulled off three amazing tricks and deserved to win but one never knew until all the scores were calculated. Even if she were somehow able to pull ahead of him, his tricks would likely give him the win. She didn't want him to push too hard and crash so she did something that showed she had a lot of class. She raised herself out of her tuck position and stood up.

This resulted in her catching quite a bit of wind and immediately slowing down. Billy could sense some sort of movement behind him and sneaked a quick peek behind him. He was very surprised to see Carmen-Lynn standing up. Billy was finally able to relax. Billy began to increase the distance between her and crossed the finish line a good 10 yards in front of Carmen-Lynn.

It took Billy another 30 yards to stop and he jumped off his board and raised both hands in the air. He didn't know if his tricks were better than Carmen-Lynn's but he was confident he had an excellent shot at winning.

Carmen-Lynn came riding over to Billy and patted him on the back. "You got it Billy! Your speed was better than mine and your tricks were better than mine. Congratulations!"

"Thanks Carmen-Lynn!"

Just then Phil crossed the finish line and the crowd roared again. Carmen-Lynn and Billy walked over to Phil who was smiling and taking off his helmet.

"Great race Phil!" said Billy.

"Which of you two won?" said Phil.

"Billy's got it this year," said Carmen-Lynn, "but I'll be after him next year."

"Where's Devin?" asked Billy.

"Have I got a funny story to tell you both!" said Phil and they gathered in close.

The Awards Ceremony

Thirty minutes later the awards ceremony began. The crowd had all stayed and was anxious to see the winner announced. Mike and Julie were on stage with the race marshall and Uncle Frank. There was a small table covered in red velvet and in the centre was a very large trophy about four feet high. The trophy had three levels and at the top was a person riding a skateboard. The base of the trophy had a large golden plate with "Annual Boardzone Competition Champion" written on it. There was one additional plate on the trophy that said "that said "Winner – Ben Holt".

Ben whispered over to Billy, "By tomorrow there will be another plate on that trophy and it will have your name next to mine."

Uncle Frank spoke into the microphone. "Welcome everyone to the awards ceremony for the 2nd Annual Boardzone Competition. Mike and Julie want to thank everyone for coming out today and enjoying the competition with us. Did everyone have a great time?" The crowd roared their approval. The sound was deafening. "OK, OK…I get the message. Mike wanted to say a few words before we announce the winner." Uncle Frank waited for Mike to step forward and he gave him the portable hand-held microphone.

"Uh…I am almost speechless right now. I don't really know how to say 'Thanks' but I'm going to try. The Annual Boardzone Competition is not about making money, it's about boarding and having fun."

The crowd began to yell and cheer again. Mike had to wait a moment to let the noise die down. "This year is really important to me. The money we raised will be going to try and finance a new skate park for everyone in Exton to enjoy." The crowd cheered even louder. "I want to thank all the professionals who took time out of their busy schedules to be with us here today. You guys drew in a lot of people and didn't charge a dime to do it."

"You haven't received my bill yet!" yelled Muska from the crowd. Everyone roared with laughter.

"I also want to thank the band for playing, you guys did an awesome job today and we are all looking forward to your final set tonight."

There was more cheering and the band played a bit of "We are the Champions".

"To all the dozens of volunteers who helped to make this day successful, I want to say thank you. Whether you were putting up posters – thank you Ben, Jim, Christyn, Scott and Billy – sweeping the course or driving people from the parking lot to the front gate – thank you Orion Oldsmobile. You all are great. Last but not least I want to thank someone who is the main reason this event was so successful. Julie can you join me over here please?"

Julie was smiling at Mike and felt a tad uncomfortable being in front of thousands of people.

"Julie, you show me every day how important it is to have someone special in your life. I know you and I have been through a lot and I wanted to do something special for you." Mike reached into his pocket, pulled out a ring and bent down on one knee. He looked into Julie's eyes and said "Julie Jones, will you make me the happiest man alive and marry me."

Julie couldn't believe her ears. She was totally shocked but regained herself long enough to say, "Yes!"

The crowd went crazy and the band started playing "The Wedding March". Someone threw a bouquet of flowers up onto the stage for Julie to catch. She looked at the flowers, looked at Mike and threw them back into the crowd like she would do soon enough on their wedding day.

Uncle Frank took the microphone back and stepped forward. He pulled an envelope from his jacket pocket. "Congratulations you two. Now let's get on with announcing the winner! We saw some incredible competition today but there can only be one winner for the day. The point totals are as follows and they are in no particular order. Phil Toutges – 278, Devin Snively – did not finish, Carmen-Lynn Ashton – 305 and Billy Brandt – 325." The crowd was screaming in delight. "The winner of this year's competition is Billy Brandt. Billy come on up to receive your award.

Jim, Ben, Scott and Christyn all pushed Billy toward the stage. Billy was smiling so much his cheeks were getting red. He clambered up the stairs to the stage and walked over to Uncle Frank and Mike. Mike shook his hand and handed him the envelope. Billy looked inside and then held up the cheque made out in his name. The crowd roared and in the background, a large set of fireworks was set off sending red, blue and green rockets into the air. As the rockets reached their full height of about 300 feet they exploded with a deafening thunderclap.

The band started playing and the whole crowd went back into party mode. Everyone was cheering for Billy and he was enjoying every moment. Looking over the huge crowd of happy faces all cheering for him made him feel like he was king of the world, at least for the day. He looked down at his friends and they were all lined up clapping. He would never forget this day for the rest of his life.

The Mayor Makes a Decision

The next day was a busy one for Mike and Julie. They had come home late from the competition and were very surprised to get a message from John, one of the city workers. He was the guy who had let them know about the earlier problem with the city councilors and the trip to the Bahamas.

When they played the voice message they found out that the city council meeting had been mysteriously moved back to Aug 1. Mike and Julie knew that they had $100,000 freshly raised from the competition but they would need at least two more weeks to raise the remaining $50,000 the City required. They were hopeful that the Mayor would extend them some time seeing as though they had $100,000 to give the City right away.

Mike left a message for Ben letting him know about the meeting at 10:00 a.m. Mike knew that Ben would mobilize the kids and they would be there too.

Sure enough when Mike and Julie arrived at City Hall, the kids were waiting to greet them in the council room. Mike was happy to see them and told them he wasn't sure why the council meeting date had changed again. He wasn't happy about it. He did bring a cheque for $100,000, hoping that would be enough for the Mayor for now.

"I don't know, Mike. Did you see the notes on the agenda?" said Ben.

"What agenda?" said a puzzled Mike.

"Here, read this," said Scott passing him a paper. When the kids had first arrived a city worker was giving everyone who entered a list of the discussion topics for today's meeting.

The chairs for the Mayor and city council were empty but the meeting was scheduled to begin in 15 minutes and they would soon enter from the side doors. Billy had been here once before as part of his Social Studies class. They were observing how government works and Billy had enjoyed listening to the Mayor talk even though he wasn't sure what the guy was saying most of the time.

Mike looked around "Where's Jim? Is he sleeping in?"

The kids looked around. "He was here a little while ago, I'm not sure where he went."

Mike and Julie continued to read the agenda and you could tell Mike was getting angry. "It says here that the only agenda item the Mayor is going to listen to today is arguments in favour of foreclosing on Land Lot #144668," said Julie.

"That's our land!" exclaimed Mike.

"They can't do that, can they?" said Billy.

"I don't think so!" said Uncle Frank and Ron who had just walked up behind them. We just heard about the council meeting change.

"I now know why they wanted to change the date of the meeting!" said Mike, fully understanding something he didn't previously know. "They know I need more time to raise the money for the land so they moved the date of the meeting to cut me off. If I don't have the money, the land goes back to the City and someone else gets to buy it."

"Someone like Philmore Snively!" said Ron.

"That guy is such a rat, just like his son...or vice versa," said Christyn.

At that moment the big doors at the back of the room opened with a bang and in walked a large group of people headed up by Philmore Snively. He was surrounded by all types of people some carrying briefcases, some carrying calculators and some writing feverishly on notepads. All looked like weasels scurrying around Snively's feet. Philmore Snively walked to the front of the room where everyone could see him and then he stopped and surveyed the seating. He selected a group of seats that was already occupied by an elderly couple and he burned a look of disgust at them. They quickly got up and moved back a couple of rows. Snively stuck out his arms and one of the weasel people quickly jumped forward and carefully removed his overcoat. Snively and his crew sat down and began to wait. Snively was not a patient man and began to look at his watch every few minutes.

Finally the council doors opened and in walked the Mayor followed by his 18 city councilors. The councilors were not pleased with the Mayor for calling a last-minute meeting but when they saw there was only one thing on the agenda, most of them didn't mind getting the meeting out of the way so they could get ready to call an early summer recess. They all took their assigned seats.

The Mayor sorted through some papers and then banged his gavel. "The City of Exton Council meeting is now in session. We have one agenda item to cover today. Who is first to speak?" Mayor Carter knew exactly who was first to speak but didn't want anyone to know he was in on it.

"Philmore Snively to speak first," said Snively as he rose and began to walk towards the podium.

Mike wanted to get up and yell something, anything, but Uncle Frank grabbed his collar and told him to be patient.

Philmore Snively cleared his throat and without the benefit of any speaking papers or notes began to present his argument. "I am a respectable business man in the City of Exton and I employ over 1,300 citizens. I am doing my best to add value to this city and would like to be able to take advantage of an opportunity that has been, shall we say, elusive so far."

Mayor Carter was getting annoyed with Snively's tone. "Please make your point quickly Mr. Snively."

Snively ignored the jab from the Mayor. "Last year I attempted to purchase a parcel of land so that I could turn it into low-cost housing and a day-care facility for the people of Exton. Instead my proposal was rejected in favour of a plan to build a skate park."

"That's not how it went and his plan never called for a day-care centre!!" fumed Mike.

"Easy, Mike. You'll get your turn," said Uncle Frank.

Snively continued, "I understand that the City gave the go ahead for the skate park as long as the successful bidder was able to raise the required money to buy and clear the land. This has not been done and today is the deadline. The rules state that if the bidder cannot come up with the money, the next bidder is eligible, which would be me."

The Mayor reviewed some papers and addressed the crowd. "The successful bidder is Mike Holt. Mike, are you present today?" The Mayor hoped he wasn't present so this thing could end quickly.

Mike stood up, "Mike Holt present."

The Mayor sighed. "Please approach with your presentation."

"Mr. Mayor, with all due respect, I was just informed of the meeting last night and have no presentation prepared."

"Are you going to speak at all then?" said the Mayor not really sounding concerned.

"Yes I will," said Mike and he walked toward the podium.

Philmore Snively stepped off the podium and sneered at Mike as they passed each other.

Mike stood in front of the podium and addressed the Mayor and Council. "I too am a business man in the city. I do not employ as many people as Mr. Snively but I do have plans to turn this piece of land into a skate park for the youth of Exton to enjoy. This new skate park will provide a safe place for every boarder to use. Riders will no longer have to worry about cars and with somewhere to go, it will keep them busy doing something they like."

Some of the councilors were nodding in agreement.

Snively saw this and glared at them too. The councilors were not impressed with Snively.

"That's a very nice plan Mr. Holt but the documents clearly state that you have to come up with the remainder of the money by the August City Council meeting which is today. Do you have a cheque for the full amount?"

"Mr. Mayor today I have a cheque payable to the City in the sum of $100,000," explained Mike.

The Mayor checked his papers again. "It says here you owe $150,000. If you can't write a valid cheque today for the whole amount I will be forced to foreclose on you and give Mr. Snively a chance to bid on the land."

202

The crowd of people in the Council room started talking and the Mayor was quite annoyed at the noise. "Quiet in the audience or I will clear the room," said the Mayor banging his gavel a few times on his desk.

"I need a couple more weeks to arrange the financing for the final $50,000, Mr. Mayor. The council meeting was not supposed to be until Aug 15 and that would have given me the time I need," said Mike.

"Well, Mr. Holt, the Council meeting is obviously today and you are out of luck. Without the full amount I do not have a choice in this matter."

Mike looked back at Julie and she had a tear in her eye. How could this be happening they both thought.

Philmore Snively was smiling broadly.

"As Mayor of Exton, I hereby…"

There was a loud bang at the back of the council room as the doors flew open. Two men and a boy came running down to the front.

"Hold it, hold it, everyone," said Jim.

"What is the meaning of this?" cried the Mayor.

"Excuse us for being late Your Worship," said one of the men.

The Mayor liked to be called "Your Worship," it made him feel even more important. He smiled at the man. "Please proceed. What is your business?"

Philmore Snively was not sure what was going on. The smile had vanished from his face. He looked over at his group of weasels and a few of them began to scurry and talk on cell phones. He had no idea for what reason.

"Your Worship, I am Richard Daly, Vice-President of Sales for Quiksilver."

The crowd started buzzing again.

"I would like to make a special presentation to a group of courageous young people from Exton. They are Jim Brandt, Ben Holt, Christyn Middlehurst, Scott Wilson and Billy Brandt. As everyone is fully aware, these fine young people were instrumental in helping to break up the nation's largest counterfeit skateboard and snowboard operation. It was personally costing my company at least $400,000 dollars a year in lost sales. I am pleased to present a cheque to the kids for $50,000 as a way to say thank you from all of us at Quiksilver."

Jim was smiling because he was the one who had arranged the whole thing. Christyn, Scott, Ben and Billy were all staring at each other. Jim stepped forward to the podium. "On behalf of the young people, I would like to accept this money."

The Mayor was not exactly sure what was going on but he knew from all the noise in the room he was losing control. He began to shout and bang his gavel again.

"Order, order!" he shouted. "Mr. Daly, this is all very nice but what does this have to do with City business?"

"Everything, Mr. Mayor," said Jim. "We'd like to add this cheque to the money from Mr. Holt and you can consider the parcel of land paid in full."

Mike jumped up and ran over to Jim. They put their cheques together and presented them to the Mayor. The Mayor reached down and took the two pieces of paper.

The other kids ran forward as well. Mike said to them, "Are you all willing to put your money into the skatepark like this?"

There was a resounding "Yes" from everyone.

"Well consider yourselves part owners in a skatepark now," Mike announced proudly.

"Does this mean we get to skate for free?" said Billy. Everyone laughed and hugged.

Philmore Snively was furious and stormed out of his seat. His entourage was scurrying behind him trying to keep up but no one really wanted to get too close to him right about now. Mike looked over at Julie and she was beaming with happiness. Uncle Frank and Ron had positioned themselves near the exit so they could say a few words to Philmore Snively. As Snively approached the exit doors, Uncle Frank said to Philmore, "Looks like you lost the battle and the war, Snively."

* * * *

The next day Mike assembled everyone at Boardzone. All the kids were there. "First thing I want each of you to do is pick out your favourite board, trucks and wheels." The kids cheered. "Then I want you to help me build our skatepark."

The kids cheered some more and hugged Mike. Julie smiled at the sight of the group hug and knew that things were finally back to normal.

Glossary

Kick-flip	A skateboarding trick where the rider uses a single up and down jumping motion to flip the skateboard into the air while it completes one rotation (the board spins one time from left to right) and the rider lands back on board and continues in a forward motion
Heel-flip	Similar to kick-flip but uses different starting foot placement
360-flip	Similar to kick-flip except the whole board spins around 360 degrees
Nollie heel-flip	Similar to heel-flip except foot placement is at the front of the board
Ollie	Trick used to pop the board up and over an obstacle
Darkslide	Trick where skateboarder flips the board upside down and slides along the ground on the grip tape side before flipping the board right side up to continue forward motion
Complete	A skateboard (board, trucks, wheels)
Board	The wooden deck a skateboarder stands on
Trucks	A metal piece that attaches the board to the wheels
Wheels	Made of polyurethane, spin using bearings
Tuck	When a rider crouches down low on their skateboard
Heat	One race during a competition
Darkstar	A skateboarding company that sells boards, trucks, wheels
Powell	A skateboarding company that sells boards, trucks, wheels
Hook-ups	A skateboarding company that sells boards, trucks, wheels
Girl	A skateboarding company that sells boards, trucks, wheels
Element	A skateboarding company that sells boards, trucks, wheels

ISBN 141202367-X

9 781412 023672

Made in the USA
Lexington, KY
20 December 2009